Oh, Susannah!

By Kate Wilhelm

Oh, Susannah!
Listen, Listen
A Sense of Shadow
Better than One (with Damon Knight)
Juniper Time
Somerset Dreams and Other Fictions
Fault Lines
Where Late the Sweet Birds Sang
The Clewiston Test
The Infinity Box: A Collection of Speculative Fiction
City of Cain
Margaret and I
Abyss: Two Novellas
The Year of the Cloud (with Theodore L. Thomas)
Let the Fire Fall
The Downstairs Room and Other Speculative Fiction
The Killer Thing
The Nevermore Affair
The Clone (with Theodore L. Thomas)
More Bitter than Death
The Mile-Long Spaceship

For Eula, Barbara, and Libby
with love

Oh, Susannah!

1

In which Susannah learns the true meaning of "fool's paradise"

The scene: Florida, St. Petersburg and the outlying beaches, in late June when heat rises shimmering from the highways and sidewalks and all native life moves at a slow pace, while the tourists hurry, scarlet, feverish with sunburn, anxious not to miss anything, darting from air-conditioned shop to shop, speeding to the beaches, cursing the stop-and-start traffic, in which eight out of ten cars bear out-of-state license plates.

A slender young woman emerges from the shiny black library building. Her sun-bleached hair is swept up on her head, leaving her neck uncovered; her arms and legs are bare also, and her skin is the same red-gold suntan everywhere it shows. She is smiling the tender, secret smile of a bride and she appears oblivious of the heat, the traffic, the wheeling pelicans overhead, as she gets into her VW bug and starts to drive. By the time she reaches St. Petersburg Beach she is drenched with sweat.

She turns off the highway on to a side street that curves as if deliberately turning its back on the vulgar commercialism of Highway A-19-A with its endless traffic and motels and boutiques and restaurants. Here, the street says, by turning so quickly, is serenity and comfort, here is quality, the good life. The street twists and curls around luxuriously landscaped yards, with houses spaced in such a way that no one is directly across the street from another; from no point can more than two or three houses be seen, and they are all different. If you follow the curves and pay attention, a feeling of déjà vu creeps over you, and you wonder: Did I already pass that house with the bowed windows? or Is that the same arched entrance I saw a second ago? If you observe enough, you come to realize there are four basic designs and the differences are in the trim, the facings, the plantings. Where one has arches and curves, the next has straight lines and right angles. A Spanish motif is next to English Tudor, vertical stained siding next to horizontal white clapboard.

There are no sidewalks. No one walks here. No children are at play in the street or the front yards with their silk-carpet grass. Even now, sprinklers are coming on, untouched, untended. Water starts to run in the gutters, to swirl down the storm drains.

She does not know anyone on this street where she has lived for the past six months. She sees the red Bricko house and slows to turn into the next driveway. In her yard the sprinklers have come to life. One sprinkler, out of synch, is spraying the garage door.

The house is expensive, a U-shaped stucco building painted soft gray touched with a rose tint. White houses reflect the glare of the sun enough to burn the eyes. Gray and pastels of every hue are the norm. The wet garage is shiny, darker than the rest of the house.

Dense hedges of oleander with red and yellow flowers border the sides of the property and divide the exposed front yard from the very private back yard, isolating it. A great white heron rises from the lawn as the woman approaches the garage and breaks the silence with one tap of her horn. The garage door lifts, dripping water; the car rolls forward and the door slides down again. It is as if she has entered the mouth of a whale.

The house is cooler than outside, even though the thermostat is set on eighty-five; as she passes it, she moves the control to seventy-five. She discards clothing as she walks through the silent house. From the foyer, arches lead into the living room, the dining room, the bedroom hallway. The dining room has a glass wall with sliding doors that open to a patio floored with red tile; there are potted plants and trees set in among the tiles, and lawn furniture with umbrellas, chaise longues, tables . . . The two arms of the house enclose the back patio and part of the swimming pool.

By the time the woman has reached the sliding doors she is naked; she opens the door, walks out to the pool, and dives in, causing hardly a splash.

This is a ritual with her. It is as if she has to immerse herself in water to wash away her working persona — the librarian — in order to become Jimmie's wife. She swims laps evenly, without effort, like an athlete.

After the swim and a shower, with her hair wet on her back and shoulders, she picks up and puts away her clothes. She looks over the mail that has collected in a basket under the slot in the door. There is a card from her parents, somewhere in Greece. They are well; next stop Egypt, then Argentina, Australia . . . Three days after her wedding, which they had despaired of ever witnessing, they left for a round-the-world trip. She always knew it was planned, but the swiftness with which they put the long-delayed departure into motion seems even now a message not at all subtle.

Her parents are not rich, but their thrift and long-range plans and her father's early retirement made the trip possible. Her father is eighteen years older than her mother, and sometimes when she thinks of that an uneasy feeling creeps into her mind and she pursues another subject hurriedly. She has not yet consciously wondered if she was attracted to Jimmie in the first place because he is sixteen years older than she.

As she makes her dinner she notices her fingernails and decides to polish them. Jimmie likes nail polish. He likes glamour. For two weeks before their wedding, and one week after, he shopped with her, selected for her the clothes he liked — soft fabrics, flowing lines, sensuous colors. Her old jeans and tailored pantsuits were all put away then and are still put away.

She is looking at the clock frequently now. It is only seven and he won't be home until ten-thirty. Her nails are done; her hair dry and soft. She is wearing a short terry cover-up and she is barefoot because she really does not like the high heels that she will put on later, and she would feel silly wearing a floor-length dressing gown while she putters around the quiet house waiting for him. She reads for five minutes and puts the book down. When Jimmie is away she reads a book a night usually, but she seldom reads when he is home, neither does she swim naked. Jimmie is not a reader; he likes to do things, to watch television, listen to music, go to movies or the theater. He needs mindless things, he says, to relieve his tension. Jimmie is a pilot for TWA, captain of a B747, and right now he is over the Atlantic Ocean making his approach to JFK Airport. From New York he will fly to Tampa, and from Tampa drive home in his silver BMW.

She gazes at his picture on the bedroom chest of drawers, kisses her finger and touches his nose with the kiss. He is very handsome in his uniform, steadfast, reliable, earnest.

It is ten minutes after seven. This is always the hardest part of their marriage, the last few hours before he is due home again. She is used to living alone; she likes her job at the library, and she loves books. Only these few hours are a burden.

She switches on the television with the sound turned very low. If there is an airplane crash bulletin, she will hear it, and unless there is, the sound will remain below her conscious level of attention.

Hers is a fairy-tale life, she sometimes thinks with pleasure. Jimmie wants her to work and keep her own money in her own account, to do with as she pleases. When they are together, they sail in his boat, they dine out in very good restaurants, they dance, they make love repeatedly. He gives her expensive and lovely gifts. He is grateful to her for bringing him happiness after the tragic death of his first wife. And as soon as he pays off the debts her long illness brought about, he will not have

4

to be away so much, fly so many flights. They will go together and he will show her some of the places in the world that he especially loves. She can see nothing looming in the future to mar her happiness and she knows she was right in waiting, that there is a particular man for every woman, that a successful marriage is possible without sacrificing oneself.

She knows that every woman who is aware of her lifestyle, her husband, her house is jealous of her, and after several years of having felt their seldom-concealed pity, she rejoices in her own smugness. She has it all — the college memories, a career, health, looks, freedom, a husband who is passionate and tender . . . If she were writing her own book, she would end it now with the line: And they lived happily ever after.

❖❖❖

At seven-thirty the doorbell chimed, and when she opened the front door, she was blinded momentarily by the sun in the western sky.

"Miss Susannah Rivers?"

She blinked and shielded her eyes enough to see a woman's outline and gradually her features. A dark-haired woman, olive complexion, very beautiful. She was carrying a box.

"Yes. I'm Susannah Rivers."

"I have a package for you. Sandals. From Sorrento. Jimmie ordered them."

She had an accent, her voice was deep. Neither woman moved for what seemed a long time to Susannah. A blast of heat had struck her when she opened the door, but suddenly she felt chilled. "Who are you?" she asked finally.

"Anna Maria Lucia Rivers. I think I should come in, no?"

Susannah moved and the woman stepped inside the house. Her eyes were hidden by sunglasses, which she took off; her eyes were very green. She swept Susannah with a quick glance, then examined the foyer, walked into the living room, and looked that over carefully. "But I think you are not *Miss* Rivers," she murmured with her back to Susannah.

"And you're not dead," Susannah whispered.

The woman might not have heard. She began to talk rapidly. "Poor Jimmie, burdened with a crazy daughter he must guard from the world. Poor Susannah, clinging to her father pathetically, teetering on the verge of hopeless madness." She crossed the room to scan the dining room and kitchen beyond. Her gaze lingered on the pool, then she shrugged. "Our villa is nicer, I think."

Susannah had forgotten how to move, how to speak. Anna Maria Lucia came to her and looked at her hair intently. "Mine is longer, and prettier when it is down. You should wear a hat in the sun." She thrust the package toward Susannah. "Your sandals."

"What do you want? I don't believe you," Susannah said, holding the package.

"I say to him, 'Jimmie, why can I not go to the States with you?' And he say, 'Poor Susannah, she needs me. Every minute I must give to her.' Poor Susannah see her mother raped and killed; she is raped and left for dead; she go crazy and must have special care, nurses; and her father, when he is home, he must spend every minute with his poor child. I weep for poor Jimmie and buy for his crazy child sandals and boots and purses. I light candles for the poor child and pray for her." She spoke faster, and her accent grew more pronounced; she walked around the room examining the furniture, the pictures on the wall, everything. Now she stopped. "So I come to see the poor little girl, to be a mother to her perhaps. Who knows?"

Susannah shook her head. "I don't believe you. You knew when you saw me. You weren't surprised."

Anna Maria Lucia laughed. "You are right. I know Jimmie is lying for a month. Ever since I hear him on the phone talking to his wife from my house. I know."

Again Susannah shook her head. "He never called me from Italy."

"His other wife, Mrs. Ingrid Rivers, in Stockholm." She started to move toward the kitchen. "I make us a drink, okay?" At the arched entrance to the dining room she paused and added,

"Ingrid's hair falls to her ass. But Okani's in Japan is shorter than mine." She went through the dining room, on into the kitchen.

Susannah did not move. She could hear the hum of the air conditioner and over it the muted garble from the television, and from the kitchen the sounds of ice hitting glasses, water being run.

"Why can't I go with you?"

"Honey, just as soon as I get out from under, you'll be with me. Anna Maria Lucia's mother is sort of dependent on me right now, you know? She's very old and she doesn't understand that life has to go on. It nearly killed her when her only daughter died. and, I don't know, I feel sort of obligated. It's silly, I guess, but give it a few months, okay?"

Poor Jimmie, she had thought, and hugged him fiercely. How good he was to take care of his dead wife's mother!

"Honey, it's tough right now because I'm flying these extra runs, you know, taking other guys' flights whenever I can. Won't be forever."

"But we spend so much money! We could save more. And there's my money just sitting in the bank!"

"You keep it there, sweetheart. This is my debt. I'll handle it. And you should see how I live when I'm gone! Let me have a little fun here, okay?"

Anna Maria Lucia returned, carrying two glasses.

Susannah moistened her lips. "Japan? Stockholm?"

"My detective say that's all." Anna Maria Lucia put the glasses on the coffee table and then took the package from Susannah's hands, sat down on the couch, and started to open it. "The sandals are very nice. He have good taste."

Susannah followed her across the room and stood by a chair.

Anna Maria Lucia glanced up at her. "I think he must be smuggling. Four expensive households! My God! Even he can't afford that on his salary."

Abruptly, Susannah sat down and reached for the glass. "I don't believe a word of it! Not a word!" She drank deeply. Anna

7

Maria Lucia had used sweet vermouth with gin. Susannah banged the glass down on the table and glared at the other woman, who was pulling a pair of shoes from the package. They were old shoes that Susannah had not been able to find for weeks.

"For size," Anna Maria Lucia said, dropping them onto the floor. She took out the sandals and held them up thoughtfully, then extended her own foot, clad in an identical high-heeled sandal. "Your feet are bigger than mine, but you are taller also. American women tend to big feet, I think."

Susannah picked up the repulsive drink and finished it. "Do you have any proof?" she demanded. "I think this is some kind of con game you're playing. I don't believe a word you've said!"

Anna Maria Lucia smiled and began to rummage in her nice leather purse. Susannah had one just like it on a shelf in her closet.

It was nine o'clock. Susannah had prowled the house for half an hour, and now sat staring at the ivory-colored carpet in the living room. Everything in the house was off-white or glass or pale polished wood. No colors anywhere, no disorder. A photographer for a slick magazine could walk in at any time and start taking pictures for a ten-page spread: the good life in Florida.

She thought of the three-room apartment she had lived in before she "married" Jimmie, and with the thought came a terrible yearning to be back there amidst the clutter of books, posters, potted plants . . . The plants in this house had been furnished by an interior decorator — a six-foot-tall rubber tree, an even taller palm tree in a white planter . . . What she wanted was a trailing geranium with pink flowers and a few dead leaves. It was important to have a few dead leaves, something to watch and trim and nurture . . . She found herself blinking away tears and furiously she stood up and marched into the bedroom where she yanked open the bottom shelves built into one side of her walk-in closet. She ignored the pretty soft dresses, the silk blouses, the many pairs of high-heeled shoes as she rummaged in the drawers, and finally pulled out a pair of blue jeans, then another, and the top of her favorite pantsuit. She tossed the clothes onto the bed and kept looking until she had found most of the things Jimmie had not liked enough for her to want to wear. Shoes, she thought. Where were her old shoes?

Off the utility room was a storage room with luggage, fishing gear, surfboards, and on a high shelf, a box of her old shoes and purses. She yanked it down and retrieved her sneakers, flat sandals, a pair of loafers.

For an hour she worked, sorting, packing, throwing things she did not want on the floor or the bed, anywhere. She felt satisfied at the mess she was making. When she finished, she had filled her old big suitcase and a small overnight bag that Jimmie had given her — pale blue with her initials in silver filigree. She hated it now, but she needed the extra space. She took the big suitcase out to the VW and stuffed it in behind the driver's seat; she left the little one at the garage door. Sometime during the hour she had pulled her hair back with a rubber band, and she was hot and felt grimy and tired. She had worked hard that day, too hard to have to put up with moving in the middle of the night.

She deserved it, she decided; she was past the age to believe in Prince Charming, and yet she had believed. She recalled Bobby Gresham who had wanted to marry her five, six years ago. She should have done it. She would be living in a neat little subdivision now, maybe with a child or two . . . Or Harrison Allan, back in high school. He had wanted her to wait until he got through MIT. She might be a professor's wife now . . . In fact, there had been nothing wrong with her life as a single. She had had friends, male and female, had traveled on her vacations, and had gone to two ALA meetings for the library. The last meeting was the cause of her present distress, she remembered. She had met Jimmie on her way home from New York.

He had sat by her, and when they hit a severe storm over the Carolinas, he had reassured her in such a way that it had seemed natural to agree to have a drink with him after they landed, and to see him the next day, and to marry him a month later.

She had fallen in love with a reassuring voice, and hair specked with gray at the temples. She had fallen in love with his movie-star handsome face, his muscular, square-shouldered body. She had fallen in love with his uniform. He had inspired in her the same confidence his transoceanic passengers must have felt every time he made his obligatory appearance among them in the middle of their trips. Fairy-tale stuff, she thought, every bit of it. Soap opera stuff. The stuff of adolescent dreams.

She heard the car in the driveway and braced herself against the arched opening between the foyer and living room. Jimmie unlocked the front door and came in, carrying his flight bag and a small suitcase, a mate to the one she had left by the garage door. He dropped both bags and reached out for her.

"Hey, honey, you're cute as a bug in that get-up!"

"Jimmie, I have to talk —"

He pulled her to him and kissed her thoroughly, one hand creeping under the loose garment, up her back, down again to rest on her buttock.

She pulled away. "I have to talk to you —"

"Honey, you just put a bottle of that good champagne on ice and when I get back we'll talk and talk. Okay?"

"Now, Jimmie! Anna Maria Lucia came to see me today."

He was already moving away toward the bedroom, stripping off his jacket.

She could not see any change in the way he walked; there was no hesitation, no start of surprise or apprehension, nothing to indicate that Susannah might have seen the ghost of his dead wife.

"Now, honey, I know this must be confusing to you, but believe me I can explain . . ."

His voice had changed; it had become the voice of an airline captain whose plane has hit clear air turbulence, or who finds himself on a collision course with another craft. His voice reflected the successful completion of an air captain's speech-training course in Kansas.

She heard: "*Just relax and sit back and we'll be out of this area of thunderstorms in a few minutes . . .*"

". . . soon as I get back. You'll see."

He had taken off the uniform and donned a pair of slacks and a short-sleeved pullover. He had emptied his pockets, leaving neat piles of stuff on his bureau, and now he glanced in the mirror and ran his hand over his hair, smoothing it down. "You just chill that wine, honey, and relax until I get back, no more than an hour."

"Where are you going?"

"I told you, I promised to deliver that suitcase to Mac. Flight papers and stuff. Up in Clearwater Beach. Be right back, honey."

She moved aside as he strode from the bedroom, down the hallway, out through the garage entrance, lifting the overnight bag as he passed it. She found herself sitting on the side of the bed. He would explain it away, she thought in wonder. He would try to explain it away.

She had seen proof, photostats of licenses, pictures of the various wives at his side in various settings, even one of herself with him, and if she told him all that, he would try to explain it away.

Suddenly she moved again, this time with a fury that startled her. She went to the bathroom to shower, stared at her reflection, and then yanked open a drawer, withdrew a pair of scissors, and began to cut off her hair. If it had been short when they met, he never would have given her a second glance, and she had worn it short most of her life. The only time she had let it grow out, he had come along. She cut it quickly. The tiny wastebasket was full of hair when she finished, and, unthinking, she picked it up and marched to the incinerator with it.

After she showered, with her hair tight about her head, she nodded at the image that stared back at her from the mirror — as glamorous as a soggy pretzel. She dressed in faded jeans and a shirt, picnic clothes, hiking clothes, boyish clothes. He hated them, just as he hated the barefoot sandals that she slipped on with satisfaction. She wriggled her toes a few times and nodded at them, as if in greeting.

Finally she picked up a too-long plaid jacket with stretched-out pockets and draped it over her arm, and with her purse over her shoulder, she took one last look at the bedroom. She had strewn clothing everywhere, dumped her jewelry — his gifts — on the dressing table in her search for her old watch, a trusty Timex that she had paid twenty dollars for. The watch had vanished. Now her glance rested on the neat stacks of things Jimmie had taken from his pockets, and she saw a stack of money. She picked it up without counting it and stuck it into her purse. Wherever she ended up that night, she would need money. No credit card, no check, nothing for him to use to find her.

She visualized the scene in a cheap motel: The police break down the door and swarm in to find her hiding in a closet. They arrest her and manacle her and drag her to jail, accused of grand larceny.

She hesitated a moment, then remembered her rings and took them both off. The engagement ring had a very large diamond and several smaller emeralds in an ornate setting; the wedding band was studded with tiny diamonds. She held the rings and looked for a place for them. Her search ended when she came to the figurine of a dancing Shiva on Jimmie's bureau. The god was dreamy-eyed, reaching out to someone, moving erotically. His penis was erect. Carefully she slipped both rings over the penis, and glared at it. That summed it all up, she thought. She had been his live-in call girl.

By the time she left the bedroom, marched down the hall to the garage door, she was so furious that she considered smashing lamps, glasses, anything. Not enough time, she decided. He could get back any minute. She saw her overnight bag by the front door, retrieved it, and left, slamming the door as hard as she could.

She passed three motels with NO VACANCY signs, and at the

fourth one she saw the airport limousine pull up and stop at the front entrance. This motel had a NO VACANCY sign also. She jammed on her brakes, made the turn into the parking lot, and hurried from her little car, leaving the keys in the ignition, taking her jacket, purse, and the small overnight case. She ran for the limousine.

At the Tampa terminal she bought a ticket to Chicago, and when the man behind the counter asked her name, she said, Irene Cory, and only later, on the plane, realized that one of the men in the limousine had been called Mr. Cory by the driver. She also remembered her big suitcase in the back of the VW, and she bit her lip in exasperation, and stared glumly at the bourbon and water she had ordered and did not want.

Still later, she wandered through O'Hare studying the flight boards of one airline after another. When she came to TWA, she walked straight past without a glance. At United she bought a ticket to San Francisco, and an hour later she was airborne again.

The plane stopped at Denver, and for two hours she paced the terminal, light-headed with fatigue and sleepiness. It was daylight when they flew over the Rockies and nine in the morning when they landed at San Francisco. It seemed to take her a long time to find out where to catch a bus to the city but finally she did, and the next time she began to walk, it was with her jacket on, purse over her shoulder, blue bag in her hand. She had no idea of where she should go, where she could find a hotel.

She walked slowly. The air was cool, the sunlight pale, filtered through high clouds. Already the streets were very busy, traffic heavy, pedestrian traffic thick. She saw three teen-agers and the fact registered that she had seen them before, back at the bus stop, two boys and a girl lounging indolently, eyeing the passengers. She dismissed the youngsters and was entranced by a cable car that rattled past and started up a hill that seemed to climb into the sky. She continued to walk. Ahead, she caught a glimpse of a hotel sign. It would do. Anything would do.

She came to an intersection crowded with people waiting to cross, and she saw the teen-aged girl again, this time alone, and she knew the girl was watching her. Suddenly she was pushed hard from behind, and as she flung out her hand to catch something, a foot caught her leg, and she sprawled forward to the sound of screams, honking horns, squealing brakes. For a moment she saw a dark green car close, too close, and then she and the car collided.

2

"Life don't mean a thing
When your lover has gone."

When Jimmie wound his way out of the subdivision, he turned south toward Sarasota instead of north for Clearwater Beach. Anna Maria Lucia, he thought admiringly. Some woman! He drove well within the speed limit, not wanting to attract any attention. He would think of something, he knew, something that would satisfy Susannah and pacify Anna Maria Lucia. Something to do with business for Anna Maria Lucia. She understood business, money, the entangling complexities . . . He would tell her that Susannah was his business partner, his fence, and he would say that Susannah had insisted on the mock wedding in order to account for her recent affluence. He made a left turn at the ghastly pink castle that was the Don Cesar resort hotel, and now, off the beach road, traffic thinned and he drove faster. He went over the story, smoothing out details until it was plausible, and he knew that Anna Maria Lucia would accept it. She possibly would not believe it, but she would accept it. Business was important; making money was important; and she knew that their marriage was real, no bogus there. He nodded to himself and started up the steep ascent of the Skyway Bridge.

The same story could not be used for Susannah. He had discovered to his astonishment and delight that she was unaccountably honest. She even kept track of her personal phone calls to her parents and out-of-state friends and paid for them with her own money. He left the bridge and Boca Ciega Bay behind, and now thick jungly woods pressed in on the road from both sides. Nothing came to mind that Susannah would accept. He could say . . . a crazy cousin of his deceased wife . . . a marriage and annulment too painful to discuss . . . mistaken identity . . . He had blankouts, moments of insanity . . . Anna Maria Lucia was insane, would kill anyone he grew fond of, and she refused a divorce. He tried that one with variations as on the sides of the road the thick woods gave way to scrub, then to farms, and ahead the first lights of the outskirts of Sarasota started to flicker in the darkness.

He would think of something on the way back, he knew, and slowed down as he came to the speed limit sign. He drove directly to the Bide a Wee Wile Motel and parked next to Felix's car. As soon as he turned off his headlights, one of the doors opened a crack; he lifted the overnight bag, walked to the door briskly, and went inside.

"Jimmie, come sit down," Felix said softly. "Drinks are cold and ready. I trust you had an uneventful trip, good tail winds all the way."

Felix was a retired pilot with thirty years of service behind him. He could have passed as Jimmie's older brother; he had the same straightforward, earnest look, the same square-shouldered build, and when he spoke, the same inflections, the same intonations.

On the bed was a cardboard carton. "How many?" Jimmie asked, putting the blue bag beside it, accepting the drink that Felix was extending.

"Three dozen pairs of jeans! And, Jimmie, lean back and belt up for this one. One dozen pairs of Gloria Vanderbilt! On sale for fifteen bucks a pair."

They touched glasses happily, then drank. Only then did Jimmie reach inside a pocket and withdraw an envelope, Felix's share of the profits of his last run. Jimmie knew it was too much, a quarter of the money, but what the hell, he thought, Felix did all the shopping, and he was a good shopper, and Felix got rid of the stuff that Jimmie brought back to the States. He deserved it.

Felix counted the money with an embarrassed grin and then turned to the blue bag. "Key, please," he said. But the case wasn't locked. He raised one of the catches as he spoke, then the other, and turned a reproachful eye upon Jimmie. "Really, you should be just a bit more . . ."

Jimmie yanked the bag away from him and pawed through it. Old faded blue jeans, knit tops, sneakers . . .

"It's the wrong suitcase," he said, so pleasantly that Felix clutched a chairback for support.

They drove back with Felix following closely behind Jimmie's BMW, and at the house they found that Susannah had indeed taken the other blue bag. Jimmie stood in the bedroom surveying what looked like the aftermath of a tornado.

"What're we going to do?" Felix asked, joining him.

"We'll just go down the beach and find her. She's gone to a motel to cool off, I expect."

"What if she finds the, ah, merchandise?"

"She won't. No way." He visualized the case with its beautiful watered-silk lining quilted in a floral design. The stitches that held it to the case were false in one corner, but no casual, or even not-so-casual, glance would reveal that. The corner could be pulled down easily enough, the merchandise removed, the whole thing restored, this time with a permanent glue, and no one would ever be the wiser. There was no reason for her to fool around with the lining. Nothing showed.

Neither reacted visibly when the doorbell chimed. Jimmie went to open the door and Anna Maria Lucia flew in as if a strong wind had propelled her forward.

"Jimmie, my darling! I have come to be with you. To share your burdens. My husband!" She threw her arms around him, kissed him passionately.

"Not now, Anna Maria Lucia," he said carefully, unwrapping

her from him. "Later. I have a little problem at the moment, nothing serious. We'll be out of it in no time. So just relax . . ."

"You poor darling! Your little problem has flown away, betrayed, rejected, humiliated. I see her fly away."

"Where did she go, Anna Maria Lucia? Did you see that?"

"Of course. To a motel. To be alone. To brood. To think. To plan. Poor little girl!"

"What motel, Anna Maria Lucia?"

Now she looked from him to Felix, back to him. "But . . . it is serious? That she has flown?"

"It is very serious," Felix said, sounding just like Jimmie.

"I show you."

She drove them to the motel where they found the VW with the keys in the ignition, the big suitcase jammed in the back. Felix went to the desk to find her room number and came back quickly.

"She's not here," he said. "No one checked in tonight after ten. No vacancy after ten."

Beyond the parking lot, five feet down and thirty feet away the surf mumbled in the receding tide. The water gleamed from the lights of the many motels down its length here.

"She's drowned herself," Jimmie said slowly. He could see her walking away in the water that slowly rose about her, covered her. Brave little girl, he thought. Honorable little girl. She had done the only decent thing. He stared at the water and lifted his head, chin up, shoulders back.

"Ah, Jimmie," Felix said softly, interrupting his farewell, "remember that I've got twenty thousand tied up in this deal. I want to find that suitcase, Jimmie."

Jimmie turned to look at him and heard the sounds of doom in the well-modulated words.

Just then Anna Maria Lucia came to them, put her hand on Jimmie's arm. "An airport limousine depart at about the same time she come. Naturally she leave on it. Now we go back to the house, I think, and we talk very much. Oh, very much. And I call my detective friend, I think. Come on. Back to the house."

3

*"And for every fatality there are
countless others whose lives are changed . . ."*

There are people who should never be allowed behind the
wheel of an automobile. They invariably find themselves in the
wrong lane when they have to turn off a highway; they never see the information signs that say SACRAMENTO RIGHT
LANE, BERKELEY LEFT LANE, ROAD NARROWS, or STOP
SIGN AHEAD, or anything else. They are confounded by one-
way traffic patterns. They never remember the route even
though it may be one they drive daily. Always they prefer to
drive in the left lanes where they feel they have more space.
They stop far from a corner that has a red light, or else they
fail to see the light until they are part way through the intersection and then they stop. They are erratic in their considera-
tion for pedestrians: they may stop in the middle of a block to
permit one to cross, or, equally likely, they may fail to yield
at a pedestrian crossing.

Their passengers learn that to talk to them while they are
driving is to risk terrible consequences. If one of them becomes
preoccupied at the wheel he may easily drive many miles, hours
even, out of the way without noticing that familiar landmarks
long ceased to rise and vanish before him. They usually carry
local maps and need them and probably not a single one of
them has ever made a successful cross-country trip alone.

Often they keep their automobiles in excellent repair because they heed the manufacturers' rule books about servicing at so many miles, and if they have good mechanics, they never even consider what is under the hood. There is no test to screen them out, to prohibit their acquisition of drivers' licenses. When they concentrate, as they do during tests, they function admirably if a bit cautiously.

Bradford Hale was such a driver. Brad was twenty-seven, with the build that some people describe as spindly, but in his case would be wrong. He was quite muscular, without an ounce of fat anywhere, so that he was bones and muscles and skin, and in those places that muscles do not cover, he was bones and skin. His wrists were knobby, his ribs showed when he took off his shirt, and his face was angular. His angularity made him appear taller than he was.

That morning he had planned his route carefully: He had to pick up a book at the library, had to go to the bank and withdraw money, had to go to the post office to mail a package that a friend had left at his house by mistake, and finally had to go to the Embarcadero and meet Donna and have lunch with her. She had something scheduled for the afternoon, but he had made no note about that since Donna would be in charge. It was all straightforward and fairly simple with one stop on the way to the next, no zigzagging or backtracking, nothing like the awful days when he had to drive to Berkeley and back. He had allowed enough time to accomplish everything, with time to spare if there were delays.

But somehow he had found himself in Chinatown hemmed in by trucks and tourists, and panic had set in. He had flashes of memory of another time when he had found himself mysteriously shunted onto a freeway with no exits for miles; and flashes of fantasy, careening down one of the hills out of Chinatown with no brakes. At every corner he stopped, looking for a way down, a way not too steep, not heavily populated with traffic. Behind him a cacophony of horns blasted every time he touched the brake pedal, until in desperation he made a turn and started downhill. He had the car in first gear and drove with his foot in the brake, touching it now and then, jerking along. At the first intersection the light was green and he sighed his relief and crept through. He slowed even more when he saw a red light at the next intersection. It changed as he eased down the hill; people cleared the street and he continued haltingly, and then it happened.

He had just started through when a woman appeared before him, arms outstretched, head down in the configuration a diver assumes on leaving the board. She seemed to be moving faster than he was. He hit the brake and stopped almost instantly, but too late. He felt the jar as they collided.

"I've killed her!"

◇◇◇

Donna Murphy was using up the entire lounge area of her mother's shop with her furious pacing. It was twelve-thirty and Brad should have been there by twelve.

"I'm afraid you've been stood up, darling," Marlene said, dodging as her daughter made a swing in her direction again. "If you'll just let me get into the fridge a moment . . ." Donna spun and marched back to the other side of the suddenly-too-small room.

"I haven't been stood up!" she said grimly. "He wouldn't think of standing anyone up. He's forgotten!"

"Maybe that's even worse," her mother murmured as she took a bottle of Tiger's Milk from the refrigerator and started to shake it. Marlene was only five feet tall and weighed no more than one hundred pounds. She kept her hair a soft beige — champagne she called it — and the clothes she wore were advertisements for her own fashion shop. If she were married to a prominent man, or held a high office herself, she would have made the ten-best-dressed list year after year. One had to get very close to her and examine her thoroughly to spot the small signs of age that she had learned to conceal.

"Or he's lost," Donna muttered darkly. She was six inches taller than her mother and twenty-five pounds heavier, sleek looking with shiny black hair and beautifully soft, cream-colored skin.

"I don't see the attraction," Marlene said. "He gets lost on his way to the bathroom. Darling, he would drive you insane in a week."

"Mother," Donna said sharply, "do you realize how many books his father has in print? That doddering old fool has thirty-six books in print! Thirty-six! Do you have any idea how many little kids get his books every Christmas, every birthday, every time dear old Aunt Ellen or Uncle Charlie comes to visit?" She paused to catch her breath.

"Think of all those innocent little brains rotting under the influence of Pinkie Wink, and Rouse Mouse, and Hoy Boy," Marlene said with a shudder.

"Think of all those royalty checks!" Donna cried. "Royalties twice a year on thirty-six books and a new one every fall in time for the Christmas trade!"

"Who would have thought that nice old man had so much crap in him?" Marlene murmured.

"Jesus! Mother, stop that! Brad is coming over tonight for dinner and you'd better behave. If you even mention his father, or his books, or any of those characters again, I'll . . . I'll . . ."

Marlene waited with interest, but Donna's imagination failed to produce a terrible enough threat.

"Just behave yourself," Donna finished.

"Honey, behaving is something I've been meaning to bring up with you. I don't think Hoy Bo — Bradford, that is — intends to do a damned thing about changing the status quo, if you know what I mean. And frankly, darling, I'm getting damned tired of feeding his face." She began to drink the Tiger's Milk.

"Are you suggesting that I should drag him off to bed? Is that any kind of advice for a mother to give her daughter?"

"As my mother used to say, if you get a fish on your line, you'd better pull it in," Marlene said complacently when she finished drinking her lunch. She started to rinse the empty bottle. "Because once it's caught it's going to be eaten by someone, and it might just as well be the hooker."

Donna glared at her mother who smiled sweetly and said,

"I'll call the bakery and order a pie. God, I'm sick of watching him eat pie. I've served more food for your Hoy Boy than I ever did for your father." She went to the door that led into the shop. "Actually, you know, once you let them creep into your tent, they tend to lose interest in pie for a time."

Donna waited, fuming, until one, and then she stormed from the shop, retrieved her little MG from the parking lot, and drove directly to Brad's apartment in Haight-Ashbury. Donna was determined that Brad would be hers; he was her investment, the big investment her instructors had talked about in school. She had known him for two years, but not until this past Christmas had she realized that Bradford Hale was the only child of Michael Berryman, and that Michael Berryman was considered to be one of the richest, most successful writers of the century. He had come to San Francisco to do a benefit for children and there had been interviews and television appearances, all the hoopla that successful writers created. One of the articles had mentioned his son, Bradford Hale Berryman, and Donna had frozen, staring at the name. She knew him! She had met him at a party in Berkeley.

Donna had known all her life that she would manage money in one way or another. When other little girls played nurse, or played with dolls, or turned tomboy and played ball, she had played with Monopoly money; she had cut out stock reports and made a scrapbook. She had made a portfolio, using funny money at first, then her allowance, and her earnings at the shop where she worked on weekends all through school. She now was an investment counselor and her dream was to see her name on the list: Merrill Lynch, Pierce, Fenner, Smith, and Murphy.

Everything she bought was an investment: her clothes, her car, the apartment that she shared with Marlene. And she had invested six months in Bradford. Time, she knew, was even more precious than money; to invest time was to invest the self, and she refused to lose a day that she had put in on this project, just as she refused to lose a penny. It was not that she expected to have the money for herself: she was not greedy or extravagant; she had no use or need for exhibitionism, conspicuous consumption. She simply wanted to manage his father's estate, to put idle money to work, see it multiply, see it blossom and scatter its seeds, which would also grow and bloom. She thought of herself as a successful gardener of greenbacks. The thought of Brad inheriting that money and being at the mercy of the IRS and other frauds made her shudder.

That love never entered her long-range plans did not seem strange to Donna. She did not believe in love, although she had great faith in the power of sex. She had planned her strategy carefully upon completing her investigation of Bradford Hale, and she knew that he was either shy or afraid of entanglements. The women he slept with, he left; there had not been an affair that had lasted more than a few months, and he had always been the one who backed off. She, accordingly, had not gone to bed with him, had, instead, talked disparagingly of promiscuity, and had kept him so occupied that he had no time to relieve his frustrations with anyone else. Scrupulously she had put aside her own sexual needs until by now they were both as horny as toads, she thought with great bitterness.

No one had said it would be easy, she told herself, climbing the stairs to his second-floor apartment in the remodeled Victorian house that she detested. It had proved to be ridiculously difficult. She had two immediate goals and she did not care which came first: he had to be reconciled with his father, and he had to propose, or else say yes to her proposal. Both had to be done this summer. When school started again in the fall, he would bury himself once more in his stupid twelfth-century literature studies and not surface again until the midwinter holidays.

She let herself into the apartment and glanced into each room without dismay at the disorder everywhere. He was not home. Although she was fastidious, she accepted that Brad was not. Because this was business she could overlook his bad habits — the stacks of books on end tables, on chairs, the unmade bed, his clothes draped here and there on furniture in the bedroom, the breakfast dishes in the sink, his desktop covered with papers in no particular order that she could see. She could overlook all this in Brad although at home she became furious if Marlene left a spoon on a countertop, or a sweater on a chair. She had no trouble keeping her business life separate from her personal life.

She heard the window creak in the living room and turned to see the cat, Exxon, enter. She looked at it with hatred.

It was a loathsome cat. Its head had the short sleek fur of a Siamese, its neck sprouted a ruff of dark grayed orange and its body seemed hidden by an ill-fitting, mottled-brown bear suit. Its legs were trim, obviously from the same genetic pool that had shaped the head, but the pool had run dry before the feet were formed. They were too big, too hairy, with too many toes. And the brown tail was too long; it looked more like a snake than a tail, a broken snake. There was a permanent kink in it several inches from the end. Raised, it looked like one of the spyscopes that children send coupons away for — See around corners, over walls! It was a conglomerate cat, a poorly conceived corporation of cat ideas. It went with the apartment, perhaps it owned the apartment. It belonged to the original lessor and was dutifully passed on from sublessor to sublessor. It trusted no one, liked no one, was arrogant and demanding, had no redeeming virtue, and it was hypocritical. It pretended affection when food was being prepared, or if people were snacking. It demanded a certain amount of lap time, and stroking.

Someone had put a glass pane on a pivot that allowed Exxon to enter and depart when he chose. Now he sat on the windowsill and stared at Donna through slitted yellow eyes.

Donna looked for something to throw at it; before she could carry out her intention, which had become a ritual whenever she was alone with the beast, she heard a key in the door and turned to see Brad enter. He looked ghastly, ashen-faced, and shaking.

"Darling, what happened? You had a wreck!"

"I killed a girl," he said in a harsh whisper. "She'll die any time. I hit her with the car."

"Dear God!"

They stared at each other. Exxon flowed from the windowsill and went to Brad to weave infinity patterns around his legs, purring.

Donna moved finally. She took Brad's arm and guided him to a chair. "Tell me what happened," she demanded.

"They took me to a police station and asked questions. There were papers to be signed, stuff like that. I don't know where the car is. She's in the hospital, unconscious."

"What did you sign?"

He shook his head helplessly. Exxon leaped to his lap and automatically he stroked the cat. Exxon's purr filled the silence.

Donna looked for whiskey and found only wine. She shook her head in disgust and made coffee instead. Brad was stroking the cat like an automaton, staring fixedly into space. She called her mother and told her to find Wayne Hunter, jerk him off the golf course, do whatever she had to do, but get him, and bring something to drink, for Christ sake!

It was two hours before they arrived, Marlene carrying several bottles in a shopping bag, Wayne Hunter looking annoyed at being called out on Saturday afternoon. He was a slender, middle-aged man with steel-gray hair that had been carefully styled and looked quite artificial, like a very expensive wig. His eyes were nearly the same color as his hair, and just as false looking.

"Well, where is he?" Hunter demanded. He put his briefcase on a table, pushing aside papers and books with it as he did so.

"He's taking a bath. I thought it might relax him. He's in shock or something," Donna said. "Did you find out what happened?"

Hunter told her what he had learned. "There are witnesses. The hoodlums were not apprehended, but there are good descriptions. And the woman he hit is still unconscious. A slight concussion seems to be her only injury, and a few scrapes and bruises. Nothing serious."

"He'll need a lawyer," Donna said. "She'll sue."

"It will be a formality," Hunter said. "There won't be any problem with insurance. I looked at his statement. He's covered."

"Of course she'll sue," Donna said firmly. "He hit her, didn't he? She won't be willing to settle for a pittance!"

"Some might say she hit him," Marlene murmured.

"Keep out of this," her daughter said, watching Hunter. "I've told him a hundred times to check his brakes."

"They impounded the car to test it. It's okay," the lawyer said uneasily.

Donna shrugged. "He probably wasn't paying attention. Anyone who's driven with him knows he's a menace."

"I thought you wanted to marry him," Hunter said coldly. "Why are you taking the adversary role? I don't understand."

"I do," Marlene said. "Brad has no money. If she sues, he'll have to turn to his father."

"Exactly. And I'll be his strength, steadfast and loyal."

"You realize, I trust, that if she presses a suit, it's the insurance company that is at risk." Hunter's voice was heavy with disapproval.

"You realize, I trust," Donna said sweetly, "that because it wasn't his fault the insurance company may be difficult, especially if she asks for more than his coverage allows."

In a bus one hundred miles south a girl stared out the window, seeing a broad avenue with marquees that flashed her name in brilliant lights: Dawn Skye. On the rack above her was a pale blue suitcase with the name Dawn in gold ten-cent-store letters. The letters just covered the holes that had been left when she prized off the silver initials. In her purse she had three hundred dollars, her stake, her reward. She was fifteen; she had never been so happy in her life. Today she had been born, she had risen like the dawn. Although she visualized the glittering white way, she did not really want the theater, or even movies. She had set her sights on television. She would become a television star, have her own series. She was on her way.

They had wanted her to hock the suitcase along with the purse, but she had clung to it, the first beautiful thing in her life that was hers alone.

4

"Do you know me?"

She awakened to see a woman in white looking down at her. "Come on, time to take temps. Open up." Something was thrust into her mouth and the woman held her wrist. She released it, wrote on a note pad, removed the thermometer, wrote again, and went away.

Susannah tried to get up, but when the bed began to rock, the room to tilt first one way, then another, she put her head down and closed her eyes.

"You awake, honey?"

This time it was a different woman, younger; she too was in white. "Admissions," she said cheerfully. "Paperwork time." She dragged a chair close to the bed, pulled curtains between this bed and the next one, and then sat down. "We just need some information, honey." She was clipping a form on to her board; when it was ready she fished a pen from her pocket and said, "Name."

"What?"

"Your name, honey."

"Oh. Josephine LaCroix."

The woman spelled it out loud and looked up for confirmation. "Address."

"One twelve Harness Street. New Orleans."

"Married."

"Widow."

"Children."

"No. He was killed on our wedding night during Mardi gras. Three pigs shot him dead . . ."

"Pigs? Police?"

"No. Pigs. You know, pigs."

The woman was no longer filling in blanks. "Oh! Mardi gras! Men in costumes!"

"Pigs."

"Okay, pigs." The good humor had left, now she looked cross. "Let's get on with this. Insurance."

"Insurance?"

"Yes. Do you have any?"

"Of course. He was very wealthy, you know. The insurance was a fortune. That's why the pigs shot him, so I could get the insurance and they could steal it from me. That's what they did, stole it from me."

"I mean, do you have *medical* insurance?"

"Will I be allowed to have some breakfast sometime? I'm awfully hungry. And I'm really thirsty."

"I'll get you some water." The woman put down her clipboard on the foot of the bed. "Be right back."

When she returned, carrying a small plastic pitcher and a glass, the patient was sound asleep. She put the water on the bedside table and left.

The next time she came awake there was a man in white standing over her. "Well, well," he said. "Let's have a look at that bump. How're you feeling?"

"Hungry, I think. I'm thirsty."

He poured water into the glass and handed it to her. She spilled more than she managed to swallow.

"Well, Miss LaCroix, you've had a good sleep, haven't you?"

She was concentrating on getting the glass back to the night stand and did not respond.

"Miss LaCroix?"

There, it was back. She could feel cold water running down her neck and rubbed it with the pillowcase.

"Let's have a look," the man said, and he felt her head gently. He peered into her eyes and ears, down her throat, listened to her heart and then stepped back as if ready to leave. "You're fine. You may feel a bit weak for a day or two. Concussion does that sometimes. Do you remember the accident?"

She started to shake her head, winced, and said no.

"That happens frequently. Don't worry about it. Headache?"

"No. Just sore. My shoulder is sore."

"A few bruises. Do your friends call you Josephine?"

"No."

He waited a moment, then smiled distantly. "What do they call you?"

"Frankie."

"Frankie. Josephine Frances LaCroix? Is that right?"

"No. Frances Ivers."

"Your name is Frances Ivers?"

"Yes."

"But you told Admissions . . ." He reached behind him and pulled the chair in close, sat down. "Where do you live?" He opened the file folder he had picked up from the night stand.

"Twenty-eight thirty-six Meadows Avenue. Indianapolis."

"And how long have you lived there?"

"Four years, seven months."

"Where did you live before that?"

"Paris. I was born in Paris. My mother is dead. My father is . . . he's a famous painter. I can't tell you his name. I'm not allowed. They weren't married, naturally, and he has never accepted me as his daughter, but there's proof . . ."

"I'm sure there is," he said acidly. "When Admissions comes back again . . ." She was watching him candidly, as open as a child, as guileless as a saint. He felt a tingle then, the same kind he had felt the year he bought the sweepstakes ticket and won two hundred dollars. "Miss Ivers," he said softly, "do you know where you are?"

"No. What is this place?"

"It's a hospital. What city are you in, Miss Ivers?"

She did not even hesitate. "Chicago."

"And when did you arrive in Chicago?"

"Last month. I came for a job. I'm a dancer and there was an ad in the papers. I sent in my picture and talked to Mr. Solomon on the phone, sent him my portfolio, and he said I could try out."

"Did you get the job?"

"No. Mr. Solomon is a white slaver or something. He does dirty pictures of women and men, children too, and if his clients like them, they hire the actors and actresses to do the same things in person, live, in foreign countries. It would have paid very well, but I didn't like the idea. You know, fucking with strangers in front of cameras, all that. I went to the police and talked to a detective, and actually I got a job, but a different one, for the police department. It's undercover work, except there aren't any covers usually, and that's all I am allowed to tell anyone. Maybe that was too much, but you don't even know Mr. Solomon, do you?"

He shook his head. "Do you know what day this is?"

"That depends. How long have I been in here?"

He glanced at his watch. "About twenty-four hours."

"That's why I'm so hungry," she said. "It's Tuesday, November nineteen, one thousand nine hundred seventy-two."

"Okay, Miss Ivers. I'm going to send you in some food, too late for breakfast, though. You slept through that. Maybe they can get you an early lunch. And you rest. Try to sleep after you eat. Okay?" He had made one note on the chart: "Amnesia/ confabulation?"

◈◈◈

And so it went. Whenever they asked her who she was, the answer was intricate and different and false. None of the addresses was real, none of the names in any phone books they were able to check.

◈◈◈

"That's how it is, Mr. Hale. It's real amnesia, total amnesia for her past. It would take a psychiatrist and days of testing to find out exactly what all she does remember, but she has language and manners, she's clever, probably rather intelligent."

Brad stared at the cat Exxon and listened with horror, the telephone slippery in his hand, which had become wet; he was cold and sweaty at the same time. It was true. He really had killed her. "How long will this last?" he asked unsteadily.

"No way to tell. Her memory could come back gradually in bits and pieces until most or all is filled in. She could snap out of it all at once. She could have a partial recall suddenly. Or nothing, ever. No predictions on how it will go."

Brad made a meaningless noise and the doctor continued: "When she does recover her memory, most likely she will lose everything that has happened since then. What I mean is that by remembering her life before the accident, she'll forget everything following it. That's how it usually goes."

"You said confabulation," Brad said suddenly. "What does that mean?"

"It's rare, but sometimes the patient doesn't realize she's forgotten who she is. She doesn't know she has amnesia, you see, and so she answers readily when asked questions about herself, and the answers are all false. She isn't lying in the usual sense; she really doesn't know she's making it up."

"Oh God," Brad moaned.

"In her case it seems to be triggered by a direct question about herself. She remembered me when I went back to see her this afternoon, and she remembered that she's in the hospital, the nurses she's seen during the day. It's tricky, Mr. Hale. We'll keep her another twenty-four hours to make certain, but I think I've told you everything I can about her."

"What do you mean, keep her for twenty-four hours? Then what? You can't just turn her out!"

"We have no choice really, Mr. Hale. She doesn't require hospitalization, not in the usual sense, and we can't hold her against her will, now can we? She isn't legally incompetent. The police don't have a missing person bulletin on her. We'll steer her to a halfway house for women, and they'll help her get a job, settle down somewhere. That's about all we can do."

Brad hung up after another moment and stared dully at the telephone. Amnesia! Total loss of self, past, everything. What if she had children? A husband? A little boy out there crying himself to sleep because his mother had not come to tuck him in, to kiss him good night? He started and yelped when Donna touched his arm.

"Well? What did he say?"

"She's Jane Doe," he said, and told her the rest of it too lost in his own gloomy fog to notice the spurt of interest that came into her eyes; he did not realize that she closed her eyes hard and hugged him fiercely in order to hide herself from him. He felt simple gratitude for her loyalty.

Perfect, she thought. It was perfect. Wayne Hunter wouldn't handle it for her, but that toad Conover would.

◆◆◆

They had brought her a hospital robe, blue striped, down to her calves, big enough to wrap around her almost twice. The scuffs they had brought had fallen off her feet, and she slipped on her sandals instead and walked around the room carefully. Minute by minute the weakness was receding, she was feeling fine.

"Hey, that's great!" Melissa cried from her bed. Melissa had one leg in a cast, in traction. She was forty-three, had four children, a man she hated, three cats . . .

Susannah went to the window and looked out at the city. San Francisco, she thought. I'm in San Francisco.

Carrie, in the third bed, watched her broodingly. She had not said a word. In the last bed Mary was sitting up working a crossword puzzle. She was in for tests, on a clear liquid diet that she cursed. Occasionally technicians rolled machinery to her bed, closed the curtains, and did mysterious things to her. She did not say what they were. Probably she did not know, Susannah thought. She liked Mary the best.

"I ain't signing nothing," Mary had said emphatically to the intern who had brought surgery orders to her bedside. And she was maintaining her stance. Susannah thought she was quite brave.

Actually there was nothing to be seen from these windows, only the red brick wall of another building across an alley. She stretched, trying to see the length of the alley; the windows were too deeply set in, nothing was visible. She could not even see the sky.

"Jane Doe?" She heard the voice without realizing she was being addressed. Someone touched her arm and only then did she remember that she was Jane Doe.

"Yes?"

He was a little man, no taller than she, fussily dressed in a gray-striped suit, with a silk tie, pointed pink handkerchief sticking from his breast pocket. He smelled of perfume.

"I wonder if there's someplace we could talk a moment?" he said. "My name is William Conover. I'm an attorney."

"Attorney! Balls! Shyster! Ambulance chaser! Greenback sniffer!" Mary muttered angrily. "Honey, don't you sign nothing either!"

"Do you know me?" Susannah asked, not moving from the window.

"No, but we have a mutual friend. She asked me to come see you."

Mary looked at her crossword puzzle and said, "He means he slipped the admissions clerk a couple of bucks for the tip. He smells money."

"We can't talk in here," Conover said. "I'll just need a few minutes, Miss Doe."

"If he knows someone who knows you, how come he don't know your real name?" Mary was looking at the little man with hatred. "Know your type, I sure do. Like a hog snuffling for truffles."

Susannah was shaking her head at him now.

"Of course," he said smoothly. "You're probably tired. Let me just give you my card. See this number, that will reach me. And here's cab fare, if you decide to pay me a call." As he spoke, he took a bill from his wallet and handed it and the card to her. "You'll need help in finding a place to live, a job, all sorts of things," he said. "I've been hired to render you that service. Give me a call when they release you and we'll talk about it."

The women all looked at the card after he left. It was expensive, they decided; the firm had one of the best addresses, and Carrie, breaking her silence, said grudgingly that it was a high-priced firm. She had heard of them before. She became silent and turned her head away following that one comment.

"Good firm!" Mary said in disgust. "It's like pussy, they're all the same, do the same thing, some just charge more."

Susannah tucked the card and the bill, which was a twenty, into her pocket. What he had said was true, she realized. She did need a place to go, a job, something. What did people do? How did they get food, clothes? She looked at her hands. What could she do?

At ten the next morning the same doctor who had examined her before came back. He went through the same routine — the bump on her head, her eyes, ears, throat, heart.

"I don't know your name," Susannah said.

"That makes us even, now doesn't it?" He laughed. "I'm Ralph MacElroy, resident here at the hospital. If you want anything, need help, I'll be here for the next year and a half."

She nodded.

"I'll sign the release form," he said. "One of the nurses will come to check you out."

"But who's paying my bill? I don't have enough money . . ."

"Don't worry about it. We'll probably bill the insurance company. There shouldn't be a problem."

"I don't know my insurance company, or if there is one."

"Not yours. His. Bradford Hale's. He's the one who hit you. Didn't anyone tell you?"

She shook her head.

"I'll look up his address. Leave it at the desk for you. You'll want to know for your insurance eventually." He started to walk away, came back, and said, "I almost forgot. I'll leave the name of a place where you can go. They'll take you in for a while, until you know what you want to do."

After he was gone, she dressed and told the other women goodbye. Mary and Melissa gave her scraps of paper with their names and addresses — just in case she needed something after they were out. At the nursing station one of the nurses gave her a copy of her release forms, the name and address of the half-way house clipped to it, and a separate slip of paper with Bradford Hale's name and address.

"Take a taxi," the nurse said. "They'll pay for it at the house. Dr. MacElroy called them and made the arrangements. Tell the driver that. Okay. Here's your ride."

"Hop in," an aide said. She was tall and thin, worried looking. She was pushing a wheelchair.

"Why? I can walk."

"Regulations. You want to leave, don't you? Get in."

She went down in the wheelchair and outside the main entrance the aide took the chair away and left her standing on the sidewalk alone. She took a deep breath; it was like being born full grown. Everything was new, unfamiliar. Even the air smelled strange. She recognized a taxi when it rolled to a stop at the curb and that gave her confidence; at least she knew some things, knew what was expected of her in some situations. She felt in her pocket for the halfway house address, and forgot that it was clipped to the release form that she had folded up and put in her jacket pocket. When she got inside the taxi she was fumbling with several slips of paper, the lawyer's card, the twenty-dollar bill.

The cab started to move, stopped at the end of the drive. The driver half turned to ask where to, and she searched through the papers looking for the right one.

"You have to tell me where," the driver said, grinning in an amiable way, "or we have to sit here. And if we sit here too long, the cops get sore." He was young, with a full black beard, and bright blue eyes that studied her frankly.

She felt a wave of panic and held out one of the slips, the one with Bradford Hale's name and address, along with the twenty-dollar bill. "Is that enough?"

He glanced at the address and nodded. "Yep." He made a

U-turn against traffic and eased into a space between two delivery trucks. "Nice neighborhood. Not far from the park. You know the park?"

When she said no, he took it as an invitation to give advice about the city. "You'll want to wander through Chinatown," he said. "And have a dim sum brunch. Skip breakfast that day, and go with three or four others. And if you like hot food there's the Hunan restaurant, but for really hot stuff, try Thai . . ."

She was scarcely listening. Everywhere she looked there was something new that dissolved and became familiar as she examined it. *Bakery* was a blur of letters at first, then flipped and was a known word, a known concept. Bakery: bread and rolls, cakes, pies, cookies. *Jewelers, Antiques, Furniture* . . . One by one they passed from the unknown to known category. But there were other things she did not understand at all. Why the driver was talking, talking.

". . . skip the new piers, though. Tourist stuff. The old Fisherman's Wharf is still okay."

She leaned forward and touched his shoulder. "Do you know me?"

He glanced at her, shook his head. "Why?"

"I thought maybe you did." She turned to look out the window again. Strangers talk to each other, she thought, and did not know why she was bothered by the observation. She watched three young boys on skate boards and nodded: She knew skate boards. Only then did she realize that it bothered her that strangers talked because she had nothing to talk about, nothing to say.

". . . really one of the best," the driver was saying. "Some of the oldest houses in the city, built around the turn of the century. Down farther they're town houses. Victorian town houses, for heaven's sake! Cheek by jowl Victorian town houses!"

He came to a stop and pointed to a tall fancy house with balconies and cupolas and sharp spires. He started to count out change, but she was already leaving the taxi, walking toward the house. He shrugged, shifted gears, and left.

Susannah climbed the wide stairs slowly. The front door had

a stained-glass diamond in it; the door opened easily. Inside there was a short hall, another flight of stairs. She glanced at the slip of paper she still clutched. Apartment 2A. She went up and stopped on the second floor with her hand outstretched to knock. And she wondered what she would say, what she would talk about.

◆◆◆

Bradford Hale sat on the floor with a stack of books on one side, notebooks on the other, and an open book before him. He had stopped looking at it some minutes past, and was staring at the end of a eucalyptus tree branch that dipped, scratched his window, straightened again and again. It was beckoning him, he thought, calling him to come outdoors, walk in the sunlight while he had a chance, before the fog rolled in. Walk in the park, go down to the bay, watch the ships, watch the sails. The truth was that Brad no longer wanted to read twelfth-century literature, and wanted even less to read the long, convoluted articles about it, the critiques, the tortuous labyrinthine commentaries.

Sometime during the spring break he had awakened one morning to hear his own voice saying, Damn them all! And he had meant his instructors, the authors of the books he had to read, the musty, even older books on file with the Library of Congress, all of it. Where before he had sought out all the work he could cram into an eighteen- to twenty-hour day, without a thought for the outside world for days, weeks at a time, now he had to trudge in doggedly, with great effort, and any sound distracted him. The wind called to him, the branches tapped on his windows for attention; when all else was silent, he willed the telephone to ring, willed a drop-in visit by anyone.

His dissertation was nearly completed, needing no more than a month's additional work, and most of that to be done in the Library of Congress, where he would check sources, read a dozen more articles. It was nothing of consequence, what work remained to be done, and yet, and yet . . . He sighed and looked again at the open book. It might have been written in Phoenician, he thought. Greek he could have handled, or Latin, or Old French, or Old English.

The trouble was, he thought clearly, there was nothing else he could do; school had equipped him for one thing only, to teach medieval literature. He examined the thought in his head, aghast. It made no sense, he told himself firmly. This was all he had ever wanted to do, and now he was nearing the finish. It was a premature letdown after ten years of work.

This was the first free summer he had allowed himself since . . . junior high school. And this summer was free only in that he was neither teaching nor taking a class; every day he spent hours writing on his dissertation, or doing research for it, or rewriting what he had done in the past year and a half. When was the last time he had taken time off and done nothing? A week here and there, one year he had taken two weeks and had felt guilty. No wonder he was feeling burned out, numb. Still, the words on the open page of the book refused to make sense and he turned once more to the window to watch the grayish-green tip dance in the slight breeze.

He thought idly of all the things he could not do: business, law, medicine, anything mechanical, anything in the building trades, anything to do with cars, sports . . . He knew he could not be an editor, or copy editor, or journalist. His spelling was atrocious, and he always got the details wrong when he tried to tell anyone else an event that he had witnessed.

All he could do, he admitted glumly, was teach medieval literature and write incomprehensible articles for obscure journals. That was his fate, one he had chosen quite deliberately years ago without, apparently, realizing that the day would come when he actually would have to do it. Promises to be redeemed so far in the future shouldn't count, he thought.

Exxon stood up on the rocking chair where he had been sleeping. He leaped off it, leaving it rocking gently, and went to stand at the door. A second later the bell rang.

Brad opened the door and looked at his caller without recognition. She looked like someone from school in a vague sort of way — the same somewhat dirty jeans, a shirt that was torn, a jacket slung over her shoulder, no makeup, her hair short and windblown, ragged.

"Hello," he said.

She looked at the cat and knew the word *cat*. And the man's name, Bradford Hale, she knew that. She smiled at him, grateful that she knew his name, glad that he had a funny cat. "Hello," she said and stepped inside the apartment. She did not know what to talk about, and she remembered that strangers talked, but something would come to her, she thought, and if it didn't, then he would start a conversation just as the driver had done.

"Is there something you want?" Brad asked helplessly, still holding the door open.

"I don't know," she said after a moment's thought. "I guess so."

Brad waited, but she said nothing more, was instead looking about the apartment with interest. Exxon was stropping himself against her legs.

"Maybe we'd better start over," he said finally. "What do you want? Who are you?"

5

*"The ancient shaman fixed
his baleful gaze upon her . . ."*

My name," she said, "is Ingrid Morgan. Perhaps you've heard of my father, Harold Morgan. He's a rather famous archaeologist. I was in school in Davis getting my Ph.D., teaching, every summer going down to the new city they had found to work with him for several months at a time. Then I met Maria Apac." She paused, as if considering, or sorting through memories, then continued. "She was very young, a student in one of my classes. Peruvian. Very beautiful. We became friends, and now, of course, I know it was her intention all along, but at the time it just seemed to happen that we decided to go to the Andean city together at the end of the term."

She told about the terrible trip to the newly found city that the archaeologists were unearthing laboriously day by day.

Whenever she paused, Brad said, "Go on." Or he asked a question: "What's an *arden?*"

"It's a garden on a terrace. They terraced the whole mountaintop, built retaining walls and filled in with good rich dirt that was brought up in baskets from river deltas, sometimes a mile down, seven thousand feet straight up and down at places."

At the site of the new city, Kevin, who had made the actual discovery, was in charge of the Indian diggers and other laborers. Also at the site was a stranger, an old Indian man, dressed

41

in a mixture of outlandish clothing: a pale blue oxford-cloth button-down shirt, a bowler, green twill trousers tied at the waist with a scarlet sash, sandals. The Indians treated him with deference, as if he were a god, or at least a great sorcerer. A *brujo*, Kevin said, as if explaining his presence. Kevin was restless, tired of the digging; he was anxious to leave the ruins and go wandering in the forest, the only place where he was happy.

"And one night," Susannah said, "the old *brujo* entered our shelter. Maria and I were together in one of the buildings on an upper-level *arden*. He came in and spoke with Maria in a dialect I didn't know, not Spanish. Kevin arrived also, and I knew the old sorcerer had arranged the party. It was all his."

He had made plans, he told them, to conduct the group out into the forest where Kevin would use his special skills to locate the next city in the line starting with Cuzco, going through Machu Picchu, then the new city, and finally the last one still hidden in jungle. Kevin said no, Ingrid Morgan said no, but the ancient shaman fixed his baleful gaze upon her, and the next morning before dawn they were on the way, a group of five Indians, the sorcerer, Maria, Kevin, and Ingrid. One of the Indians was Luis, Kevin's long-time friend who had accompanied him on many explorations; he was clearly very frightened.

Luis whispered what he knew to Kevin, who passed it on to Ingrid during the next awful days of forced march through jungles no one had ever penetrated before.

Maria Apac was the *accla*, an Inca princess, bride of the sun. It had been foretold that when this city that Kevin had found rose to the sky again the *accla* would travel to the final temple hidden deep in the jungles, where she would become impregnated by the sun and bear the Inca who would reunite his people in a new kingdom.

Ingrid's role was messenger of the god; she was destined to remain by the princess's side until her pregnancy was assured, and then, by sacrifice, be returned to her god in the heavens.

"We started to make plans for our escape, but we were too closely guarded, and every day we moved ahead, now by river in long swift boats, again by land where every step was tortuous and filled with danger."

She talked for nearly an hour and he listened, now and then asking questions that she answered without hesitation. During that hour they moved into the living room, seated themselves in the facing overstuffed chairs; Exxon claimed her lap and purred in contentment as she spoke, and idly she rubbed his ears or scratched his neck.

"It's all a lie, of course," Brad said finally when she paused. "I don't know why you came here to tell me such an incredible story, but it is a lie. I don't believe a word of it."

She shrugged, then yawned. "Do you have coffee?" she asked. "I'm falling asleep."

"I'll make some. Be right back."

He made the coffee and found clean mugs, sugar and cream, neither of which he ever used, then searched futilely for napkins, which he also never used. When he returned carrying the steaming mugs, she was asleep, curled up in the chair with Exxon in the hollow between her thighs and stomach. He put the mug down on the table at the side of her chair; she came awake and sat straight up.

"I'm sorry," he said. "Didn't mean to wake you up. There's your coffee."

She looked at it blankly.

"Then what happened?" he asked, sitting down again.

"Happened? When?"

"You were in the jungles, remember? You found the second city exactly as Maria said you would. How did you get out?"

She was regarding him as if she feared he might pick up a knife and start wielding it. Shaking her head slightly, afraid of offending him if she moved abruptly, she started to ease out of the chair, upsetting Exxon who stalked away indignantly.

"Wait a bloody minute," Brad said angrily. "I told you before I didn't believe it, but you can't leave it at that point . . ." He stopped and at that moment he knew who she was: Jane Doe, the woman he had hit with his car.

"Holy Jesus!" he muttered and sank back into his chair. "Jane Doe! What are you doing here? Why did you come here?"

"I don't know. Maybe to talk to you."

He closed his eyes for a moment. "Did you come here for money, is that it?"

She shook her head. "I don't think so. Do you want to give me money? I don't have any, you know. Do people give each other money? I know they talk to each other, people, strangers, but do they give money away?"

"No. I thought . . . They told me that you were going to a halfway house for women."

"Yes. But I got here. I must have been sent here instead."

Sent? He blinked at the word. Sent! She had been sent? "Drink your coffee," he said. The word spun around in his head, echoed hollowly, rang, boomed, faded, returned. Sent?

They would get her a job, he thought, find her a place to live. A job doing what? She was educated obviously, well read, probably knew Spanish. She knew more about South America, jungles, and the Incas than he did. She probably really was an archaeologist. What kind of job would they get for her? Nothing dealing with the public, they would not dare expose her to questions about herself, and they could not guard against it in any kind of public job. What were they equipped to do anyway? They were not an employment agency. She had no references, no credentials. They would get her a menial job; he was surprised at the rush of anger that came with the thought. Scrubbing floors somewhere safe, or washing dishes in an institution. Somewhere out of sight where she could keep to herself, not be an embarrassment to anyone else.

He visualized her in a steaming kitchen, her arms plunged into a sink full of hot soapsuds, sweat running down her face, down her neck, and endless piles of institutional crockery everywhere. Someone yelling at her to speed it up, a conveyor belt bringing in more dirty dishes. Someone asking her who she was, laughing at her answers, jeering at her . . . And it was his fault; he had put her in this position.

Not all strangers talk to each other, Susannah thought sagely,

44

watching his expression change from dark to darker: this one obviously had no need to fill the silence with chatter. She felt a great relief. If he did not have to talk all the time, neither did she. She picked up her coffee and sipped it, watching him closely as he struggled with his silent broodings.

They could not have her, he decided. She could stay in the second bedroom of the apartment for a few days and he would ask around for another solution. Ask whom? He turned away from the question quickly.

"Look," he said aloud, "I have a spare room here. My cotenant graduated and left. You can sleep there. I'm going to write up what you told me and see if you can find any clues in it about . . . You know. And every day you should write down everything you've done, what you've thought about during the day. I heard that sometimes that helps. And anyway, later you'll want to know."

Later? she thought. Later than what? When later? Know what? His words made little sense to her, but then she remembered that there were things about herself that she could not remember. Remember, not remember, later. It was all too confusing to think about any longer.

"I have the name of a lawyer," she said, remembering the card. "Mary said he'll want to sue you for a lot of money, because of what you did to me. Do you mind?"

Brad groaned. "Don't worry about it. I'm going to write up what you told me. I'll find you a notebook to use . . ." He rummaged on his desk and came up with a notebook that had only a few pages scribbled on. He ripped them out and handed it and a pen to her. "Just keep a diary," he said. "Whatever you can think of." An article he had read that morning said that one of the hardest parts of amnesia was snapping out of it and finding there was a new blank. The hospital, this visit, it would all be gone and she would wonder what she had done, where she had been, whom she had been with. He shuddered and yet felt nearly envious. If only he could rub out whole stretches of life like that.

❖❖❖

Brad worked on her story all afternoon, only vaguely aware when she put down her notebook and wandered about the apartment looking at his books, looking in the kitchen, the two bedrooms. He forgot her again.

She learned much about Bradford Hale. Some of his books were familiar, some so strange she did not even know the language they were written in. She found his dissertation and started to read it, and after a minute or so, she picked up a pencil from his desk and started over, this time correcting his spelling as she went.

Late in the day, Brad stopped and leaned back in his chair. His stomach sounded like a drum rehearsal and he remembered that he had not eaten lunch that day, and probably she had not either. It was nearly six then.

"Let's go out to eat," he said. "Do you like Mex—?" He stopped, then said, "There's a small mom-and-pop Mexican place around the corner. Pretty good food. Hungry?"

"Starved. Are you finished?"

"No. I'll let you read what I've done so far while we wait for our order. Ready?"

What was there to do to get ready, she wondered, and glanced down at herself and for the first time knew that she was in dirty clothes, that her shirt was torn, either from his car, or from the street. That was where she felt soreness in her shoulder.

"Like this?" she asked in a small voice.

He looked at her in dismay. "After we eat, we'll shop," he said finally. Marlene would be open until nine, he thought. She would know what to give them. He put the pages he had typed in a large envelope, waited until she had slipped on her jacket that was less disreputable than her shirt, and they went out together for dinner.

The restaurant was small and cheerful with red-plaid table-cloths, a bustling owner/waiter, who was obviously glad to see them, and a short, hand-written menu. Susannah looked at it and asked Brad to order something for her. None of the words looked familiar. As soon as he had done this, she started to read the story he was working on.

The waiter brought guacamole and chips, and they had just finished it all when she turned the last page.

"Then what happened?"

"It's your story," he said.

She shook her head. "What else did I say?"

"You talked about the terrible trip through the jungles, down the mountain to a river, with daily deluges, mud slides, snakes — fer-de-lances, chicotillos, the famous flying serpent of legend, you said." He was watching her; there was no sign of recognition, of memory of the fantastic tale. "Kevin and Luis got more and more nervous as the group got deeper into hostile Indian country. When Kevin asked how they knew which way, Maria showed him on her map. A straight line drawn from Cuzco through Machu Picchu, through the new, unnamed city, and now on to the next city. Earth Magic, she said, the lines of force, that's where they had built their cities."

Their food arrived and they learned that Susannah liked Mexican food very much. She ate ravenously. With her mouth too full to be polite, she asked, "Then what happened?"

He sighed. "After weeks of hell, they reached a place in the jungle where they told Kevin to start looking for his drain canals. For two days they had been climbing, not very steeply, but upward in an area that Kevin knew from his maps. And his maps did not show the hill, not even a rise. The jungle was so dense that one could see only an arm's length away. He and three of the Indians left the others and started to search for the channels that would lead them to a city up higher, a city he did not believe in. And of course, they found the city, eventually. And in the city they found the marriage stone. They had to work to clear it of jungle, naturally, but finally they did, and now the *brujo*'s plan was put into execution. You and Maria had been closely guarded from the start. You were her companion, her confidante, her slave actually. Maria was the virgin *accla*, and it was written that she would be impregnated by the sun, the true bride of the sun. Her son would be the new Inca, the new ruler of the Inca nation that would be reformed under his guidance. And you, chosen for your golden hair, would celebrate her impregnation by being sacrificed."

Susannah was no longer eating. Her eyes were large, blind to the restaurant, blind to Bradford retelling the story. She was seeing the black jungle, the marriage stone, and then the virgin bride being tied down to it in the black before dawn, with chanting priests on all sides, a torch-light procession of the priests. The sun would rise over the trees, the first rays penetrate her . . .

"You aren't eating," Brad said, and she roused from her reverie. "You and Kevin and Luis had to escape before you were all killed."

"Then what? How did we?"

"I don't know. That's where you stopped."

"But I got out!"

"Good God! It's a story! You were telling me a story! I want you to finish it."

"I don't know anything about any of that."

"Neither do I."

They looked up at each other helplessly. Then Brad said, "We could cobble up something, I guess."

She nodded. The waiter was clearing the table by then, and they were ready for dessert.

6

Flicker, flicker, little star.

Three black, three brown, a chink, and four wasps. That was Hank Carlton's shopping list. Faces never seen on TV before, or movies, new faces, kid, get it! That was his marching order, and in a savage mood, he waited for the bus to pull into the station. Bushnell wanted them new and green. He'd deliver them so green they'd have to take a lawn mower to them.

He knew the kid with the blue suitcase was his as soon as he saw her. A runaway, but he didn't give a damn. Underage, but she could lie about it.

He made the contact, gave her the address and time, and only then asked her name. He could not suppress his groan when she said Dawn Skye.

"Yeah, well change it, kid. Fancy names are out. Use the name Mama gave you, or something like Juanita, or Maria, or Rosita. They're good names. When you show up Monday morning we want a good Chicano name, or Puerto Rican, get it? Just keep it pronounceable."

She nodded, big-eyed. She had stayed a safe distance from him, not believing anything he said at first. She had heard stories about men who met the bus and picked up girls, turned them into whores, gave them dope, beat them. If he had asked her to go anywhere with him, she would have screamed and run. He didn't.

"Blue jeans, T-shirt, sneakers. We're trying out for a new series set in a summer camp. Don't do anything fancy to your hair." If she came loaded with makeup, they'd scrub her face, he added to himself, and knew she would come made up like a commercial for Mabelline.

She nodded again, staring at him numbly, in disbelief. She kept watching him until he vanished among the many people in the bus station. Then she looked at the card he had given her and suddenly put it to her mouth and kissed it again and again and she laughed.

She had to buy blue jeans and shirts, shoes, everything. She had to find a room, get some decent makeup, a blow dryer. She would need taxi money, get a manicure . . . She looked at the blue suitcase speculatively: Twenty-five, thirty dollars at least. She started to walk, looking for a pawn shop.

7

Marlene and Brad waited in the shop while Jane Doe tried on the clothes that Marlene had delivered to her in the dressing room. Marlene was in a deeply thoughtful mood, staring pensively at the champagne-colored carpet. She had taken measurements and had seen the all-over suntan, the pale strip left by a wedding ring; she had seen underwear so expensive it had made her catch her breath. The jeans were from Sears, the shirt from a chain shop, the sandals handmade, the underwear from Paris. And the haircut was a butcher job, done in her bathroom with household scissors.

"She's very pretty," she said absently. "A perfect nine. I could use her in the show Saturday, if she wants a temporary job, that is. A one-day job actually."

"What show?"

"I told you. A fall preview of West Coast designers' fashions. It's going to be in the Hyatt, a luncheon show."

"Modeling? I don't know . . ."

"Darling, it's better than washing dishes in an institution, isn't it? You're right about her, she needs a job. She's going to need money."

"I think I'd better just give her a few dollars . ." he mumbled. The truth was that he had no more than a few dollars to give anyone, and his next check was not due for ten days or more. His father had set up a trust for his education many years ago and the bank was punctilious about mailing his monthly checks on the tenth, and unreachable if he wanted an advance, or ran over expenses.

"Don't be ridiculous," Marlene said firmly. "It would look bad. Someone might even suggest that you were trying to buy her off, prevent a lawsuit, something horrible like that. I'll lend her some money, a formal loan to be paid back when she's working, or else when she recovers her memory, whichever comes first. It has to be cash, of course. A checking account might be difficult . . ." She stopped when Susannah reentered the shop, dressed in a navy pantsuit with a pale blue shirt. Marlene said in satisfaction, "Yes indeed, I can use her Saturday."

For the next hour Marlene fussed with her, until she had an adequate wardrobe to see her through the next week or two. She pressed three hundred dollars in cash into her hand, realized she needed a purse and some makeup and added them, and finally they were done. Susannah wrote Jane Doe on the IOU, and signed for the clothes, and they all got into Marlene's car and she drove them home.

Marlene went inside with them, and watched Susannah walk down the hallway with her boxes and bags. "You aren't going to get . . . involved with her, I hope?"

Brad looked shocked. "She's sick! Any minute she could wake up and I'd be a total stranger to her!"

"She's married," Marlene said. "Or has been until very recently. A husband might take offense at any hanky-panky."

"You think we should put her in a hotel or apartment of her own?"

Marlene shook her head. "I think you're doing exactly the right thing, keeping her here." It gave her the shudders to think of someone else taking over, leading Jane Doe away, possibly misusing her, taking advantage of her. She was an heiress, or the wife of a wealthy businessman, or oil tycoon, or something like that, she felt certain. That underwear . . . Someone would claim her, someone was probably at that moment conducting a very discreet inquiry about her, and that someone would be grateful to anyone who took good care of her while she was lost. She patted Brad's arm and went to Susannah's door and tapped, calling out, "Honey, I'm leaving now. Brad will bring you around to the shop Saturday at nine. See you then. Good night."

◆◆◆

Brad lay in bed trying to think of an ending to the story she had told. That morning he had read articles and had talked with a friend, a psychologist at school, and had learned that possibly within the stories of amnesiacs with confabulation there were clues to their identity, or what they were fleeing. It was a defense mechanism, his friend had said; there was something too terrible to deal with, too traumatic to handle . . .

Seeing her friend tied down to a marriage stone, knowing she was doomed to suffer a bloody sacrifice, would be traumatic, he thought sleepily and came awake. Shit! It was a story! It needed an ending. He started the whole process over again.

On the other side of the wall she lay awake also. When she admitted that sleep would not come soon, she got up and pulled on a heavy robe that Brad had lent her. They had forgotten to buy her one in the shop. She opened her balcony door and stepped out onto the tiny space fenced in with wrought iron, barely big enough to turn around in; she leaned on the rail and stared moodily at the city lights. Somewhere out there someone must be missing her, pacing the floor wondering where she was, when she would come back. Somewhere a job was not getting done, papers stacking up perhaps, or reports not written, a deal falling through because she had not turned in a vital paper . . . Maybe a man out there was turning restlessly in his bed, lonely, reaching out for her in his sleep, finding a cold pillow . . . Maybe a friend had waited in a restaurant, waited, finally ordered, finally had dinner, finally left, feeling hurt, neglected, feeling resentment at her carelessness.

You can't just leave without someone noticing, she thought.

Didn't anyone out there miss her enough to call the police, to demand an investigation, to shout: "Find her! Bring her back!" Had she been so unloved, so alone that no one even knew she was gone?

"I'm someone," she whispered to the lights. "I am someone!"

The wind turned chill and she went inside and closed the door, got back into bed. Deliberately she turned her attention to the fantastic story she had told Brad. They had to think of an ending for it. She tried to ignore the stinging in her eyes, but after a moment, turned her face down into her pillow and wept.

◇◇◇

"Okay," Brad said. "We agree they have to get through the jungle to the river again and go downstream until they join the Amazon. Right?"

She nodded. They were still at the table with the remains of breakfast, drinking coffee. "It seems simple enough to me. A page or two is all it would take."

"What grows in the jungle?"

"Trees and vines. I don't know."

"That's the point, you don't know and neither do I. But the first part has all kinds of names for things, and they sound pretty good to me, authentic. The rest has to sound authentic too."

She shrugged. "Why? Why not just leave it alone now?"

"I think you can sell it. Maybe you were a writer. Have you thought of that?"

She shook her head. "You did the writing. I couldn't have put in all that detail, dialogues, everything. Actually, you're a writer, aren't you?"

She was astounded at his reaction to what was really an idle question. He turned pale, blushed a deep red, paled again. He got up abruptly and began to clear the table with brusque motions. "I'm a few months away from my Ph.D. in twelfth-century literature. I'm a teacher, not a writer." The words were clipped.

Wordlessly she stood up and helped him clear the table. She filled the sink with water and added detergent. "I'll wash up," she said. Then, looking at the suds, she muttered, "If neither of us is a writer, I don't see how we'll ever finish the story anyway."

"I have to go claim my car, and then I'm going to school and get some books on Brazil, the Amazon basin, and a map," he said. "We'll finish," he added grimly. He had found an extra key to the apartment that morning, and he tossed it down on the table. "There's a drugstore around the corner, a grocery, fruit stand, stuff like that, if you want anything. You won't get lost, will you?"

He knew he still sounded angry, and felt helpless to do anything about his tone. Any fool could finish that story, he knew. Anyone who could put words together to make sentences could write stories, and everyone who had gone through high school presumably could do that. If they couldn't put the words on paper, they could put them in a tape recorder and let some other idiot transcribe them. There was nothing to it. He had seen the process often enough to know that much about it. "Any fool," he muttered, "could get rich doing just that, putting words on paper."

❖❖❖

When he returned a couple hours later he found her sitting in the middle of the living room floor surrounded by newspapers. There were newspapers on the chairs, opened, torn apart, more on the table, also pulled apart, sections abandoned here and there all over the room.

Exxon was diving under one tented section, growling. She had pulled out the classifieds, he realized. Job hunting? There were ink smudges on her face; her hands were black.

"What are you doing?"

"I'm looking for me," she said. "In the Lost and Found columns." Exxon began to stalk a comics section.

"Good heavens!" He looked at the mess and sighed. "It wouldn't be under Lost and Found."

"Listen: 'Lost, Doberman, black, answers to Spiky. Reward!' Or this: 'Female cat, tan with white stockings, Pucker. Reward.'

You'd think if people cared enough about animals to advertise, they'd at least put in a notice or something about a person."

"People don't get lost, except little kids. And crazies. If it's in the papers, it would be under Personals."

She turned pages and stopped. "Here it is. Listen: 'Wanted: Genteel, educated, open-minded woman under thirty to share alternative lifestyle.' What does that mean?"

"Never mind. That isn't you."

"I don't know what any of these mean. 'Couple desires French-educated lady to share home and experiences.'"

"That's not you, either," he said, and tried to see what paper she was reading.

"What's bondage?"

"Look, you're not going to find anything in there."

"It seems to me that we're on the right track, though. At least these ads are for people, not animals and wallets and things."

"Those are ads for people who . . . They like kinky sex, stuff like that."

"And how do you know I don't like that! I don't know myself what I like!"

He choked back his response and said reasonably, "If one is for you, it'll say something like: 'Connie come home. We miss you.' Would that mean anything to you?"

She shook her head, and when he began to gather up the papers, she did not interfere.

"Okay, let's get to work. I've got a stack of books on Brazil. What I want you to do is start going through one and jot down exotic names. Plants, animals, birds, whatever might fit. I'm going to try to find the location, see where the rivers are, what they're called." As he spoke, he finished gathering up newspapers and took them out to the trash in the kitchen. He hurried back and began to stack up books and notebooks spread out on the dining table. He dumped them onto the window seat, nearly blocking Exxon's escape hatch. On the newly cleared table he laid out his maps and began to make lines, using a plastic ruler, muttering softly as he worked.

Susannah watched him, then took the four books over to one

of the comfortable chairs and began to read. From time to time she glanced at him, now catching him bent over the map, again seeing him staring off into space, his pencil poised over the map, or scribbling hastily. Once he threw down his pencil and paced back and forth, finally stopped before her. "Where did you get satellite maps? Are there such things as you described?"

"I don't know," she said helplessly.

"Oh yeah, I forgot. There must be, though." He started to pace again. "NASA," he said. "Or JPL."

Susannah put down the first book, a technical treatise on the flora and fauna of the Amazonas. It was hard going, giving her a headache. She stared at the next book she picked up, and for a second it seemed to waver in and out of focus. The moment passed and she put it down without opening it, picked up a different one. She started to read again, now and then jotting down a note. And so the afternoon passed until the phone rang at five-thirty.

Brad scowled at it and when he answered, his voice was clipped, almost rude. "Sorry, but I'm swamped with work. I'll get a bite to eat later and work on through. Yeah, I remember. Saturday, dinner. Yeah." He hung up and went back to his map. "Donna," he said, as if she knew what he meant.

Donna hung up the phone and looked murderously at her mother. "He's working too hard to see me!"

Marlene shrugged. "Isn't he always working too hard to live like a normal human being?"

"Yes, but not with a woman in his apartment! What is she doing while he works too hard to see anyone else?"

"Maybe she's baking a pie, or washing his windows, or looking up dates in the almanac, or rewriting his dissertation, or mending his clothes, or painting his walls —"

"Oh, shut up!" Donna went to the window wall and stared out at the city; she began to crack her knuckles.

Marlene groaned.

"You're sure about her underwear? How expensive they are?"

Donna did not wait for an answer. Her mother would never make a mistake about something like that. "What are you planning?" Donna asked then, turning from the magnificent view that she seldom saw anymore. "You don't want her money, if there is actually money. What do you want?"

That was the question that Marlene had no answer for. She was not certain what it was that had interested her in that lost girl. Her first reaction had been that someone would be grateful if she helped take care of her, but when she had thought about what she meant by grateful, she had not come up with a financial reward. Gratitude, simple gratitude for taking care of a lost child. The way she could imagine her own gratitude if someone had taken care of her lost child, when she was still a child, and if she had ever been lost. Looking at Donna she tried to remember what it had been like when she was a child, but it seemed to her now that Donna had emerged from the womb a schemer; her cleverness, her ability to manipulate, her unerring instinct for weaknesses had been perfectly honed from day one.

She sidestepped the question. "You know as well as I do that Brad will not take advantage of her in any way. I talked to Dr. MacElroy this morning about her, and he thinks that she'll snap out of this amnesia rather quickly. She wasn't injured enough to account for it, and whatever happened that she wants to forget couldn't be that terrible or there would have been news of it. A slain husband, brutally murdered children, anything like that would have been in the papers. Probably she and her husband had a quarrel and she walked out and doesn't want to think about it right now. But it will pass. A few days of rest, boredom, watching Brad eat, that will cure her and she'll remember and go back home."

And then sue the living shit out of Brad, Donna added silently. It worried her, though, because she knew how long it had been since Brad had had a woman, and she did not trust his overlay of gentleman training to be stronger than his instincts and needs. But what if they did fuck, she thought clearly.

What if they did? What possible difference could it make once the amnesia was over with? In fact, if she was keeping a diary as Marlene said she was, it would make everything even worse later, worse for Brad, because it would appear that he had taken advantage of her helplessness. Her husband would have a legal cause for action, ask for punitive damages, or whatever. She considered the idea from all sides and could see nothing wrong with it. Eventually Jane Doe would be gone, Brad would be floundering in legalities, and she would be his life-support system. Nothing was changed. She admitted silently that she welcomed a few days off; most of the time Brad was a noncommunicative bore.

◆◆◆

Diagonally across the country Jimmie was saying, "Now, Felix, be reasonable. This is my profession, after all. I have to avoid any suspicious deviation from my routine, and that means that I have to make my already-scheduled flight to Paris. But, old friend, it is not routine to be accompanied by my wife and my best friend. That is simply not in my previous pattern of behavior, you understand. You can't travel to Paris with me, old buddy."

"I guess I can, though," Felix said just as slowly, just as carefully. "I guess I don't intend to let you out of sight, Jimmie, not until we get this little matter settled."

"You know the detective is working on it, Felix. He'll come up with something, I'm sure. He's a good man, thoroughly trained, years of experience behind him. Why don't you just relax and let the professional handle it, old friend."

"Is there another woman in Paris?" Anna Maria Lucia demanded. "Is that why you so afraid of company?"

"Now, Anna Maria Lucia . . ."

"I tell you this, Jimmie. I stay with you, Felix stay with you. We make the, what you say, *ménage à trois*, no? If this darling Susannah show up, I take care of her, no?"

Felix looked at her in shocked disapproval. "We don't want

any trouble with the girl," he said carefully. "We just want the little blue bag, ma'am. I think you really should go home and wait for Jimmie and me to take care of this little matter, just relax and leave it all up to us."

"And I think you are idiot! You and Jimmie both, idiots! They plan to meet in Paris, no? Is that not right? In Paris?"

The two men talking in low measured tones, the woman shrill and excited, they departed the expensive house in the suburbs and started the drive to the Tampa terminal, en route to Paris.

"That detective, he too is idiot!" Anna Maria Lucia cried. "Three leads! Bah! One woman alone at night and no one notices nothing. Bah!"

❖❖❖

Susannah and Brad returned to the Mexican place and he told her about the area he was mapping out. It was a blank on the map, he said, probably unexplored; they could do anything they wanted with it. Even put in a low mountain. He had made a map for their purposes, including the known rivers; he had added an invented one, the one the three escapees would use. They would get to the Amazon, risking rapids, a waterfall, piranhas, the pursuing Indians . . .

How excited he was, she thought. Like a boy making his first great discovery about life. Remembering his reaction to her suggestion that he was a writer, or should be, she wisely did not ask why he was so excited by a piece of fiction. Despite his statements to the contrary, it obviously had nothing to do with finding clues about her. She sensed that there was a mystery at his center, not like the simple mystery that surrounded her, something deeper, more meaningful, something too sore to touch.

"What will you do with the story when it's finished?" she asked later.

"We'll have to use a pseudonym," he said so quickly that she knew he had given it much thought already. "Not your name, because it isn't your real name. Certainly not mine. We'll make up a good third name and use that, share everything down the middle. That okay with you?"

"Of course. You think someone will publish it? How will you go about that?"

"I know an agent," he said evasively. "She'll handle the business end."

They finished the story before lunch the next day. "Can you type?" Brad asked, and shook his head quickly. He kept forgetting that she didn't know things like that. "Why don't you see if you can," he said.

She tried and they learned that she could probably type her letters, but nothing more complicated than that. She made frequent mistakes and was not a touch-typist.

Brad sighed. "Okay, I'll type the final copy. You go over it for spelling mistakes and stuff like that."

She was wandering restlessly about the apartment and now she objected. "I feel . . . very strange. I don't know how to describe it, but I need to do something, walk, run, ride a bicycle, swim, something physical. My muscles are twitchy."

Another clue? He frowned. He knew of no swimming pools, and he detested jogging. He hoped she was not a jogger. "A walk?" he asked hesitantly. She nodded and they went outdoors and headed for the park, and he felt only contentment. A walker. He usually walked miles almost every day, more often than not ending up lost, but unconcerned about it because no matter how lost one was in the city, it was always possible to get back home. There was always someone to ask, or a familiar street name, or something; it was not like getting lost in the countryside, or in the car where the landmarks came and went too fast to take advantage of them, and the streets all were one way — the wrong way — and other drivers had incredibly short tempers.

They walked in the park and he found himself talking about his childhood, something he certainly had not thought of telling anyone, had not thought about, in fact, for years.

He realized as he talked that she was the one person he could tell anything, everything, because she would forget it again, as soon as she recovered her memory. That night, tomorrow, next week, she would return to another life, forget him totally, forget anything he told her.

There was an ice cream vendor in front of the science museum. He bought them both ice creams and they wandered across the way to the pond before the de Young Museum and sat on the stonework watching the ducks. There, haltingly at first, then faster and faster, he told her about his father.

"You probably read some of his books when you were a kid," he said. "Funny pictures, funny creatures, nightmare stuff tamed into comical animals. They were very popular from the start. When I was born, we lived in New York City, but a couple of years later, before I was two, my mother got a divorce and he moved to a farm upstate. I stayed with him during the summer months, with her in the winter for the next three years until she got married again. Then I went to him for good and only saw her for weekends, sometimes for Christmas, that kind of stuff."

He began to toss bits of his cone into the pond; the ducks streaked over to squabble for them. "He took pictures of me endlessly," he said, watching the ducks. "He'd buy me stuff — a tractor once, big enough to ride — and then take hundreds of pictures of me trying to master it. The same with a tricycle, a bike later, pictures of me learning to swim, climbing trees, everything. I didn't think anything of it. He was a camera nut, simple as that. One of the things he bought was a desk with a typewriter, a portable that really worked. I was delighted with it, played with it for hours at a time, making X's, soldiers, making pictures with letters. He showed me how. And he took pictures of it all. He even set the stage for them a couple of times, crumpled papers and tossed them onto the floor, stuffed a wastebasket full of junk from his office, put a dictionary on the desk, really set a scene."

He put his hand down into the water, making waves, and the ducks fled, squawking furiously at this betrayal. "I never gave it a thought," he said. "When I was eleven or twelve it all stopped, no more pictures, no more setups. I was getting too big. And when I was fifteen one of my friends showed me a big glossy article about him in one of the women's magazines, how he worked, his inspiration, everything, and there I was. Picture after picture, first of me in the flesh, then how he had used that picture to draw his characters. It was always me — in a gorilla suit on a tractor, or in a dog suit typing, or with pretty curls, or something else, but it was me every time."

"*Hoy Boy, Rouse Mouse, Pinkie Wink, Draggin' Dragon . . .*" Susannah said softly. In her mind's eye she saw the covers, the illustrations, and they were all Brad.

"You've read them," he said in disgust. "I guess everyone's read them. He's still doing them, one a year. And it's still me." He stood up and wiped his hands on his legs. "This fall there will be a new one, and it'll be me, too."

He did not think to ask her how she knew children's books well enough to remember the titles when some that she had mentioned were less than ten years old, published at a time in her life when she would have been reading D. H. Lawrence or Henry Miller. She did not think to question that memory of the books, covers, inside illustrations. They started to walk back toward his apartment in silence, and neither of them noticed that she was leading the way.

8

*"The region of Turgenev,
where everyone lives . . . forever."*

Marlene looked Susannah over carefully and nodded. "Very nice," she said. Her hair had been styled beautifully, her makeup was perfect, she looked lovely. "This is Laurie," Marlene said, introducing a tall, strongly built woman with jet-black hair that was in bangs, cut short all over so that it clung like a shiny black cap. "And that's Martha," Marlene continued, indicating a younger woman who had on an apron with many bulging pockets. "They'll take over now," Marlene said. "I'll see how the house is filling up. Be right back." She rushed away to inspect the restaurant where the show would be held.

They were in Marlene's shop in the Embarcadero complex. Floor-length mirrors had been set up, and makeup tables arranged. Susannah had already met the other three models, and now she watched in fascination as each model in turn became wooden at Laurie's approach. No one moved, no one would dare, it was obvious. Laurie studied Rhonda first, walking all around her slowly. She adjusted a belt, arranged a lock of hair so that it lay on her cheek, accentuating her fine cheekbones. It was like that with them all, and each in turn submitted to the pats, the tugs, the adjustments without expression, apparently without awareness. When Laurie came to Susannah, she unbuttoned her sleeves, turned up the cuffs, then undid one more button on the shirtfront, opened it farther down. "Fix her finger," she said. Martha rushed over, drew out pancake makeup from a pocket, and applied it to the narrow white strip on Susannah's ring finger.

Susannah tried to remain as impassive as the others had done, but when Laurie touched her hair, involuntarily she recoiled. Martha hissed, "Hold still!" And Laurie gave the lock a sharp yank.

Marlene opened the door and said without entering, "Are you ready? It's a full house, girls. Extra tables in the rear. It might be a little crowded back there. Just watch out for the damn waiters, yield to them every time. Remember, you yield to them. They'll go around you. Pause, make an extra turn, or something. Let's go!"

The models were ready, the customers in place, the announcer in her raised seat, a three-piece ensemble playing softly. Marlene's models walked to the holding room, chatting easily, including Susannah in their small talk; they seemed at ease, relaxed, but Susannah sensed that they were nervous, more so than she was, and she wondered at her own lack of nervousness. She had nothing to lose, she thought then; this was not her job, not her future. She did not expect to be discovered and hired to pose for a magazine cover. She said nothing and knew that their chatter was a screen and she felt sorry for them in spite of her admiration and near envy for the way they walked, the way they held their heads, the way they wore the expensive clothes.

The promenade began and presently it was her turn to walk among the tables, stop at certain points, turn slowly, continue. "Don't make eye contact," Marlene had said. "That makes them uncomfortable, as if they're expected to comment or something. Today they're just looking. They're buyers, shop owners, fashion writers, people like that. They won't buy today, just take notes." She walked, noticing the many luncheon salads hardly touched, the many Bloody Marys, the wineglasses, the plants growing down the walls from the ledges of the upper-floor balconies. She finished her first walk and hurried back to change. This outfit was a two-piece dress suit, high heels, scarf fluttering behind when she moved. Her next costume was a three-piece pantsuit, the jacket to be worn over her shoulders casually. Laurie and Martha helped her into it, made adjustments, and went on to the next model who had come back. Susannah returned to the holding room, and presently was on her way again.

There were eight models for this section. They were showing professional women's clothes: suits, dresses with jackets, jumpers, sweaters and skirts . . . They entered in pairs and split up while the announcer talked on and on about fabrics, pointing out details . . .

Brad had not planned to attend this madness; until he actually walked inside the Hyatt lobby he had thought he would go to one of the small bars and wait it out. Instead he was standing outside the rail that separated the walking traffic from the diners, and he looked for her. He saw her as soon as she entered and it pleased him that her mimicry of the other models was so perfect that no one would have guessed that until that day she had never modeled a thing in her life. Or had she? She did it well enough to be a professional. She looked remote, withdrawn, somehow apart from the crowded dining room, apart from the stares, the merciless probing examination the patrons gave each model in turn. Mannequin, he thought, that was exactly right. They stopped being human and became things. He opened his fists and a moment later found them clenched again.

Susannah looked at the musicians, a woman in a long black skirt playing violin, a man in a tuxedo with a cello, a very heavy man seated at the piano. They played well, classical music, muted in order not to interfere with the announcer's running monologue, not to interfere with the rise and fall of murmurs, conversations, orders to waiters. She watched out for the hurrying waiters, froze whenever one came her way.

She made her stops, turned, continued, and then she saw Brad and a smile came to her lips; she lowered her gaze almost instantly, remembering Marlene's instructions. They were supposed to remain impersonal, make eye contact with no one, walk, stop, turn, walk, not see anyone, not notice if anyone was drawing sketches, making notes. Impersonal. When she looked away from Brad, she found herself gazing into the eyes of a woman seated just inside the rail. She was immobilized by the intensity of hatred that was glaring up at her.

The woman was over sixty, her hair colored an impossible black, her eyes shrouded with shadow, false lashes, her eyebrows peaked with carefully applied pencil. She wore a pink linen suit, gold jewelry, earrings, necklace. Money, money said everything about her. But good clothes, hair color, makeup, jewelry, none of it could change her age, and none of it could conceal the fact that she was seventy-five pounds overweight.

Susannah moistened her lips, unable to look away from the woman's malevolent eyes. "Why do you hate me?" Susannah whispered. "Do you know me? What have I done?"

The woman, Mrs. Leonora Beam, snarled, "Slut! Hussy!"

"It's not me, though, is it? Not really me. It's . . . all this . . ." She swept her hand up and down to indicate the clothes, everything. "Because I am young, pretty."

Mrs. Beam leaned forward furiously. "How dare you talk to me like that! I'll have you fired! What's your name?"

Susannah drew in a breath and now she too leaned inward, spoke in a low voice, conspiratorially. "Nadia Leontov. Don't tell, for God's sake, madam, please don't tell them you met me, where I am. My father was a distant relative of the czar, a prince, and now only I remain. But always they search for me, others like me who escaped the terror. Ah! The things I saw! My mother, my beautiful mother . . . And my father! Three times they threw him from the window. Too strong to die. They couldn't kill him! How his eyes blazed at them! Always I remember the fire in his eyes. He would tell them nothing, nothing."

"This is preposterous!" Mrs. Beam cried, looking past Susannah for help.

"My father was a scientist," Susannah said. "You've heard of the region of Turgenev, where everyone lives, it seems, forever? That was his work, to find the secret. I lived there as a child, but then the revolution ... Ah, madam, the things I saw!"

"You're too young!" Mrs. Beam was staring fixedly at Susannah now, forgetful of the surroundings, of the patrons at nearby tables watching the whispered dialogue curiously, unaware of Brad's frantic gestures to Susannah to stop, to go away.

"There my grandmother was like my sister, my mother like a girl always. My father, Prince Alexander Stanislaus Tolstoi Leontov, world famous for his work in genetics, he find out why, and they torture him, beat him, throw him from the window many times, and he . . . He refused to tell."

"What did he find out?" Mrs. Beam had half risen from her seat now, clutching the table with both hands.

"The water," Susannah whispered. "From a spring deep in the mountain. And the B foods."

"Vitamin B?"

"No. B foods. Broccoli, beets, Brussels sprouts . . ."

"Barley?"

"Most assuredly. And bleu cheese and beans . . ."

"Beef?"

"Never any meat! Fish: bream and blue fish, bivalves."

"Jane, dear, it's time for your next change," Marlene said, taking her arm, tugging it gently. She looked at Mrs. Beam to apologize, but she was staring into space with a stunned expression. Susannah leaned forward and whispered to her once more and she squealed and fell back into her chair and started to fan herself with her menu.

Marlene pulled Susannah away then, but she turned once more and said softly over her shoulder, "Bananas and butternuts." Marlene was mystified at Mrs. Beam's grateful nod.

Behind the rail Brad had a notebook out and was scribbling furiously.

Marlene waved Laurie and Martha away when they drew near to undress and redress Susannah. "She's finished for now,"

Marlene said. "She's been ill, you know. Let her rest in the lounge for a while, and get her own clothes on." She drew Susannah back to the rear room and gently pushed her into a chair. "Rest a few minutes, dear. I can't stay, but I'll be back later."

Susannah whispered to her, "You won't tell them where I am? They would take me back. They think I know the secret."

"I won't tell them," Marlene said. "I promise. You just rest a minute." At that moment she wanted to hold this lost girl, cuddle her, make her well again. She acknowledged these surfacing maternal instincts with a mixture of glee and derision.

Susannah leaned back with her eyes closed, her head against the wall, and presently she opened her eyes and blinked. It must be time to get into the next outfit, she thought, and stood up, started to undress. Martha rushed in and helped with the designer clothes, darted out again. "You're finished," she said. "Get your own things on."

Susannah dressed slowly; she heard Monica come in and change, heard the whispers that were hardly comprehensible: "She insulted Mrs. Beam, or did something to her. She left almost instantly. Someone said she went straight to a travel agent in the lobby."

"What could she have said to her?"

"God knows."

Martha peered in at Susannah once, started to speak, changed her mind, and became busy with Rhonda.

Susannah remembered. Slut, hussy, hatred. Slowly she walked from the shop, hesitated when she did not see an outside door, then turned and walked the corridors looking for a way out of the Embarcadero. Slut, hussy. Hatred. Pitiless hatred. Why?

She walked, a solitary figure in the wide corridors, past men's wear shops, children's clothing, toys, a book store . . . She passed people who knew where they were going, hurried to arrive; and she passed others who loitered aimlessly and looked as lost as she was, but she did not speak to any of them, did not ask directions. Once she went up an escalator, and later she went down one; once she found herself walking in the sunlight, but still within the sprawling development. And finally she went through a doorway and found herself on a sidewalk with traffic in the street, and sky overhead, and she knew she had escaped the maze.

She walked, hardly noticing the shops, the offices, the construction going on. Later, a man fell into step beside her and whispered in an inaudible voice. She glanced at him indifferently and continued her steady pace. He whispered louder and she caught some of the words: suck those pretty titties . . . stick it up your ass . . . five dollars . . . It seemed to have nothing to do with her and she did not look at him again, but kept thinking of the woman in the dining room, wondering why that woman had hated her, and wondering most of all what had happened. There was a blank. She had been looking at that woman and then she had been back in the shop and she did not know anything that connected the two memories. The man touched her arm and she came to a stop and looked at him. T-shirt, jeans, thirty years old perhaps.

"Do you know me?"

"I want to know you," he said in a whisper. His hand tightened on her arm and he started to pull.

She yanked free. "Go away. I have to think." She turned her back on him and started to walk again, already immersed in her thoughts.

For a few seconds he watched her, unable to comprehend her lack of fear, her lack of anxiety. He looked for someone else, spotted a redhead and started to walk toward her. She saw him and hurriedly crossed the street; he followed happily. She was almost running.

Susannah knew that something terrible had happened. It was like the story she had told Brad in the beginning, she thought. Sometimes she seemed to lie outrageously and at great length, and she did not know why, did not remember doing it, or what she said. She took a deep breath. She was getting very tired; she did not know how long she had been walking, or where she was. She looked at the buildings now, shops, an Italian restaurant, and next to it a Chinese restaurant. A theater with pornographic posters of Chinese women with no clothes on. A fenced-in building, set back from the street, a public building of some sort with wide stairs and many people going in and out. Most of the people going in were women; she slowed her pace to examine the building. There was a placard: A ROOM OF ONE'S OWN. Virginia Woolf, she thought. A women's room, a place where she could sit down and rest a few minutes and get directions about a bus.

She followed the other women inside and saw another smaller sign with the same words and an arrow under it. Most of the women were heading in that direction, and she did too, thinking only of a chair.

"Are you preregistered?" someone asked in a pleasant voice.

Susannah saw a woman seated at a card table covered with papers. She shook her head. The woman was near double doors through which Susannah could see into an auditorium with what looked like a scramble of chairs instead of orderly rows.

"Okay," the woman said, and fished a plastic badge from a cigar box. She was very handsome, middle-aged, with graying hair, and little makeup. Her eyes were bright blue. "The workshops are for preregistered participants only, I'm afraid. But there are several open discussion groups. There's Problems with Reentry, and You, Your Job and the Law, and Identity Crisis." She smiled at Susannah and waited for her decision.

"Identity Crisis," Susannah said, and watched her write a large number two on the badge. The woman handed her the badge and turned her attention to someone else. Susannah, holding the badge, entered the auditorium.

Now she could see that the chairs were arranged in circles, eight or ten chairs in each group. At the other side of the large room there was a food counter with many women milling about getting fruit juices and cookies. Other women were talking in small clusters, or wandering idly looking at amateur art on the walls. There were young teen-aged girls and women past sixty, but most of them seemed to be in their twenties or thirties. The apparel was as varied as their ages — everything from jeans and T-shirts to expensive dresses and suits.

"You new here?" a voice asked close to her ear. She turned to see a teen-ager in a leather jacket and jeans tucked into boots; her hair was cut so close to her scalp that it stood up like newly sprouted grass. The girl was carrying a chain that she thwacked against her hand over and over.

"Yes," Susannah said.

"Thought so. You look sort of lost. What's your number?"

Susannah showed her the badge and the girl said, "That way, near the stage. The whole fucking meeting should be about identity crisis, you ask me." She thwacked her hand softly.

"Why are you carrying that chain?" Susannah asked.

"Any guy so much as looks cross-eyed at me, he gets it."

"You give him the chain?"

"Right across his ugly face. Or maybe in the balls. Depends."

"Oh, you hit people with it!" She took a step backward.

"Not people. Men."

"Why?"

"Are you kidding me? All they know is violence! I've seen how they knock women around. Wham, bam, and thank you ma'am, and take that. You give them the right to knock you up, they think they have the right to knock you down." She swung the chain; it whistled in the air.

Taking another step backward, Susannah said, "One knocked me down. Out in the street."

"See! Violence! Knock you down, bat you around, bam, pow, all they know. What did you do?"

"Nothing. I was unconscious."

"After you came to."

"I couldn't do anything. I was in the hospital. At first they thought I was crazy."

"Sweet goddess! See what I mean! You get raped and it's your fault because you had on shorts, or a dress, or tight pants, or none of the above. You were out when you should have been in. You get knocked out, land in a hospital, and you're crazy!

72

Crazy for not crawling back into a hole and waiting for the prick to come do it again maybe. Where's the fucker now?"

"Home, I guess. But I don't want anyone to hit him with a chain. I can't let you do that. It wasn't his fault. I don't blame him. There were two or three others who started it; they told me all about it in the hospital. He couldn't really stop himself."

"Couldn't stop himself! Out of control! Uncontrollable passion! Sweet goddess! That's what they always say!" She was watching Susannah intently and suddenly she let the chain fall, and winced as it smacked her leg. "You live with him, don't you? Don't you?"

Susannah was trying to walk backward without giving the impression that she was moving. She nodded. "In his house . . . I don't have anywhere else . . ." She bumped into someone who caught her by the shoulders.

"Don't be frightened," the newcomer said. "Marly isn't going to hurt you." She was very tall and elegant, with a soft gray chiffon dress and an emerald in the side of her nose. "You're new, aren't you? Well, this is the Women's Room and we meet every Saturday. I'm Patricia Lundquist. Sometimes there are lectures, sometimes workshops, for coping with jobs, children, separatist theories and practices, whatever our members want." She was gently leading Susannah away from the furious girl who was twirling her chain in wide circles.

"She's married," Marly shouted after them. "And he beats her! She's protecting the fucker! Women like her deserve to get beaten unconscious in the street!"

"Do you need help?" Patricia asked in a low voice. "We can help you. There are places you can go if you're afraid."

Susannah shook her head. "It isn't like that," she said. "But thank you. Marly didn't understand what I was trying to say."

"The very young are so uninhibited, aren't they? I find it refreshing much of the time, but it can be a trial ... Marly sincerely believes that if a woman loves a man, she has betrayed the cause." She had led Susannah to one of the circles near the stage. "They're already getting themselves arranged," she said.

"Just take a chair and in a minute you'll all introduce yourselves and get started. I'll talk to you afterward, if you like."

Susannah nodded. She would like to talk to this woman, ask her advice about a job, about everything. She felt that she would be given good advice. She was grateful that she finally had a chair; for a while she could relax and rest and not have to try to understand anything.

Almost as soon as Susannah was seated, the leader began:

"I'm Marianne," she said softly. "I'm a social worker in family planning, and I'm gay. I was chosen to lead off in this group because I started my women's work in a group just like it a year ago. What we'll do is go around and introduce ourselves, say whatever you like, and then we'll open it in a free discussion." She nodded to the woman on her left.

"I'm Kathy. For the last six months I've been living in a women's commune in Marin County, but it's time to go back to work, and I don't know what I want to do. I was trained to teach elementary school, but I don't want to go back to it. And I'm divorced," she added, then looked to her left at the next woman.

"Wanda. Gay separatist. Busted for demonstrating at Sacramento. Put in a mental hospital for observation, four months." She turned to look at Susannah with a hostile scowl.

Susannah said nothing until Marianne prodded gently. "Just tell us who you are, where you're from."

Susannah nodded and took a breath. "My name is Oshana, and I'm from a planet called Arretxul."

Beside her, Wanda muttered, "Bloody Jesus! And I was put away!"

Marianne hushed her with a glance. "Go on," she said.

"Yes. I was sent here to tell you about our world. To prepare you. We live in shelters that are organic, we grow them and they care for us, give us food — fruits and nuts and sweet saps to drink. Everyone paints and writes poetry and dances. We have no wars, no injustices, no wants. There is perfect equality for all."

"And what are the guys doing while the women are sitting around in Eden?" Wanda asked harshly.

"There are no men," Susannah said, looking at her in wonder. "I thought you understood that. When the males are two years old we weed them out; we keep and maintain only the strongest and healthiest, the ones with the most desirable genetic qualities. The others are sacrificed to the Holy Mother who nourishes our shelters with them. At fourteen at the latest the selected youths donate their sperm to the ice caves and they join their little brothers joyously, to sustain our shelters. There are no adult males. As soon as the boys start to show the signs — facial hair, odors, the strange vocal changes, all the manifestations of approaching bestiality — we know it is time."

No one was moving in the circle; they were all watching her, some with wariness, some with absorption. "We were sent here and to other worlds by the Holy Mother," she went on. "It is time to liberate her daughters. She instructed us about the worlds we would see, the hideous injustices done to our sisters in the name of the fallen, false god, who was at one time Her consort, but who became totally corrupted by power. He knows that when he hurts one of Her daughters, She suffers and he heaps on the hurts, the insults and humiliations. This is the final battle. Males are learning the secret of reproducing themselves through cloning, and when that process is fully understood and implemented, they no longer will want women since they regard themselves as the ultimate perfection. If the Holy Mother acts now to free Her daughters, remove them to worlds of their own, like my beloved Arretxul, the males will be defeated, and in a short time the universe will be freed of their violence, their corruption. Without the aid of their females, they will not be able to perfect the cloning process. They will wear dirty clothes, be driven to distraction by mismatched socks, become fat, flabby and weak from high-cholesterol fast foods. They won't be able to find anything at home, or in their files. Their teeth will fall out because they will forget to make dental appointments. They will have to stay home to tend the beastly boy children because the schools will be closed for the lack of teachers." She paused for breath and someone began to clap; others joined in.

"When is the Holy Mother going to take us away?"

"I don't know. She needs a sign that you are ready, that you accept Her. A small temple in a clearing. White. It must be all white. She will see it."

Just then the double doors burst inward with a crash and a deep voice called out, "Where the hell do you register for this meeting?"

Four men stood in the open doorway; one of them was smoking a cigar.

"You can't smoke in here!" someone yelled at him.

"Yeah? Who says? Call the fire marshal and have him tell me that."

"Gwendolyn! Where the fuck is my wife? I want to sit in with my wife! Any law against that?"

While the shouting was going on, the women had left their circles and advanced on the men at the doorway. Many of them were yelling at once, drowning out the male voices until only occasional oaths were clear enough to be heard. Near the food counter, Patricia Lundquist mounted a chair and beat a pan with a spoon for attention.

"Please, please! Everyone! Please take your seats again . . ."

"Yeah! Sit the fuck down!" one of the men shouted in the comparative silence and the screams and shouts started again, louder than before.

Susannah had stayed near her circle, but as the crowd near the door swelled, she began to edge around the room, keeping outside the milling swarm. She moved warily until she was near enough to the doors to dart outside. Men and women were rushing toward the auditorium from both directions. She ran past them to the main entrance and out to the sidewalk, kept running to the corner where she stopped to catch her breath. She held up her hand and a taxi stopped for her. She climbed in and sank back with her eyes closed, taking deep breaths.

Before the driver could pull out into traffic a police car appeared, siren wailing. Susannah and the driver both turned to watch it stop halfway down the block; two uniformed policemen leaped out and raced inside the building.

"Wonder what's going on," the driver said.

"I don't know."

When he asked where she wanted to go, she told him Brad's address and wondered again what had happened at the fashion show.

Another police car hurtled past them, and a moment later a third one.

"You must have just missed it, whatever it is," the driver said.

She nodded. "I'm glad. I don't like crowds and riots."

"Yeah, me too." And he began to tell her in exquisite detail all about the Berkeley riots of a few years back.

Another siren screamed nearby and Susannah turned to look once more at the building where they were converging. She had been there, she remembered. She had been looking for a place to sit down and rest; more of it came back to her: Marly and her chain, the circles. Abruptly there were no further memories of the building or the women's meeting. With a wrench she realized that she had done it again; she curled her fingers into fists to keep from trembling.

9

*"If you can't trust
your mama, who can you trust?"*

Carlos Castillo drove slowly through the village, eight miles west of Tucson. He waved to Manuel and Maria who stood in their open doorway, and then he waved more vigorously to his mother who was on her porch rocking gently. On the passenger seat of his seventy-one Ford truck the blue suitcase slid back and forth as he braked and went through one pothole after another. His own house was on the outskirts of the village, and it, like the other two- and three-room buildings, was adobe with a tin roof; the yards were dirt and sand with a straggly orange tree here, a Joshua tree there, a cluster of pecan trees with limp leaves unstirring in the heat.

Serena was standing in the doorway of their house, smiling happily at him when he ran up the one step, crossed the porch.

He caressed her hair and stroked her neck and kissed her many times. "I was so worried about you," he murmured. "I dreamed that you went to the hospital alone, that you had four sons."

She laughed softly. "Never! I waited, but soon, very soon." Her pregnancy was near term; her face was thin; her eyes were radiant.

"I have a present for you," he said then. He ran to the truck and brought the suitcase in to her and together they marveled at its beauty. She emptied the plastic shopping bag on their bed and refolded the few things that spilled out. Baby clothes that she had made, a pretty gown for herself, a handmade housecoat from her sister. She carefully packed everything in the new blue suitcase.

"I will take off that other name," Carlos said.

"It doesn't matter. It could be a name, or it could be what it says, Dawn, a new day." She looked at him. "You sold all the . . . everything?"

He nodded.

"But no more. You promised. No more."

He said nothing. Every evening at dusk, when visibility was poor, when sounds carried far, he went out onto the desert, dug up the stinking cactus plants, and wrapped them carefully in burlap; when he had enough, he drove to the city with them, met with men who bought them and put them in their shops and resold them to the landscapers and the home owners who wanted a piece of the desert. He did not deal in Tucson where he was known, and probably watched; he drove across the desert to Los Angeles to conduct his business.

"If they catch you," Serena said, more as if speaking to herself than to him, "I will die. If you leave me, if they put you in prison, you will die, and I also."

He was thinking of the doctor in Tucson, and the hospital, and the priest who would christen the child, and the price of gasoline, and rent and beans and tortillas. He said nothing.

The next day Serena's sister Margarita came to stay until the baby was born and Serena was well again. "It is the prettiest suitcase I ever saw," she said truthfully.

"Yes. But Carlos needs the tire. The money should have bought a tire, not that."

"Okay. I'll buy it from you, whatever he paid. When you come home from the hospital, I'll buy it."

"I wish you were not going to Chicago. You'll write every week, won't you? It is so far!"

"Not that far. Think, Serena, my own room with a bath! Two

days a week off from work, to do whatever I want! I'll save so much money, and soon I'll come home again."

Serena shook her head; it was not for her. For her, the only life was with Carlos in their little house, with the baby soon to join them, and the little garden out back to watch, and the pig and the chickens. That was life, not in someone else's house in a distant city, cleaning someone else's floors, making their beds, cooking their meals. She thought Margarita was loco.

Anna Maria Lucia talked to her mother from a phone booth in Charles de Gaul Airport while she and Felix waited for Jimmie to check in.

"What did you tell her?" Felix asked, when she hung up. "You didn't mention anything about our little problem, now did you? There's no reason to worry anyone else about it, you know. We can handle it."

"You, Jimmie, bah! I tell my mama everything. I always tell my mama everything." She swept past him looking for the bar where Jimmie said they would meet. It was true that she told her mother everything, but not some things, not, for instance, that Jimmie had married other women. Her mother would tell her cousin three times removed, who would tell his brother, who would tell someone else, and finally a distant relative would pay a call on Jimmie and shoot him dead for dishonoring their family. Because she did not want Jimmie dead, she did not tell her mother every single thing. But she had told her about the suitcase and its hidden fortunes and the business partner who had run away with it, threatening ruination for her and her husband. And her mother would tell her cousin three times removed, who would tell his brother, who would tell someone else, and finally a distant relative would find poor little Susannah and recover the lost suitcase and return it to Jimmie who would pay off Felix and get rid of him and use what was left to take Anna Maria Lucia to many exotic places and treat her very well.

"Uh, Anna Maria Lucia, you want to tell me exactly what you said to your mother? I mean, we don't want just anyone looking for that little suitcase, you see. It's not worth bothering anyone else with, such a little matter."

She looked at him scornfully. "You think I am born today? You think I don't know nothing? What is worth twenty thousands of dollars to you? National secrets? Dope? What? No, I don't tell the policia, I only tell my mama."

"Well," Felix said slowly, doubtfully, "if you can't trust your mama, who can you trust?"

10

In which Brad dines out — twice

When Brad heard her key in the door he rushed across the room only to stop a few feet short as she entered.

"Where were you? I looked everywhere. I was worried. I have to call Marlene. She's worried too."

"I'm sorry. I didn't think . . . I was walking."

"All this time? It's been hours! I thought you were lost or something."

"I am lost," she said. "I'm awfully tired. May I sit down?"

Helplessly he moved aside and allowed her to come into the room. He called Marlene as Susannah wearily sank down into one of the big chairs and eased her shoes off.

"You have a date, don't you?" she asked, when he hung up.

He sat opposite her. "Not until seven. Are you all right?"

"I think so. I was thinking a lot. Part of the time I was somewhere, a public building of some sort, a women's meeting, but I don't remember most of it. And then I was in a taxi. I'm . . . That isn't normal, is it, not to remember where I went, what I did, the people I talked to?"

He shook his head. "But it's part of your amnesia. When you get over this, that will be okay too."

"What if I don't get over it?" she asked, rubbing her foot, looking at it intently. "I'm empty inside, like those models are when they're working. People are made of bits and pieces of their past — here a scolding, there a hug, a birthday party, all those things. First-grade fears, teen-ager anxieties, how they got through them, things their parents taught them, things they learned from watching other kids. People are the sum of everything they've done, everything they've thought, everything others have done to them, things they weren't even aware of at the time. All of that defines who you are right now, at this moment. If you tap real people, all that comes spilling out. If you tap me, there's nothing. I might deflate, be nothing but a piece of skin on the floor. Or else, I'll tell you an incredible lie. It scares me to lie like that, not be able to stop, or even know I'm doing it. And then not know what kind of lie I've told afterward. I think I did it again," she said in a subdued voice. "In the women's building. There was a riot."

"It won't last," he said, feeling more helpless than ever. A riot? He saw her being hit with a bottle, being knocked down, trampled on by a mob, being hauled away by the feet by policemen... "It won't last," he said again. "And until you're well, please just stay with me, here in the apartment, or at dinner, shopping."

"I know it won't last," she said, almost too low to hear, "and when it ends, all this will vanish."

She waved her hand, indicating the apartment, the cat on the windowsill, Brad. "I want to go somewhere else," she said. "An institution, something like that. I'm not your responsibility and I shouldn't be. It isn't fair for you to have to worry about me."

Brad stood up and moved aimlessly about the room. "No. That's the worst thing you could do. You're... In a funny way that I can't even begin to explain, you're doing me a favor. Don't ask how, or what I mean, because I don't know. But you are. Please believe me."

She jumped up and said angrily, "And that's part of my problem! I don't know enough to believe you or not believe you. I can't compare what you're saying to anything in the past. How many men have said to me, please believe me? How many times have I wished I hadn't?"

He shook his head. "I don't know. There's no real reason for you to trust me after what I did to you, but I wish you would. In a couple of weeks I have to go to Washington. Will you just try to trust me that long? We can decide then what you should do, if you still have amnesia."

She picked up her shoes and walked toward her room. "All right. But we have to try to find out. A picture in the paper, something like that. Someone must know me! You can't just lose a person and not realize it! I must have parents, a family, someone who misses me, or at least knows I'm gone."

At the hallway she stopped once more and looked at him gloomily. "What if they're just glad I'm gone? What if I was so terrible that they're sighing with relief right now? Maybe they just hope I'll never show up again."

"I'll never believe anything like that!"

"But we can't know. There's no way to know."

"... and he actually came to the office and plunked down one hundred dollars in silver! I said, 'Mr. Ryder, do you realize the value of silver right now?' and he said, 'Girlie' — he always calls me Girlie — 'if I didn't know I wouldn't have given it to you.' Brad, are you even listening to me?"

Brad brought his eyes back into focus and looked at Donna across the tiny table from him. She was lovely that night, with a shiny silver dress off her shoulders, her hair done up somehow, like a black crown with a glitter here and there. "Sure," he said. "Something about a stock split, something like that."

"That was half an hour ago. Oh, just eat your pie."

He looked at his plate in confusion. They were still on the entree; veal something or other smothered in sauce was getting cold. He took a bite and chewed methodically, not tasting it.

"When you go back east," Donna said, "you have to look up Hiram Wakeley, at Columbia. I mentioned you to him, remember? He's very interested, and I'm sure there's an opening at Columbia. They're really very aggressive in getting the best and the brightest for their faculty."

"I've been thinking that maybe I won't look for a job teaching right away," Brad said with his mouth full. He could not seem to get rid of a piece of gristle. He remembered then that he did not like veal; anemic beef, that's all it was. Sick and anemic and gristly beef.

"Why in the world not? What else can you possibly do with your Ph.D.?"

"Not much. I've been thinking I might take up archaeology, go somewhere and dig a few years. South America, maybe."

"You're kidding! That's an insane idea! It would take you six years of study!"

He nodded. The piece of gristle seemed to be expanding as he chewed it.

"You poor dear," Donna said, reaching across the table to pat his wrist. "You've been working so hard for so long. No wonder you feel tired and discouraged. Finish your dissertation, and then take a long rest. You'll feel differently about it after you have a vacation."

He had to get rid of the gristle; he could not chew on it forever. Finally, pretending a cough, he put his napkin to his mouth and spat out the offending lump, but then he had a napkin in his lap with a sizeable, chewed-on piece of gristle. If he could slip it onto his plate, he could hide it under a piece of the limp escarole garnish. He palmed it and eased his hand up to the table just as Donna leaned forward.

"Brad, don't you believe me? Just give it a try, will you? Finish up . . ." She took his hand in both of hers and found his clenched in a fist. "Darling, relax. It isn't that bad . . ." As she spoke she was working her fingers between his and she stopped when she felt something slimy and warm in her hand.

For Donna this was the worst moment of her life, or very nearly. She was a fastidious person, had never played in mud, or with Play Doh, or finger paints. She refused all finger food, anything that could possibly run onto her hand, like ice cream, or watermelon. She was certain that all dark corners, long-unopened boxes, shoes out of storage, and even the recesses of her own desk drawers held unspeakable crawling things that were waiting for her to offer a finger. It never had occurred to her that she had to be on guard in a restaurant like this, expensive, catering only to the socially elite. But now suddenly she had in her hand one of the monstrosities that had threatened her all her life. With a shriek of terror she flung it away, and jerked back from the table. In her swift motion, she upset the tiny candle holder, upset the candle, and spilled melted wax that was instantly aflame.

She screamed again as the tablecloth flared, and, unnoticed by her and Brad, across the room there was another shriek as something propelled through the air fell with a splash into another patron's vichyssoise, spraying fragrant soup in all directions.

On both sides of the room there was pandemonium now. Diners were shouting directions, telling Brad not to throw water on the fire, just as he emptied his glass on the flames, which danced away and burned more furiously.

"Call the fire department!"

"Let's get out of here!"

"What happened?"

Waiters were rushing in, two of them with fire extinguishers.

"They were fighting and she slapped him and he threw a glass at her!"

"I tell you something was swimming in my soup! It splashed me!"

"Poltergeist! Things started flying all over the place!"

"I know what I saw! It burst into flames, and then she screamed!"

"He's drunk! Knocked it over . . ."

Presently Donna and Brad stood on the street in the midst of the other patrons who were fleeing the firetrap. Somehow Brad's entire leg had been wet with ice water and he started to shiver. Donna had counted to ten half a dozen times and was halfway there again. The front of her silver dress was specked with fire retardant. Silently they walked around the building to the parking lot and got in Donna's MG.

"I'll drop you at your house," she said through clenched teeth.

He nodded miserably. He wanted to ask her if she knew what had happened, but at the moment he thought it wiser to ask nothing, say nothing. He had the disconcerting feeling that he had been plunged all at once into an ongoing nightmare without first falling asleep.

She drove fast, with jack rabbit starts, and hard, jerky stops. Her mother was right, he was a klutz. But damn it, he was her klutz, and she would teach him manners, house-train him, do whatever it took to make him presentable in public. And he would finish his dissertation, if she had to write the goddam thing for him, and he would teach at Columbia. They would have a Park Avenue address and she would manage his father's money and have her name on that Mount Olympus list if it killed him.

She skidded to a stop at his apartment.

"Look, Donna . . ."

"Good night!" She was starting again before he got the door closed. But, damn it, she thought furiously, what had he been holding in the restaurant? Where had it come from? She shuddered at the next thought: Maybe it was something he always carried with him.

Susannah looked up in surprise when Brad came into the apartment so early. "Is something wrong?" She put down the notebook she had been writing in.

"No. Have you eaten yet?"

She shook her head. "I had a bath and a nap. I'll find something in a few minutes. Why?"

"Let's go eat. I have to change first."

"Go where? Should I change?" She was wearing her jeans and a shirt, sandals.

"You're fine. I'll just be a minute." He dashed into his room and very quickly was back, wearing jeans also. "Let's go."

On the sidewalk she asked, "But what happened? Why did you come home so soon?"

"Oh, the table caught on fire and people were throwing fire

extinguisher junk around, and I got wet. This way. There's a pretty good all-night Italian place a couple of blocks over. Good cannelloni, great coffee."

"Fire? Are you all right?"

"Yeah. Look, about that story you told that woman today, I guess you don't remember any of it, do you?"

"No."

"Okay. That's what I thought. Let's do it the same way we did the other one. I'll tell you as much as I know and we'll knock together a finished story. Leslie Knowles rides again." He was laughing softly as he took her arm and steered her around the corner. Leslie Knowles, the new bright spot in the American literary scene, he was thinking. He had picked the Leslie part, because, he had said, it could be either male or female. She had chosen Knowles, because she thought names that started with K and sounded like N were funny, and because, she had added mysteriously, "Who is that masked writer? Leslie Knowles."

They ordered and while they waited for the food, Brad told her the story. "So here she is, a woman of what? seventy? who looks no more than twenty-five or twenty-six. And she has this terrible secret, the secret of longevity. Why hasn't she told anyone?"

"Because the water is in Russia? She doesn't want the Russians to have it?"

"Maybe. She has a real hatred of Communists because of what they did to her mother and father, of course, but that makes it pretty political."

They ate, talking, and had coffee, talking.

"At least part of the story has to be in the village, and it has to be the way it was in nineteen eighteen up through the early twenties. No highways, for instance. What do you suppose they lived in? What kind of houses?"

She shook her head, thought about it. "Heavy timbers. There would be plenty of woods there, and cold in the winter. Big iron stoves. A trading village? No, too traveled."

At one they left the restaurant and they talked all the way back to the apartment, up the stairs, talked while they both got settled comfortably. "Okay, she knows but she doesn't realize what it is she knows," Brad said. "She can't explain why she doesn't seem to get older, but she's lonesome. One by one her lovers begin to age and eventually she is forced to leave them. They think she's a witch, or some of them do. How's that sound?"

"Pretty melodramatic."

"Well, it's a melodramatic story."

Susannah giggled, then yawned. "What if she does know and has to go back periodically to renew the treatment. They'd think she was a spy or something."

"Too melodramatic," Brad said. "Makes her too calculating."

Susannah continued, ignoring his objection. "And there is a plan to dam the stream, make a huge lake for hydroelectrical power, and the water will be too diluted, joined with too many other streams, no longer magic."

Brad picked it up. "A young officer, no more than a boy, was on the scene when her mother was arrested, and he fell in love with her. Now he's the head of KGB, and somehow he sees the reincarnation of that woman whose face has haunted him all these years. He's an old man, but seeing the girl brings it all back, and he has her seized. She innocently tells him everything. But when he goes to the village he finds that only a year or two ago, they did dam the valley, the stream is gone, the villagers scattered past finding again." He looked at her and slowly she nodded, yawning.

"I have to go to bed," she said a few minutes later. "I'm falling asleep sitting here."

He had started to read an encyclopedia article about Russia, the section near the Afghanistan border, the villages there. He hardly even looked up as she left the room. A minute later when he spoke to her and she did not answer, he realized that she had gone to bed, and that it was three in the morning. He never had been so happy.

Only when he got into bed did he feel how tired he was, too tired to sleep. Their story kept running over and over in his head: he saw scenes, the villagers, the small girl being smuggled out over the mountains to safety . . .

She was his muse, he thought drifting between wakefulness and sleep. She said in the beginning that she had been sent, and he believed her. She had been sent to him. She was his muse. He drifted closer to oblivion, seeing her in a flowing white gown, radiant, his muse. Then he plunged over the edge into sleep.

11

*Thou shalt not covet
thy neighbor's wife.*

Donna hung up the phone and looked at Marlene, who was on the couch reading the Sunday paper. "He doesn't answer. I guess he's sulking after last night." She was dressed for golf, her bag by the door.

"Did you mention going out with him today?"

"No. But we've played every Sunday for five weeks. You'd think he'd remember."

Marlene turned the page and tried to read. She was concentrating on not thinking about Brad nearly burning down the restaurant. If she thought of it, she would laugh again, and Donna would have a tantrum. She stared at the paper.

"Mother, I want to talk to you." Donna glanced at her watch. If she could not reach him in half an hour, she would have to cancel their appointment with the pro. She did not care at that moment, although she had insisted that Brad learn to play. Since he did not drink, did not like bars, there was little opportunity for him to mingle with important people informally. Golf would fix that. She visualized him on the greens with the president of Columbia, with an important columnist, someone high in the State Department. She saw a foursome with herself talking animatedly to the chairman of the board of... anything. Any chairman of any board would do for openers.

"It's about that woman at Brad's apartment," Donna said, sitting down opposite her mother. "It isn't fair to her that no one's doing anything to find out who she is, where she's from. Conover won't touch it unless she goes to him herself, and so far she hasn't done that. But someone should make a move."

"You mean me," Marlene said drily.

"She likes you and trusts you. Conover said something ridiculous about invasion of privacy, something of that sort. Since she isn't a ward of the state, she's a free agent, and you can't simply publish her photograph without her consent. I think he's full of shit, but he's standing by that. But you could talk to her, get her to see that it's for her own good. And you could be the box number for people to write to. Someone would have to screen any responses that come in. You know, if she has a birthmark, something to identify her with positively, they would have to mention it in detail. And you have those pictures from the show yesterday."

Marlene admired her daughter's mind. It was like a twisting maze with cunning traps, unexpected dead ends, so devious that she doubted any rat could learn to run it. She could almost follow Donna's planning, but she never would have come up with her schemes alone. She knew that Donna was counting on her genuine interest in the girl, her concern for Jane Doe; she was stressing that it was for Jane's benefit to start some action, as if there was no other thought in her head. She would use anyone, her mother included, to gain whatever goal she had set. Marlene almost felt sorry for Brad.

"I wouldn't touch anything Conover's mixed up in," she said mildly. "He has to sleep in traction to keep his crookedness from showing on the outside."

"I told you, he won't do anything."

"And that should give you a clue. It must be as dangerous as a rattlesnake in the shoe box for him to back off."

"Not if she wants to take action. That's the whole point. She can get publicity for herself. We can't."

"I'll think about it," Marlene said, and held the newspaper

92

up in front of her face, terminating the conversation. She would do it, she had decided already, but not for Donna and her scheme. Jane Doe rather needed help, she thought, or something would get started between her and Brad, and that would be unfortunate for them both. Of course, Donna would pick up the pieces afterward, and in the end it might all be the same no matter what. Even if Brad did have an insatiable appetite, he was sweet, and he had done nothing to deserve the shattering experience of falling in love with a ghost, or a dream, that would vanish and leave no trace afterward. She had seen him at the fashion show, had been touched by the look on his face as he watched Jane Doe. He had not seen anyone else. And later, when he had come to the shop for Jane, he had been panicked to learn that she was gone, was out wandering alone. Marlene felt a great deal of responsibility for the presence of the girl in his apartment, she admitted to herself. She could have brought her home, or she could have seen to it that she found a studio apartment, or something. She regretted now that she had not even considered bringing Jane home; in retrospect it seemed the natural thing to have done. Staring at the paper, she admitted to herself that she had not thought of Brad as a real man, much less a sexual creature; he was Hoy Boy, Donna's tame robot to be manipulated and used, a schoolboy with an appetite, nothing more than that. Seeing him at the rail at the fashion show had changed him in her eyes, and she saw him now as a man who was strangely vulnerable. In her perception, he had made one giant step to maturity and he could be desperately hurt. She suspected that it would be best for Brad if he never realized that what he was feeling was love, if he kept the whole matter buried, and settled for sex and books. He was, she thought, the kind of odd person who can have only one great love in his life, and Jane Doe was as ephemeral as whipped cream, forbidden, appealing, irresistible, and destined to melt away and vanish.

And Jane, she thought sighing, what about her? She recalled with a pang how touching the girl had been pleading with her not to tell *them* where she was. How vulnerable *she* was during those insane episodes when the truth melted like snow in April. For the first time Marlene realized that Jane could be in serious danger, that she was utterly without defenses. What if she approached an unscrupulous stranger and begged him to hide her? Marlene knew it was possible, knew it could be disastrous. She would do something, she had decided, and Donna did not figure into her reasons. If Donna snagged her man afterward, so be it; that was a fair fight, but where Jane Doe was concerned, nothing was fair.

◆◆◆

They had been swimming and playing in the sand like children, building sand castles, searching for shells, trying to spot whales or sea lions, or monsters, anything that might surface.

Now Susannah was watching gulls overhead; she was drowsy after the swim in the frigid water. Although the sun was hot, the wind had a bite that was different. Like fall, she thought distantly, or early April before the heat settles in. She never had seen the waves so high except after a hurricane. Everything was wrong, she thought, almost asleep now; there should not be cliffs, that was certain, there should be palm trees and sea grapes, and smooth flat beaches. If it were March there should be porpoises out just beyond the sand bar, leaping, hitting the water broadside, with explosive cracks, drunk in their wild mating orgy.

She sat up suddenly, wide awake.

"What happened?" Brad asked, pushing himself up also, dazed from sleep.

"Nothing. I don't know. Let's take a walk, or climb the cliffs, or something." She stood up and pulled on her jeans over the bathing suit they had bought in a beach shop.

She was looking out to sea as she pulled on her clothes, and suddenly she stopped all motion. "Look! What's that?"

They had found a small cove with only a few other people in it. To the south, the cliffs met the sea, cutting off the view;

to the north, the cliffs made a wavy line that ended in mist. Behind them was a low stabilized dune with shapeless hummocks of European beach grass. The waves here were flattened a bit by the configuration of cliffs, but still they rolled in and crashed rhythmically, hurried along by an incoming tide. Beyond the surf only moments ago the sea had stretched blue and magnificent to a sharply defined horizon, but now a white wall reached from the sea to the sky, and the wall was advancing perceptibly.

"Fog," Brad said in disgust. "We'd better head back before it gets here. It'll be cold."

She shook her head slightly, staring at the wall that was beginning to show some details. At first it had appeared solid, without features, but now she could see that it was a cloud at ground level, tumbling, rolling, billowing first here then there, so brilliant in places that it hurt her eyes, so dark in other areas that it was like midday and night all together, as if somehow the cloud had warped time and mixed up times randomly.

They watched the fog advance, now and then shooting out a plume, like a snow plume on a mountain peak, or the wayward smoke from a fire. Brad touched Susannah's arm and pointed to the cliff south of them. Fog was rolling over the top, flowing down the side, piling up at the bottom as if gathering strength enough to start forward motion again.

"Let's get to the car, at least," he said, but her fascination was contagious and the cold, penetrating wetness now seemed an acceptable fee just to continue to watch the land vanish, the sea disappear, to hear the sounds of surf become muted and distant. The other people on the beach had fled, and they were alone as the fog touched the surf and subdued it, tumbled over the foam and made it vanish, poured over the dry sand and finally touched them.

Susannah drew in her breath sharply. The fog was bitterly cold after the heat of the sun, and it tasted mysterious and stung her eyes. She turned to watch it swallow the sand dune, and then she and Brad were alone in a white world with the distorted sounds of the surf the only noise. She knew the sea was behind her, but the sounds made it seem everywhere, as if she stood on a minute island in the middle of the ocean.

"Well, it's going to be slow going now, but we'd better get started before it gets thicker and slower yet." Brad had not taken his hand from her arm; he became aware of the feel of her skin, the smooth muscles, the firm flesh, the warmth, and he released her abruptly.

She was looking at him, not moving. "We'd better go," she said in a low voice.

He nodded. The fog had gathered in her hair, formed droplets the way dew forms droplets on grass, in flowers. Even her eyelashes were ornamented, and her eyebrows, as if the fog had bestowed countless perfect pearls on her. She was ethereal, a creature of sea and fog; he was sorry he had taken his hand from her arm, for now he thought he would not be able to touch her, his hand would either pass through her, or be stopped short. She had appeared in his life, had been sent, and she would vanish just as suddenly, leaving him to wonder forever if it had been real, if she had been real.

"Why are you looking at me like that?" she asked.

He shook himself, suddenly feeling the chill of the fog. "Come on," he said brusquely, and started to walk.

"This way," she said, not moving yet, waiting for him to turn, and when he did, she led the way to the sand dune, around it to the pull-off area and to the car. They got in.

He started to drive. "I want to go home and work on that last story," he said, still brusque. "There's that problem with the middle part. We haven't decided yet if she knows the secret of longevity."

"We should stop in a supermarket and buy groceries so we won't have to go out again. We should cook more meals and save money. Do you always eat dinner in a restaurant?"

"Sometimes I scramble eggs, or make a steak, something quick. Can you cook?"

She did not answer and he regretted the question. "We'll pick up a cookbook," he said, and wondered why he never had done that before. "Even I can follow directions."

"So can I. And let me pick out the cookbook. There's a supermarket."

She selected two cookbooks, an armload of magazines, and a paperback book. He started to protest at the checkout counter, but she insisted.

"I have money, remember? I'll pay for them. I'll pay you when we get back."

He tried to peek at the titles: *Cosmopolitan, Mademoiselle, Ms., Redbook,* all women's magazines.

"What are they for?" he asked, in the car again, driving carefully.

"I have to find out how to act, what to wear, what to say, all that."

"I haven't noticed anything wrong with the way you act and talk now," he said grumpily.

"I don't think you would notice, would you? Do you know how other women really behave?"

He glanced at her. "What does that mean?"

"You don't pay any attention to how people behave, or how they dress. You let me go to a restaurant in a torn shirt and dirty jeans. You didn't notice."

"What difference did it make? No one said anything to you."

"But I could be doing all kinds of things wrong and you wouldn't notice or tell me."

"You're not."

"Tell me about your date last night. What did she wear?"

"I don't know. A fancy silver thing."

"Was she in high heels?"

"Yes. No. Hell, I told you I don't know. I didn't look at her shoes."

"What did she order to eat?"

He shrugged helplessly.

"What did you order?"

"Drop it, okay? I don't know. Veal or something. It was awful and I couldn't eat it. That's enough. Those things aren't important to remember, so I don't."

"What things are important to remember?"

"Good God! Where we're going for one thing. I think we're lost."

"No, this is the same street we came on going the other way. I'll watch for where we have to turn. What else is important to remember?"

"Things that mean something. What someone wears doesn't mean anything. What they say does. I try to remember what they say."

"What did you talk about with her?"

The glance he shot her this time was venomous. "I don't know. I wasn't paying any attention. She talked."

She was frowning. "I don't understand. You don't remember anything at all, but you don't have amnesia. I can remember perfectly what I ate, what we both said, where we went, and still I do have amnesia. I think everyone has amnesia, only most people won't admit it." She pointed. "We have to turn left at that intersection, where the service station is."

He slowed for the turn without question.

"You didn't say anything about the past being important, and it is. You left it out to save my feelings, didn't you?"

"No, I didn't. I don't think the past is all that big a deal. It's now, what you're doing now that matters, not past history."

"Anything that makes you run away has to have some importance," she said thoughtfully.

He did not know which of them she was talking about. "Look, let me concentrate on driving, okay? We'll talk when we get home."

"See. Running away." She reached over the seat and pulled a magazine from the bag and began to flip through it.

She put the magazine back and this time brought forth one of the cookbooks. "Did you get a chicken?"

"Yes. And some hamburger, and pork chops. And frozen vegetables, and lettuce."

"I'll find something to cook," she said absently, reading through a recipe, then on to the next one. "I saw onions and garlic, and I think there's soy sauce."

"I'll make something," Brad said after a moment. "I thought you might want to shower and wash your hair, you know, get the sand out, and I'd be starting something." His hands were tight on the wheel and he could not explain to himself why it was important that he should cook for her, but it was important and he was prepared to argue for the chore.

She said nothing for a long time, then agreed. "But we'll take turns. It wouldn't be fair otherwise."

Neither of them spoke again until they reached the apartment and went inside. All the rest of the way Brad was busy trying to separate his reasons from his feelings, his sanity from what seemed to be a growing insanity. She was a normal young woman with a serious affliction that he was responsible for. She was his muse, his God-sent gift. She was ephemeral, a waking dream. She was a nuisance who had interrupted his well-planned life and was putting him weeks behind schedule. She was a guest and an interloper. And she was someone else's wife. Always he came back to that: she was another man's wife.

Under the shower, Susannah pondered the question of what is important enough to remember. Many things, she knew, but some more than others. One could do without childhood, obviously, although there would be blanks, areas of behavior where it would be impossible to say why the person did this instead of that. If she had been bitten by a dog at a very early age, today she might have a fear of dogs that would appear irrational unless one knew about the childhood incident. Or even if one did know, she added, glumly. People were supposed to get over those traumas, or be labeled neurotic. The magazines would help. At least she would learn what other women thought was important.

She looked at her telltale ring finger and knew that at least was important to remember. A husband somewhere — who did not care enough to file a missing person report.

Husband, she thought, running her fingers over her breasts. Making love to her. She tried to imagine his hands on her breasts, on her stomach, her thighs. No image came; she felt only a rising excitement, and she turned on the cold water full, then gasped under its impact.

She could see herself not recovering her memory. Months pass, and because she is young and healthy, she yearns for love, for the controlled violence of sex. Sees herself falling in love with a man, wanting his body to melt with hers, wanting to share his breakfasts, to sip wine by a fire and hold hands. Telling each other it's too risky, not believing it, and finally marrying. Years pass and they want a child; she wants a son like him, he wants a daughter like her, until, weeping and fearful, they try joyously to make a baby and she finds one day that they succeeded. And now the swelling womb, the feel of a heartbeat, an elbow, a knee, a movement. Their love is tender now, filled with awe. They redecorate a room, buy a crib, a basinette, diapers, and she makes tiny garments. She sings throughout the pregnancy, throughout the morning sickness, the pains, the strange cravings, and he sings with her. The trip to the hospital. No. A midwife clinic. She would go to a midwife where he could be at her side the entire time, hold her hand, remind her to breathe deeply, relax. And then the child — beautiful, perfect son with dark hair, not crying. And sleep for her. She wakes up, and it is all gone. She is someone else. What is she doing in this bed? Where is this place? She gets up and finds a phone and calls her husband who comes and picks her up and takes her home where she belongs. They have separate bedrooms and never speak unless they are entertaining; he is contemptuous of her and hates women generally and won't let her have a checkbook, or any money of her own, or her own friends. And at the clinic her child is crying, and her lover-husband is weeping. Years pass and she is a widow and meets a beautiful youth and falls in love with him. He is an orphan, he tells her. His mother died in childbirth and his father died soon afterward in an accident that was probably a suicide. She takes him home and cares for him, sends him to a fine school, sees him become a great . . . psychiatrist. That was it. A psychiatrist. They are lovers now, but he falls in love with a young woman and leaves her and sadly she looks over the meager possessions he had when he first came to her house, and among them she finds . . . the awful truth.

Susannah was dressed now and she walked to the kitchen heavily, overcome by sadness, blinking back tears.

"What's wrong?" Brad asked and when she did not respond, he hurried to her and touched her arm.

She pulled away and backed up a step, then another. "Don't touch me! Never! Promise!"

12

The joys of gentle womanhood

Dinner was quiet. Gradually the story Susannah had told herself faded, lost its immediate poignancy, and she could look at it with some distance, and even find it funny. Perhaps she had a career as a writer of sentimental tear-jerkers. Even as she derided the story and herself, she was aware of an iron resolve that had formed: she could not allow herself to become attached to anyone in this life; she could not trust her own emotions or beliefs or even her own reactions, because in this life she might be totally different from what she was in real life. She began to sink under the weight of the problem of trying to decide what was real life, what was illusory, and finally she gave it up. This felt real; the food tasted real, and across the table from her, casting quick glances her way and averting them instantly, Brad seemed very real. She ate in silence mulling over the many insoluble problems this life was presenting. One thing shone with exceptional clarity: she had to find out who she was and where she belonged, and go back there.

Several times Brad started to ask a question about the story she had told of the Russian woman with the secret of longevity, but each time he clamped his mouth shut. She had provided the bones; his job was to add the flesh, and then together they could wrap it in a nice covering of skin.

He had made hamburgers and a salad and frozen broccoli

that was still hard and barely warm. It was wondrously green though.

"I'm sorry about the dinner," he had said at the start of the meal. "I should have looked up something in the cookbook."

"It's good," she had said with her mouth full. "A little vinaigrette on the broccoli turns it into a salad, too, and that's a classy dish anywhere."

He ate moodily. Probably she was a good cook. They finished and Susannah said she would clean up and let him get to his work. When she joined him in the living room, he was at the typewriter; she went to the window seat with her magazines and a notebook and began to read and make notes. For a long time neither spoke, until he ended the silence.

"What are you doing?"

"Making a list of things I need. I'll go shopping for them tomorrow."

He looked at the open magazine uneasily. "What kind of things?"

"A hair dryer, a blow dryer, a curling iron, a manicure set and fingernail polish remover, a girdle. There are two kinds. One makes you flat, and the other one makes you round. I'll have to try them both, I guess. And there must be a hundred different kinds of bras."

"You don't need a girdle, for heaven's sake! And your hair is fine just as it is."

She looked at him pityingly, glanced at her list and went on: "a hair-setting gel, a conditioner, maybe a brightener. It's supposed to be good for light hair like mine. Bath oils and powder. Several sizes of sanitary pads and tampons, for different kinds of days. A long list of makeup, mascara, foundation cream, cleansing cream, stuff like that. A disposable deodorant douche. A razor, or maybe an electric razor. I'll have to look at them."

"Good God! You don't need all that junk!"

"And a wig, for those days that I can't do my hair and have to make a good impression. A biorhythm calculator to tell me when it's a good time for various things — like when to go to the dentist or apply for a job. A personal calendar and thermometer. Cologne and perfume. An exerciser board. A long list of vitamins, enriched with iron. A tape measure — to see what exercises I need most . . ."

"Stop! Just stop right there! Ja—" He left his chair to stand before her. "I don't even know what to call you. Not Jane! You're not Jane! Let's pick a name for you. How about Loretta?"

She shook her head.

"Althea? Janice?" This time he rejected them. "We'll make a list of names and choose one later. But just listen to me a minute. You don't need any of that stuff. Oh, maybe one or two things. But most of it you can forget. You've done without those gadgets and gimmicks for a week and you look terrific. Honestly. You don't have to rely on fakery and makeup and fancy hair-dos. I forgot to tell you that Marlene called while you were in the shower. She's dropping in later. Ask her advice about all that stuff, will you?"

"I've gone through three of the magazines," she said, "and they all seem to agree. These are the things women need and use. Why do you want me to be different?"

"Not all women, just certain ones who have so little faith in themselves that they let others tell them how to dress, how to look, what to eat, everything. What's wrong with wearing clothes you like, eating food you like, not hiding behind makeup?"

She considered this, puzzled. She did not know what was wrong with being herself, but she suspected that something was very wrong with it, she simply did not remember what it was.

Exxon pushed the window open then and jumped to the floor meowing furiously. He was wet. Susannah got up and went out for a towel. When she returned with it, Brad started to warn her, but she was already rubbing down the cat briskly. Brad watched in wonder. He would have said: Exxon never lets anyone rub him with a towel; he would bite and scratch anyone who even tried. The only evidence of Exxon's displeasure was the spastic twitching of his ridiculous tail.

Exxon had accepted her from the beginning. He chose her lap; he followed her to her room and slept on her bed; he went to her to protest if his food was running low; he greeted her first when he came home and met her halfway down the hall when she got up in the mornings. Anyone would assume it was her cat and had been for a long time.

"Another thing. When I sit down I'm supposed to make something," she said, smoothing Exxon's fur back in place. He was purring. "A rug, just a little one to start with. Or house slippers. Or furniture covers. Or redesign a dress that's out of style. There are a lot of kits. Maybe I could start with potholders. They seem pretty easy."

"What would you do with them?"

"I'm not sure. I could use one when I cook, and I guess give a few to Marlene, and some to you. I don't guess you make more than that for starters. They say in the magazine that they make lovely Christmas presents."

"Forget potholders, will you? If you want one, I'll buy it for you. Let's talk about the story. I think I've got the middle section."

"How about things to put on glasses so they won't get the table wet?"

"I don't want skirts on my glasses!"

"Macrame plant hangers?"

"Christ! Will you please stop all that! You don't have to keep busy. You have enough to do without all that."

"I have exactly nothing to do."

"Yes, you do. You have to help me with this story!"

"That's your work, not mine. Oh, all right," she said, in a pacifying tone. "What do you have now?"

"This woman is in her seventies and looks under thirty, but she notices that she is starting to have a few gray hairs, and wrinkles are forming. She's desperate and has to go back to Russia to renew the treatment..."

Susannah waved it aside. "Shades of Shangri La," she said. "You sound just like those magazines!"

"What do you know about Shangri La?"

"Remember? They take out the beautiful girl and she turns to dust right before their eyes."

"This isn't like that. She would get back and renew herself for another hundred years."

"It's exactly the same thing. Exploiting the fear of growing old, of losing your looks. Exactly the same."

"I think it's a good idea," he said stiffly.

"I think you're absolutely right," she said. She picked up one of the new paperback books and began to read.

He watched her suspiciously, but she concentrated on the book. "You just said that because you don't want to talk."

She frowned. "Of course, you're right again. I just want to listen to you talk."

"Now what?" he said, near despair. He ducked down to look at the book title. "You don't need that one, either."

" 'Perfect joy results if you're tuned in absolutely to his needs and respond to them. All day he has encountered people who belittle him and his efforts, who contradict his statements, who disbelieve him at every turn, who threaten his livelihood, as well as his manhood. Make his home his haven, his refuge, a place where he no longer has to be constantly on guard, where he can relax and find himself. That secret self is the man you want to be with, not the competitor, the fighter . . .' "

"That's bullshit!" he cried.

"You're right," she said and put the book down docilely.

"You can't just be whatever the current book or magazine tells you! No one can."

"You're so right."

"Stop that!"

"All right. Would you like coffee?"

The doorbell rang and Brad hurried to admit Marlene. "Will you talk to her?" he almost yelled into that startled woman's face. "She's driving me crazy!" He rushed to his desk and snatched up a pile of papers and notebooks, and left. A moment later his door slammed.

Marlene watched him in amazement. "Well, I had no idea

Hoy . . . Brad had a temper. Hello, Jane. How are you?"

"Fine. Marlene, we have to do something about me."

"Yes. That's why I came over." It was to be very simple. A picture in the paper, a brief item, and a post office box number. "We don't want you to have to handle any correspondence, it could be unnerving for you. I'll talk to my attorney in the morning and see if he'll handle any claim that appears legitimate, and until one does, I'll take care of it."

"What if someone just thinks it would be neat to pretend I'm a lost daughter or something?"

"We'll demand proof, honey. Would you mind if I make a mole search? Have you noticed any scars?"

They went to Susannah's bedroom where she stripped and Marlene made a note of two moles on her back, no scars. No significant dental work.

"Okay. We'll see what happens. Now, what is it that got Brad so riled?"

Susannah showed her the magazines and the list she was making, and Marlene agreed with Brad that she needed very little on that list.

"Let me pick you up around eleven-thirty and take you shopping and then to lunch. You should meet your lawyer, in any event."

"One more thing," Susannah said hesitantly. "Who will pay for all this? I already owe you so much. And Brad. And now a lawyer."

"Don't worry about it, honey. That's what insurance companies are for. When it's all over, you'll file a claim and it will be big enough to cover everything. Just don't worry." She went to the door. "I have to run. You are keeping a daily diary, aren't you? So you'll know later?"

Susannah assured her that she was, and Marlene left. Writing in the diary was the last thing Susannah did every night, sitting up in bed, alternately writing and stroking Exxon, and most of all thinking, trying to remember. She always tried to find clues in what she wrote, and failed. She picked up the magazines and stacked them on the table, and then thought about the story Brad was working on. He did not reappear and presently she turned off lights and went to her room and got ready for bed. She wrote the day's happenings, and turned again to the story about the lady who did not age.

◈◈◈

Brad was still at the library when she returned to the apartment the next day carrying a bag of groceries. She hummed softly as she put away the things she had bought. She also had a few things that Marlene had helped her pick out for herself, nothing like the long list she had made out. They had gone to Marlene's apartment for a short time and she had tried needlework there and learned that she could not do it. She was relieved; she still did not know what she would have done with a dozen potholders.

She was still in the bedroom when Brad came back and yelled at the front door.

"Hey! Are you home?"

"What's the matter? What happened?"

"Nothing. I think I've got it. Let's take a walk and talk it out, okay?"

"I think I've got it, too," she said, laughing. "Let's go."

◈◈◈

Across town in her office Donna studied Jane Doe's picture for a long time without moving. She had not met her and no one had mentioned how good-looking she was. Her mother had not told her, she thought darkly. Her own mother had put those two together, was helping that . . . woman all she could. She drummed her fingers on the desktop, cleared except for one folder, out waiting for a client who was already overdue. She would give him five more minutes, no longer, and then . . . She would go meet Jane Doe. She would get Jane Doe out of Brad's apartment, out of his life. Somehow she would do that. It was not jealousy, she told herself. It was much more important than simple jealousy. She had cultivated her fields and now a poacher had wandered onto her property and was threatening to shoot her birds. Five minutes passed and she got up and told the office secretary to tell Mr. Budorf that her time was too valuable to wait for a client, that she had left for another appointment.

It was after six when she parked down the street from Brad's apartment, and she saw them almost immediately, before she even turned off the motor. At first she thought Brad was with a young man, a student. They were walking briskly, talking with great animation, first one, then the other. They passed her without glancing at the car.

They were talking with the ease of old friends, or old lovers, she realized, and gripped the wheel hard. Brad never talked to her like that; it was impossible to get more than three words at a time out of him. And he never listened to her with that kind of intensity. She drove away slowly. She had to think. She had to have a plan.

For the first time it had occurred to her that there was a possibility that Jane Doe might not go away, she might never recover her memory. She cared nothing about the devastation Brad might suffer if she left, but it alarmed her to think that there was even a remote possibility that she might not leave. Donna had taken him and was creating a sophisticated man out of such raw material that at first her task had appeared hopeless. She had worked hard on him, too hard to risk failure because of a quirk of fate. Her intention had been to volunteer to help Jane Doe find her own apartment the next day, and to see to it that she actually rented one and moved into it, but that was no longer enough, not now after seeing them together. Across town, across the country, it would be the same as long as she was Jane Doe and available. She had to resume her life as Mrs. Somebody or other. She had to go home and forget Brad and he had to realize that he no longer existed for her.

That night while Marlene was bathing, Donna looked in her purse and found the notebook where she had written Jane Doe's description, including the moles. Although Donna went to her room early, it was hours before she could go to sleep, and when she did sleep she still had not thought of a plan that was certain to work and that would not flounder her in a backlash.

◈◈◈

On the patio of his St. Petersburg beach home Jimmie poured beer for Felix and then himself. "Cheers," he said and quaffed a long drink. "I've been thinking, Felix, old friend," he said then. "If the detective is right and she is in San Francisco, I don't think it would look right if we all three barged in on her. She's just a confused little girl, most likely very lonely by now, friendless, alone in a hotel room most of the time, not sleeping. Now, if I show up by myself and explain everything to her, why I believe I can straighten out this little misunderstanding between us without any trouble."

"Ah, Jimmie, I don't think that's a wise course. I don't believe Anna Maria Lucia would approve. What we think has to be done, no matter how much it hurts, is for you to go to her and take along the little blue suitcase, tell her you're sorry, whatever you can think of — you thought your first marriage had been annulled, or was not legal, anything — then make the switch and leave her be. I'll take care of the merchandise, just like always. And then we'll consider our future flight plans. That's what Anna Maria Lucia thinks would be a wise course."

"But, ah, Felix, there is one little problem with that procedure. You see, Susannah is ah, proper, faith in the institutions, that sort of thing. Very honest. She is surprisingly honest. She just might decide to ah, to do something not consistent with the general well being of the various parties concerned in this little enterprise."

"Well now, Jimmie, you know I've never asked you about your private living accommodations, now have I? You don't ask me, I don't ask you. How you settle your little private problems is beyond the scope of these particular flight plans. You learn real early not to bring your little private difficulties with you into the cockpit, old friend, or they'll get between you and your instrument panel. Once the merchandise is delivered, if you and the two ladies want to get together and calm the waters, that's your affair. But we take one storm front at a time, old buddy. Only way to go, one at a time."

"You're right, of course, but have you thought about the consequences of all possible actions little Susannah might be considering? I don't anticipate trouble; I think we have things under control, but it never hurts to look ahead and make a few estimates of conditions that might arise. For instance, if she consults a lawyer and decides to charge me with bigamy, there could be an investigation that might prove embarrassing for my friends as well as for myself."

With a sigh Felix poured more beer for them both and then stared moodily at the sparkling blue water of the pool.

Minutes later Anna Maria Lucia rushed furiously from the house waving a newspaper. "The delivery man, he bring it!" she cried. "Look! Look at her! Just look at her!"

They looked at the picture she slapped down on the table between them. Jimmie shook his head.

"Idiot! Look at her! It is your Susannah! Look at those clothes, that hairstyle, that makeup! Designer clothes! She wears designer clothes!"

Jimmie studied the picture and slowly he accepted that it was his Susannah, but not as he had known her. She looked distant, untouchable; she looked like someone with untold millions stiffening her spine, erecting a barrier between her and the real world.

"Now, Anna Maria Lucia, don't let's all jump to conclusions," Jimmie said mildly. "She had over a thousand dollars, remember, after she paid her airfare."

"Bah! A thousand dollars would do nothing! That suit is a Laurie original! Look at the lapel, the little *L*! And on the belt. A silk Laurie shirt! Five thousand, eight thousand! You don't walk into a shop and just buy a Laurie original, you idiot! You order it and you wait and wait!"

As she screeched, Felix read the brief caption under the picture and he sighed. "Ah, Jimmie, it says here that she has amnesia. She claims she doesn't know who she is." He sighed again, and his voice was melancholy when he added, "I'm afraid that Anna Maria Lucia's right, old friend. Your honest little Susannah's steering her own course and we're bucking in her tail winds."

"I guess we'd better head out toward California," Jimmie said, standing up. "Your detective has earned his keep, Anna Maria Lucia."

"My detective! Bah! He don't do nothing! He do only divorces and bigamies, nothing else. My cousin, he find her trail, he send picture."

Now Felix stood up also and both men took a step toward her.

"What cousin, Anna Maria Lucia?" Jimmie asked calmly. "What cousin is that?"

"Rudy, three times removed on my mother's side. He call me. He have many friends who find trail for him and he find her. Only family help when there is big trouble, that I know from childhood."

"This cousin Rudy, what does he do, Anna Maria Lucia?"

"It don't make no difference. I don't know him. My mama know him from when he is little and come to America."

Felix and Jimmie exchanged glances and Felix said, "In my opinion it would be wise if we make contact with little Susannah before cousin Rudy gets to her. Can you call him back, Anna Maria Lucia, and thank him nicely for his help and tell him there's nothing else for him to do from this point in time?"

She shook her head. "I don't know where he is. And Mama always say I never call cousin Rudy, or cousin Tony, or cousin Mario, or none of them. I call my mama and she call her brother and he call someone else who call them."

"I think you'd better call your mama," Jimmie said.

13

*The little blue bag
goes to a party.*

Margarita Portos, carrying her new blue suitcase, left O'Hare Airport on the Evanston bus only moments before Jimmie, Felix, and Anna Maria Lucia entered. Margarita was dressed in discarded clothing, gifts from her ladies; she was one of the best-dressed travelers in the terminal and she was pretending very hard that she was not frightened. She moved briskly and held her head up the way the ladies did at the health spa; she looked neither to the right nor left when she walked, and she always spoke as pleasantly as she could, saying please and thank you and would you be so kind and I beg your pardon. Not that the ladies used language like that to her, but they did to each other, and she had been an avid learner. She had met Mrs. DeKalb at the spa where Mrs. DeKalb was recovering from a nervous attack.

Although only a maid at the spa, one night when Mrs. De-Kalb was having a minor relapse, Margarita had massaged her feet, and Mrs. DeKalb had hired her.

"Just come when you can," she had insisted. "Wait for your sister's baby if you have to, but right after that. You'll have your own room..."

Mrs. DeKalb had bought her ticket, had written out instructions: first the bus to Evanston, then a taxi the rest of the way. Someone at the house would come out and pay the driver.

Margarita knew this was an important day for Mrs. DeKalb; she was having a large party, an engagement party for her son and his fiancée. She would be pleased that Margarita would be on hand to help on such an important occasion. It was lucky to start a new job with such good auspices, she knew, and tried to relax against the seat, tried to see the strange landscape out the window. Already she missed the open spaces, the stark desert landscape, the solitary saguaros. Already she was wondering what Rosario was doing, if he was thinking of her.

If she had managed to conquer her fears on the bus, there was no possibility of putting them behind again when she looked at the house where the taxi stopped. It looked like a hotel, three stories tall, with covered driveways, a covered entrance, massive eight-foot-tall double doors.

"That's twenty-eight fifty," the driver said.

"Of course. Someone will come pay you. Thank you." She walked to the door, concentrating on keeping her back straight, keeping her knees working right. Before she rang the bell, she murmured a quick prayer.

The man who opened the door was a butler. She knew from movies and television. "Mrs. DeKalb please. I'm Margarita Portos. She's expecting me, for the party."

The butler looked her over in a way not calculated to reveal the fact that he was appraising her. What he saw was a good linen frock with a short-sleeved jacket. Very good English shoes, sensible shoes for traveling. And a beautiful Italian leather suitcase dyed blue. He stepped aside.

"Thank you. Would you mind paying the taxi, please?"

"Of course," he murmured. "Allow me." He took the little suitcase and set it down out of the way. "If you will wait just a moment, I'll pay the driver and then announce you." He started out the door.

Margarita stared at the entrance foyer. It had a marble floor and large tubs with plants, a long table with a mammoth flower arrangement and nothing else on it, two paintings of important-looking men. She was interrupted in her study by the appearance of a large fat man who was red-faced and sweaty.

"Another one! By God, the party's getting off to a fine start. And what's your name, my dear?"

"Margarita Portos. Mrs. DeKalb asked me to come early if I could for the party."

"Portos? Portos?" He frowned slightly. "I'm Edward DeKalb, by the way. Have I met you?"

"Oh no. I met Mrs. DeKalb at the Edenside Resort in Arizona."

"Oh! I see! Well, come on in and meet some of the other early arrivals." The butler returned and he said to him, "Laurence, take Miss Portos's bag up. You know better than I do which rooms are empty. Any of them will do. Come along, my dear. You must meet Hilary's mother. She's a dragon, you know. We're trying to keep her from noticing the heat. She's irritable if she realizes it's hot, so we're keeping her in booze, near an air conditioner. But, by God, you can't cool off a room with fifty people in it, you know, so I'm counting on the booze. I'm feeling it already, but she's going strong. A real dragon."

He had led her through a wide hallway into a room that looked to Margarita like a waiting room for a very expensive doctor. There was white carpeting, and bowls of red roses everywhere, and pale silver striped furniture that was barely visible through the many people who were almost all standing up and moving about, talking in small groups. Several white-coated men with trays moved silently among the guests, and without pause exchanged full glasses for empty ones.

"But I should see Mrs. DeKalb . . ."

"We'll find her. Most likely she's in the kitchen giving the catering people hell. Frankly, the last batch of paté was foul, and they're not keeping up. Expect people to start falling in their tracks if they keep drinking at this rate without food to soak up the alcohol. Ah, here we are."

"Olivia, want you to meet one of Angela's friends. Miss Portos, Mrs. Blakely-Findley. Now, if you ladies will excuse me . . ."

"But, please, would you be so kind as to inform Mrs. DeKalb that I have arrived?"

"You bet. And more hors d'oeuvres."

"Thank you." She looked at Mrs. Blakely-Findley then and said, very faintly, "How do you do?"

"Not very well, I'm afraid. This heat is beastly. Chicago is such a barbaric place, don't you agree? Miserable summer and winter. Portos? Your English is very good, a bit formal, but I find that charming. Other countries do such a marvelous job with dual languages, three, four languages. They know what is meaningful. Do you know what my daughter studied at Hadley? Telephone communications. Not how it works, mind you, how to do it. How to talk on the telephone! I was appalled, I can assure you." She put down her empty glass and as if by magic a hand smoothly whisked it away and a new frosted glass appeared, steaming gently in the heated air. "We took her out as soon as I learned what they called a curriculum. We put her in that lovely finishing school outside Zurich. You know the one, of course. An old castle, so enchanting."

Several people drew in close to Mrs. Blakely-Findley. A woman sat down in a nearby chair and leaned forward eagerly. "Is it true that they're going to Oslo for their honeymoon? I can't imagine such a thing!"

A man turned to Margarita and said confidentially, "It's Henry's idea. He wants to clinch a deal there. Two birds, you know. I'm Judson Curry, by the way. Who're you?"

"Margarita Portos."

"Margarita Portos is not drinking," he said, still in a low confidential voice. He raised his hand and snapped his fingers and almost instantly one of the waiters appeared. He took a glass of champagne and held it out for Margarita.

"Oh no," she said nervously. "I just arrived. I must go change. Mrs. DeKalb..."

"Angela," Mrs. Blakely-Findley said, looking past Margarita, "what a charming little friend you have. We have just been comparing our experiences with various schools. She knows all about *l'école des fleurs pour les jeunes filles.*"

Mrs. DeKalb smiled graciously at the small group. "My dear," she said to Margarita, "come along. Edward should have shown you to your room, to freshen up a bit from your long trip." Her grip on Margarita's arm was hard and unyielding as she led her from the room, not stopping at any of the clusters of people or individuals who approached. "Be right back," she said, smiling, always smiling.

In the broad hallway she motioned to Laurence. "Tell Mr. DeKalb I want to see him in the study immediately," she said, and now her voice was not gracious or light. She was still holding Margarita's arm.

Inside the study Mrs. DeKalb stood looking out a tall window, not speaking, until her husband entered. She turned and said icily, "I've never been so humiliated in my life. You actually introduced her to Olivia. She was chatting with Judson. This is exactly the sort of thing he's been looking for. We'll be ridiculed, made a laughing stock. Give her some money and take her to the bus station. You'll have to walk through the grounds to the garage, act as if you're showing her the garden or something."

"I have to drive her to the bus station?"

"Exactly. Peters is too busy parking and unparking cars." She went to the door. "If anyone asks, we'll say she's exhausted from her trip. Get rid of her instantly, before she has a chance to do any more damage." Without a glance at Margarita she swept from the room.

"Hey, now don't you cry," Edward DeKalb said awkwardly. "It's my fault, but damned if I know what I did. Who are you?"

She was sobbing harshly and could not talk for several minutes. Then she told him.

"Well, honey, you should be glad. She's not the easiest person to work for, you see. Not her fault, not at all, but she gets nervous sometimes." He rummaged through the desk drawer and found a checkbook. "Tell me your name again, slowly." He wrote out a check and then went to the wall and moved aside a cabinet and opened a small wall safe. Margarita could not see what he was doing, but when he turned to her he had money in his hand. "You'll need something for your ticket home," he said. "Cash for that. And something to make all this up to you. Check's for that. Now we'd better get started. You ready?"

He handed her the money and the check and without looking at them she stuffed them inside her purse. "My suitcase?"

"I think the check will cover it, honey. If it doesn't, drop me a line next week and I'll take care of it."

They took their walk in the gardens and then he drove her to the bus station and hours later when she was on the plane heading back to Arizona she took out the check and looked at it. One thousand dollars! The exact amount she had determined to save for her trousseau. By the time she left the plane she was so radiant that people gazed at her with sympathy or even envy.

Edward DeKalb looked at the blue suitcase that night and shook his head. He should have paid her a bit more. It was a nice piece of merchandise. He thought of Mimi, the cook's daughter who had been visiting her mother. Mimi worked in New York, he thought, someplace like that. Maybe she could use it. She had helped out with the party and was a good sort. A little bonus and the suitcase, that should please her and her mother. It was important to keep her mother happy, best damn cook they'd ever had.

14

The family lends a hand.

Marlene left her shop early in the afternoon to stroll over
to the post office, not that she expected any response after only
one day, but you never know, she told herself. In the post office
lobby she saw a man with a sketchpad, obviously making copies
of the murals, although she did not know why. She thought the
murals were hideous. She also noticed that he watched her, and
that did not strike her as unusual either. She was used to
having men watch her; she was proud of her slight, trim body
and thought it right that people should notice. He was gone by
the time she checked the box, closed it, and started to walk back
to work. She gave him no more thought and never saw him
again, but later that afternoon Donna saw him.

Donna had invited William Conover to her apartment for a
drink and a talk. She walked up the two flights of stairs as she
always did, for her hips, and when she opened the door to the
hallway she saw someone outside her apartment. For a moment
she had the impression that he was trying the knob, but then
he knocked and she knew she had been mistaken.

She hesitated only a moment before going to the door. After
all, Conover was due any second; there wouldn't be time for
anything to happen.

"I live here," she said. "Can I help you?"

"Miss Murphy?"

"Yes." Now she looked at him more closely. Dark business suit, so-so quality, brown hair, dark eyes, nothing remarkable in any way about him, nothing memorable.

"My name is Victor Duncan. I'm a private investigator. I have reason to believe you know the whereabouts of the daughter of my client. May we talk?"

"I'd like to see some identification," Donna said cautiously, but her mind was streaking in and out of the possibilities. She would have no use for Conover after all, she thought with a twinge of satisfaction. He was expensive and indecisive, a bad combination. That woman would be out of Brad's apartment and out of his life, except for a lawsuit, that very day. She would have to be ready to take time off from work at any moment and give Brad all her attention for a short while . . .

The man had opened his wallet by then and he showed her a card that she hardly glanced at. "We've been looking for her for a long time," he said easily, replacing the wallet. "I can't tell you who her father is, not yet, not until we're sure. This isn't the first lead we've run down, you know. But if it works out, you won't be sorry that you cooperated."

Donna never did invite him in to talk, but she did tell him Brad's address, and she watched him walk down the hall to the elevator. As soon as the elevator doors closed, the stairway door opened, and Conover ran toward her.

"What did he want?"

"Who?"

"Rudy Drake. That man you were talking to. What did he want? He's one of JoJo Domino's toadies."

"Oh shit and grow turnips!" Donna breathed and did not realize she had used one of her mother's involuntary expressions when things just got too much to bear another minute.

❖❖❖

"All right!" Donna stormed later, pacing as Marlene tried again to ring Brad's apartment. "I thought it was legitimate. He showed me identification. It wasn't connected to the newspaper story at all, he said so. He's been looking for her for a long time, he said. How was I to know?"

Marlene listened to the distant ringing and finally hung up. It was nearly six. "They could be having dinner out somewhere," she said, but almost instantly she dialed again.

"They could stay out for hours! Are you going to keep dialing that number all night?"

"Maybe." She hung up. "But maybe it would be better just to go wait for them."

"Marlene, that would be most unwise," Conover said. "I tell you Rudy Drake is a bad character, but he won't do anything on his own. He'll check her out and report back. If JoJo Domino has a legitimate claim on her, there's not much you can do, you see."

"A mobster's moll!" Donna cried. "That's the kind of girl you put in Brad's apartment." She was almost certain JoJo Domino would not let his moll press a lawsuit. Everything had been reduced to a very elemental matter of survival now. They had to get that woman away from Brad, make it abundantly clear that he had not slept with her, had no interest in her in any way.

"You could call the police and claim that she stole certain items from your shop," Conover said. "If she's in the hands of the police and JoJo wants her, that's his problem. The young man would no longer be involved, and neither would you."

"Oh shut up!" Marlene said. "She's no more a gangster's girl friend than I am." She dialed again.

"JoJo Domino's base of operations is L.A.," Conover said worriedly. "I wonder if he's expanding to Frisco. That'll mean big trouble. I wonder if Ward knows . . ."

"Will you get him out of here!" Marlene snapped at Donna. "You dug him up, go bury him again."

She listened to the echoing rings of the other phone.

On Monday evening Brad had put half of the final version of the story on paper. He finished it on Tuesday morning, and as the pages came off the typewriter, Susannah had gone over them making changes here and there, correcting his spelling, suggesting a cut or expansion. By midafternoon they were finished. It looked terrible, full of crossed-out passages, penciled-in lines, corrections, but it was finished, ready for a final clean typing.

"Now we play," he had said happily. "Fisherman's Wharf, a ferry ride, a stroll through Chinatown, dinner at a Hunan restaurant. What do you want?"

"All of them," Susannah said without hesitation. "Is there enough time for them all?"

"Let's go see."

They started with the ferry ride, and he told her about the raft he had had as a child. "There was this pond, about as big as my apartment, I guess, and I used to sail around the world in it."

"I had a tree house," she said, "and I pretended it was my own private dirigible. I went around the world too!"

"You remember!" He felt himself go rigid and cold.

"No. I made it up," she said in a low voice. "It doesn't seem fair not to tell you things when you tell me about your childhood."

They both laughed suddenly and other people on the ferry turned to look at them.

And later, eating ice cream in a tiny Italian cafe, he said, "There were these two brothers who fought all the time, really fought, down in the mud, rolling over and over, that kind of thing. My father egged them on until they went to it and then he took pictures. He tried to get me to fight with them once and I wouldn't. I knew they'd beat me up and I was a coward, I guess."

"Sensible, I'd say. It's silly to fight without a reason, and you must have had enough sense to know that."

"He thought I was a coward."

"Does it matter to you now what he might have thought then?"

"I don't know."

"Maybe he didn't think you were a coward, but just wanted you in the picture. After all, you were his primary model. Sometimes it seems that certain kinds of people are so intent on what they're doing that they forget that the models are human, not just things to use." She paused with a spoonful of ice cream near her mouth. "I suppose artists have to be like that, or there wouldn't be much art."

"Yeah, but he was writing silly children's books."

"Maybe the driving force is the same for bad art as for good. Maybe it's too soon to know if his books are silly or not."

"Maybe your ice cream is going to drip all over the place if you don't take that bite."

They wandered up and down the streets of Chinatown and finally stopped for dinner, too tired to talk anymore.

"It's been a good day," he said as they finished their tea. "Thanks."

He insisted on a taxi home although they had used buses and trolleys all day. "Too tired to walk to the bus stop, too tired to wait for it when we get there. Too tired to argue about it," he said and waved at a taxi. They got in and leaned back and said no more after Brad had given the address.

"My feet are sore," Susannah said as they climbed the stairs. "Tomorrow no more walking, maybe I'll never walk again."

She stopped speaking when they reached his apartment. The telephone was ringing. Brad opened the door and they stepped inside and gasped. The place had been ransacked, furniture pulled away from the walls, the couch turned over, papers loose on the floor.

"We've been robbed!" Susannah cried.

Brad moved past her and yanked up the ringing telephone. "Hello!" he yelled into it.

"Brad? Are you all right? Is Jane all right?"

"I'll talk to you later, Marlene. We just got here and the place is a mess. We've been robbed and I have to call the police."

"Wait a minute, Brad. Gangsters are after Jane! I've been trying to reach you for hours." She told him what had happened, then said, "But if they ransacked your place maybe they don't want her, maybe they want something they think she has. Brad, call the police immediately. Do you want me to do it?"

"No. Just take it easy, Marlene. I'll call you back in a couple of minutes."

Susannah was watching him. She had not moved from the door yet; it was still open behind her. She moved finally when he went over and closed it and put the chain on.

"Listen," he said then, "does the name JoJo Domino mean anything to you?" She shook her head. "Rudy Drake? Victor Duncan?" She kept shaking her head.

"Okay, we're getting out of here. The guys who did all this might come back. They seem to think you have something of theirs."

"Getting out where? How?"

"I'm not sure yet. Let's toss some stuff in a suitcase —"

She had caught his arm, was pointing at the door. He turned to see the knob move silently, as if someone was testing the lock.

"Let's go!" Brad whispered, pulling her toward the kitchen and the fire exit.

"Wait a minute," she whispered back and yanked away, raced down the hall to her bedroom where she scooped up the diary she was keeping. Exxon was huddled in the corner, his fur straight out all over his body. She snatched him up and, holding him, ran back to Brad who had picked up the unfinished story and some notebooks. They sped through the apartment to the kitchen, out the window and down the firescape, across the back yard to the covered carport. Only then did Brad stop to consider that someone might be watching for just this, but it was too late to change now and he kept going until he had wrenched the car door open. He got in, tossed his papers on the back window ledge, and slid across the seat; she followed, still carrying the cat, her notebook and her purse. He did not turn on the lights, but backed out, headed up the alley trying not to grind gears as he shifted.

As they were leaving the alley, headlights appeared at the other end. "Shit," he muttered and pulled out into the street.

Two doors down he turned right into a driveway, and then off it onto the lawn behind a hedge. "Learned this trick in the movies," he whispered. "I'll go watch for them." He slipped out of the car, left the door unlatched, and went to the edge of the bushes where he could see out in both directions. At the mouth of the alley was a long black car. As he watched, it turned in his direction, and now he could see a man on foot; he had been talking to the driver. Brad ran back to the car.

"There are two of them," he whispered. "One's on foot. As soon as the Lincoln gets past the driveway, I'm going to take off in the other direction. Ready?"

"Is that it?"

A flicker of headlight showed through the hedge; the Lincoln was doing no more than five miles an hour. The men could not be certain which driveway he had entered; there were six or seven between the alley and the next intersection. Probably the man on foot would check them out and the Lincoln would tag along. Thank God, Brad breathed softly, there was never any parking space in this neighborhood; the Lincoln would have to keep moving.

A car with a noisy muffler came down the street and honked at the Lincoln; there were oaths and catcalls. Under the cover of the noise Brad started his car again and put it in reverse, ready.

The headlights cleared the hedge, then the driveway, and moved on down the street. "Now," Brad said, and backed up, turned, headed out again, with no lights on. Traffic was sparse on this street at this time of night, but still there were cars, an occasional truck; he had to get far enough out to see both directions, and he was afraid any motion would draw the attention of the one on foot. At least the other car would have to make a turn; it was too long to U-turn in the street. He knew he could not outrun a determined kid on a tricycle; all he could hope for was to get enough traffic between them to keep the other one helpless to act. He was already planning his route. Over to Oak, turn at the Bay Bridge intersection, off the Interstate at Berkeley, and lose him, if he still followed, in the back streets and alleys around the university. He knew that area, he thought almost smugly. He had ridden his bicycle there for the last three years and knew every tree, every turn, every blind alley, every cut-through . . . "Now," he breathed, and pulled out into the street. There was a shout, and a squeal of tires. Brad turned at the corner and merged into the heavier traffic on Oak. He sighed his relief. Temporarily, at least, they were unreachable.

"Can you see them?" he asked.

Susannah was half turned, watching. "I'm not sure. I think they turned, but it's all just headlights back there."

"You got a look? Will you know it again?"

"Are you kidding? A car as long as a football field!"

At the toll booth on the bridge Susannah said, "It's back there." She straightened in her seat and looked ahead. "What are we going to do?"

He told her his plan to lose them in Berkeley, but now he realized that was simply the first part of it. His instinct was to keep traveling east, get all the way out of the area.

"Take me to a police station," she said softly. "I don't know what all this means, but it's not your problem. It could be too dangerous. Just let me go to the police."

"What if they have some kind of proof that would let them take you away? The police can't simply keep you, no more than the hospital could."

They crossed the bay in silence. Exxon protested being held, and Susannah let him flow over the seat into the back. Brad followed a van off at the Berkeley exit. There were two cars between them and the black Lincoln. The van stopped, waited for an opening in the traffic and shot out; Brad followed without hesitation. There was a blare of horns and brakes squealing, but he was in the traffic. He cut across the lanes recklessly and turned again, this time onto an unfamiliar street that he knew was heading in the right direction.

"They probably know where we turned," Susannah said, "but we have a few minutes on them anyway."

Brad was turning randomly now, always trying to keep heading north, but after the third twist, he no longer knew which direction was the one he wanted; Exxon began to wail in a deep gutteral voice. Brad did not know where the school was, where the interstate highway was, where he was. His last turn had been onto a winding narrow road that continued to get narrower and narrower, and was climbing steeply.

Susannah had been watching out the rear window and finally she relaxed. "You did it! Brad, you lost them! I didn't think it was possible, they were so close, but you did it!"

"I think so," he said cautiously. "Exxon, shut up. I want to pull over somewhere and just sit still for a while to make sure."

"You did, though," she said firmly. "Where are we now?"

"Help me watch for a good place to pull off the road," he said, but it seemed impossible that there would be such a place. The cat's wails were subsiding; now and then he growled. The road was blacktop and so narrow that two cars could not pass unless one of them drove on the shoulder. Black woods were on the left, and he was very much afraid that there was a terrible drop-off on the right. When the road curved back on itself, they could see the lights of the entire bay area.

"There," Susannah said, pointing. A steep driveway led up through the woods.

Brad made the turn, shifted down, and climbed until they reached a level spot again. The driveway continued to a dark house. Brad pulled over enough to permit someone to pass, if anyone else was mad enough to make such a drive in darkness. Suddenly he felt lightheaded and he realized that his hands were wet; his back was wet and chilling now.

Exxon meowed hoarsely. "We'll have to let him out," Susannah said. "Will he come back?"

"I don't know. I guess so."

She opened the back door and the cat leaped out and vanished. "I'll get back there and let you stretch and rest."

"Just until Exxon comes back," he said, and when she got out, he slid across to her side, away from the steering wheel. At first his legs did not want to straighten out even a little, and his fingers seemed permanently curled, designed to clutch a steering wheel.

"It's so beautiful," Susannah said softly. The lights were far away; it was like looking at the sky below her, an incredibly packed spot in the universe, with the black ocean of sky behind, a ribbon of black separating one galaxy from another, nearer one. A spot of light drifted in the black ribbon, galactic visitors daring the unknown . . . She realized that she was falling asleep at the side of the car, leaning against it, dreaming with her eyes open, hypnotized by the myriad stars below. Tiredly she climbed into the back seat of the car and tried to arrange herself to rest, perhaps to nap a few minutes while they waited for the cat.

Brad dreamed that he was a sardine. For years he had eluded the nets of the fishermen, but now he was caught. Curiously, his worst fear turned out to have been false; it was not bad living in the can head to tail with his brothers and friends. There was a constant murmur of conversation, and it was warm and cozy. It had been wrong-headed for the elders to lie to the youngsters and frighten them with horror stories about the net, and the can. The murmurs rose and fell, sometimes became excited when they discussed controversial subjects like whether there is life on the other worlds, especially those without water. Or whether God was a sardine, or a whale, or a nonwater being. That always raised shouts of heresy! heresy! He heard a clap of thunder and he knew this was the judgment day they had talked of many times. Judgment day started with thunder. It sounded again, closer . . .

Brad sat up, hitting his head sharply on the windshield. His vision was blurred from pain and sleep, but he was reasonably certain there was a man standing at his car window, and that the man was carrying a long, mean-looking rifle.

He glanced at the back seat where Susannah was staring at the man also. Slowly, making no fast movements, Brad rolled down his window.

"Can you tell us how to get to Berkeley?" he asked.

"You just get the fuck off of my property. This ain't no lovers' lane. Get it out of here!"

"We're lost," Susannah said, scanning the yard, the nearby woods, looking for Exxon. "We couldn't stop on the road, and we didn't know where we were, so we had to do something. When we stopped, Exxon ran out and we had to wait..."

The man raised his rifle so that instead of pointing at the ground, it was now aimed at the wheel of the car. "I'm counting to three," he said, "and then I'm shooting. You'll be in the way or you won't. Up to you."

Brad started the engine. Susannah opened the rear door and called, "Exxon, come on! We're leaving!"

The man with the gun turned to regard her for a moment, then looked at Brad with contempt. "Any man would take a loonie out to screw around deserves to get shot."

"You've probably scared him to death with all your shooting," Susannah said indignantly. "No telling how far he ran."

"One," the man with the gun said.

"Oh, be still!" Susannah cried. "Listen. Do you hear that, Brad? Over there in the woods. Maybe this maniac already shot him."

"Two."

From the woods on the side of the drive came a plaintive mewing. Brad turned the car and started toward the road down the steep curving track. Susannah opened the door on the woods side and called out to the cat again, and Exxon streaked out from hiding and bounded into the back seat. The man fired the rifle and Brad raced for the first curve.

"I'll shoot that misbegotten beast on sight, you hear me! On sight!"

"I wish you could back up and run over him," Susannah said grimly. "Poor Exxon, getting shot at, frightened to death."

She stroked the furious cat until his hair lay flat again and his tail stopped twitching. Brad took the curves slowly now that he was out of sight of the man on the hill protecting his property.

"Now what?" she asked. She was in the back seat with Exxon.

"A restaurant on a back street somewhere. Breakfast. Then we'll decide."

Fog had come in during the night; looking down now all Susannah could see was an ocean of white foam. "There must be a state hospital or something for people like me," she said quietly. "You can't just give up your own plans and look after me."

"You're not crazy," he said. "I wouldn't put you in one of those places. And I don't know where I could hide you out here. I want to go to New York." He took a curve too wide and had to jam on the brakes. "Now just let me drive."

◆◆◆

They had counted the money they had between them. Three hundred sixty-four dollars. There was a sleeping bag in the trunk of the car, and that was all they had with them.

"We'll need another sleeping bag and a tarp, and a ground cover. Some pans, stuff like that, and a little ice chest. One of those cheap Styrofoam ones will do." Brad looked at the figures again and felt an unsettling doubt that he did not express. It would take about one hundred sixty dollars for six days of car travel, if they got in five hundred miles a day. There would be tolls and oil and other unpredictable car expenses. He had put it down at two hundred dollars, and that left them one hundred sixty-four for everything else. They had ruled out motels instantly. Six nights at twenty-five minimum per night. They would sleep, but they would not eat that way.

The waitress brought more coffee and they waited until she was gone to continue their planning. "I just don't see what good it will do to use all our money to take a trip to New York," Susannah said, returning to her earlier protests.

"I intend to make my father help," Brad said soberly. "He owes me something, and he's got enough money to do whatever needs doing. Just don't let him near you with a camera."

Brad paid the bill, which came to four dollars and sixty-five cents. It was the last expensive meal they would have in a long time, he thought, looking at the tip regretfully. Susannah picked up the carry-out bag, a scrambled egg for Exxon.

"I think we should clear out of this area right away," Brad continued, as they walked to the car. "We can drive over to Davis and find a Salvation Army store, or a junk store for most of the stuff we'll need. Okay?"

"Sure. Let me drive and you can make a list."

They had asked directions in the restaurant and now Susannah started the car and backed out of the parking space, headed for the highway five or six blocks distant.

"Hey! You can drive!" Brad exclaimed suddenly. "Did you remember that you could?"

She shook her head. She had not even given it a thought. It felt good to be driving, to be doing something. "Put clothesline on the list," she said. "Something light enough to make a leash for Exxon, about twenty feet should do it, plus enough to hang up our shirts and stuff every night. We'll both need one more shirt, I'm afraid."

They started the list, putting things on, discussing them, often taking them off again. Bare necessities, they agreed, and took off chocolate milk mix. They reached the highway, joined the stream of traffic, and headed for Davis.

15

Jewels, jewels, fabulous jewels!

Marlene studied the handsome man attentively — ruggedly good-looking, like a movie cowboy, she decided — and turned her attention to the older man who did not actually look like his brother, but somehow exuded the same kind of easy confidence and power. The woman was different, clearly excited, trying to keep herself in check. She was very lovely, forty perhaps.

"My attorney says that he is satisfied that Jane Doe, as we know her, is actually your wife, Mr. Rivers. I know you must be anxious to locate her, but I have to satisfy myself that I'm acting in her best interest, you understand. I'd like to know why you didn't file a missing person report."

For a second she was afraid he actually was going to say "Well shucks, ma'am," but he sidestepped that and said:

"Well, it was like this, Mrs. Murphy. We had a little spat, you see, and when I got home and found her gone, and her suitcase gone, a few clothes, nothing much, not as if she meant to be away long, why, I thought she was telling me she wanted time alone, time to think, the way some people do when they're upset." He looked at the carpet and added, "We've only been married for six months and this was our first quarrel. But I'm gone so much, it's hard on the little girl. Felix and I talked it over and we decided there was no reason to bring in the police, maybe cause a lot of trouble, cause Susannah a lot of embarrassment later. We knew we could handle it ourselves, with the help of a private detective, and that's what we did. I never suspected that anything might be wrong with Susannah. It honestly never occurred to me that anything could be wrong."

Still Marlene hesitated. They knew Jane Doe, that was certain; Jimmie Rivers had pictures of her, their marriage license, a sample of her handwriting. It was enough. And yet . . . She wished she could talk to Jane — Susannah — first, or arrange something so that Susannah would not have to go with Jimmie if she chose not to. She sighed. There was still the problem of that hoodlum, and the attempted robbery.

"Mrs. Murphy," Jimmie said sincerely, "she's my wife and I love her and want her back. You have to tell me what you can. I'll take her home and in those familiar surroundings, with plenty of rest and no worries, we'll have a safe passage back to a normal life. Believe me, Mrs. Murphy, I'll never cause that little girl another worry again. Our first little spat will also be the last."

He was so damn reassuring, Marlene thought with irritation. "You know there's another party looking for her? He or at least the people he represents seem to think they know Susannah also."

"Ah, do you happen to know who that party is?" Felix asked. He looked so relaxed and comfortable she was afraid he might fall asleep on her couch. "Obviously they're wrong," he said.

"Of course they're mistaken," Marlene snapped. "They're gangsters. Rudy Drake was looking for her. He's a gangster."

"And they traced her this far?" Jimmie said in a musing manner, as if not very interested. "Well, now, ma'am, if you can just tell us where we can find Susannah, we won't bother you any longer."

"I don't know," Marlene said finally. "They called around noon, from a place near Sacramento. I suspect Brad is taking her to New York, but I don't know."

"New York? Why? And who is this Brad?"

"Bradford Hale," she said after another pause. She did not understand her own inclination to tell them nothing. Jimmie

Rivers had paid all of Jane's debts. This was exactly what she had hoped for: that someone would come very quickly and prove that he had a reason for taking Jane Doe away and taking care of her, someone who could afford to take care of her. Jimmie Rivers wanted to do that, and she was dragging her feet for no reason that she could identify, except a vague feeling of antipathy, a feeling that he was not the man she had hoped would show up. He was too old for one thing, nearly her own age, she guessed. And he was too self-assured for a man whose wife had run away. And why were his brother and his brother's wife along? She knew she had to cooperate with him, but she promised herself that she would follow this up; she had his name and address, and after Jane — Susannah — recovered, she would get in touch with her, make certain she could leave again if she chose to do so.

"You know about the accident, I know," she said finally, with evident reluctance. "Brad is the man who hit her. When she had no place to go, he let her take the spare room in his apartment. We all thought after a day or so she would recover her memory and leave. As for New York, that's where his father lives. Financially he is able to help her with whatever care she needs, and maybe to protect her from those gangsters, if they continue to pursue her. Brad doesn't have any money, and, of course, she doesn't either. Just what's left of what I loaned her. But that's only a guess. If you'll leave a number where I can reach you, I'll get in touch when I hear from them again." She stood up and her guests did also. Anna Maria Lucia was the first to reach the door.

"Bradford Hale," she murmured, as if to impress it upon her memory.

Marlene opened the door for them and they left, but the woman turned and asked, "Do you know where Bradford Hale go to school before he come to California?"

"No. Back east somewhere. Why?"

"Nothing. Nothing at all. I find my curiosity picked. Such a good person, taking so much trouble for a stranger."

Marlene shrugged and closed the door, grateful that they were gone, unable to stem the uneasiness that kept washing over her again and again.

◆◆◆

"They've gone where?" Donna cried later. "Are you sure?"

"I'm not sure about anything anymore," Marlene said wearily. "And don't shriek at me."

"Mother, exactly what did Brad say?"

"Exactly: 'Don't say a word. Don't worry. I'm taking our mutual friend to a safe place.'"

"Jesus Christ! What makes you think he means New York?"

"Because it was a collect call and the operator said it was from Davis. Oh, yes, he also said, 'I'll call you in about a week.'"

"A week. Across the country in that heap of his, with him at the wheel, it'll take a month, or a lifetime. They may end up in Poland!"

"It's an okay car," Marlene said, but she was worried about a cross-country trip with Brad driving. "Maybe Susannah is a superb driver," she said. "After all, they did make it to Davis."

Donna glared at her and counted on her fingers. "Monday night, or Tuesday, if they make five hundred miles a day, and they won't. Say Wednesday. But I can't count on that. She may be able to drive..."

"What are you getting at?"

"Do you think for a minute I'm going to let him take her to meet dear old daddy alone? When the handsome captain shows up to claim his forgetful little bride, I'll be there. Brad will need me then."

"And while you wait you can discuss stocks and bonds and money market funds with Croesus."

"You bet I will," Donna said defiantly.

◆◆◆

"Bradford Hale! Hah! You know what I think? They are old friends, old lovers from school. They make the arrangements for her to fall down, for him to stop, he go to her all concerned and she pass to him the key to a safe place, a box like you put your things in at the airport, and while she stay in hospital, Mr. Bradford Hale, he go to the airport and open the safe box and now he have the little suitcase! That's what I think!"

"She didn't know about the suitcase," Jimmie said reasonably. "She didn't even plan to take off until you showed up and spilled everything."

"She know! You think women are silly? Dumb? She know just like I know. How you afford so much, Jimmie? A house here, a house there, presents for wife in Japan, presents for wife in Italy, presents for too many wives. She know. You think a stranger say hop in my little car and I take you to meet my papa? My papa take care of you. You think stranger say, you move in my apartment and have your own little room and I don't touch you never? Hah! Little Susannah pull sheep over your eyes! Now you tell me what little Susannah steal that cause so big fuss! You tell me or I go talk to cousin Rudy even if Mama say I never call him."

They were in a hotel room so small that if one of them wanted to move they all had to shift. Jimmie was sitting on one of the twin beds, Felix on the other, and Anna Maria Lucia was in the only chair.

"I think we'd better tell Anna Maria Lucia everything," Felix said after a lengthy silence. "We'll need full cooperation from everyone aboard if we're going to get through this little problem intact. Don't you agree, old friend?"

Jimmie nodded. He drew a deep breath and started. "You see, Anna Maria Lucia, when you fly back and forth across the sea all the time, certain people get to know you and ask you to do small favors for them, and in return they, of course, do little things for you. Just little things, you understand. A special blend of whiskey, or a perfume you're having trouble finding, things like that. And then they suggest that there are certain items in the States that they have trouble getting, again just little things. Blue jeans, for example. And it's absolutely harmless. Now you know, Anna Maria Lucia, how I feel about women in blue jeans, but on the other hand, it isn't fair if they want them, not being able to get them. I feel strongly that some regulations we live by are very unfair . . ."

"Jimmie! No more sermonizing! What did you smuggle this time? Just tell me this thing!"

"Well, now, I'm coming to that, Anna Maria Lucia. Yes, I am coming directly to that little matter. I might say though that the word *smuggle* has certain connotations that don't exactly apply." He drew back as she left her chair and advanced toward the bed with both fists clenched. "Sit down now, and calm down, and just relax, Anna Maria Lucia. Let's pretend for a minute that your saintly grandmother bequeathed to you a few little jewels, nothing much, not the Hope diamond, nothing like that. But suppose you decided you needed the money instead of that jewelry. If you sell them outright there's a whopping tax, now don't you see? A terrible tax on a gift of love. You can't tax love, Anna Maria Lucia. It's just not right to tax love. But there it is. Suppose someone told you of a buyer in a foreign country who just happened to have seen those jewels in the past, maybe has a sentimental attachment for them, something moving like that. You might have thought of coming to someone like me and asking for a small favor. You know how I feel about an injustice, how I like to help a friend if I can. So you say how about carrying these little old jewels over to my friend in the States? And you say, but because this is not exactly a deal that can be insured, because the underwriters are tied hand and foot to all those regulations, you know, you will have to deposit a small sum to be repaid in full, plus another ten percent of the value of the jewels when you deliver them. So I talk this over with my business partner, and we agree that since I am doing most of the work, the dangerous work, my financial risk should be considerably less than his, and he advances some money, and I add a little money, and I hand it over and get the little blue suitcase all fixed up in advance. And that's how it was, Anna Maria Lucia."

137

"Felix, he put in twenty thousand? You put in how much?"

"Five thousand of my own money."

"You see the jewels? Ever?"

"Well, yes, sure, when the matter first came up. And the appraisal on them. It was a good investment, Anna Maria Lucia. Take my word, it was a very good investment."

"Whose jewels are worth twenty-five thousand just to carry? You tell me that! Whose jewels? What are they worth, your money and how much more?"

"Well, Felix figured he'd be making his money back two times over," Jimmie said after some hesitation. "Yes, double or nothing, that's how it was." He glanced at Felix who shrugged lazily. "We planned to profit from our investment. Fifty thousand, split down the middle, plus our original good will money."

"I don't believe this. Whose jewels?"

"I never actually asked," he said. "You don't like to pry into other people's affairs. It was hinted that at one time they went with a Peacock Throne, but I don't believe that."

"You *touched* them? You let someone talk you into touching *them!* If they vanish you have both sides running with knives for you. First they do terrible things to your body, then they use the knife and you wish many times for the knife. Jimmie, maybe they lie about this?"

Slowly he shook his head. "I don't think so. One of them that I actually saw looked a lot like a bird of some sort, with rubies and emeralds and stuff like that in the tail. A pretty little thing, about so big."

"Why you not in torture chamber right now? Why they let you run around the country?"

"Well, Anna Maria Lucia, it was their idea, you see. The suitcases. I made two trial runs with other pieces of that set, just to see if anyone would notice how they were fixed, and when no one did, they put the goods in the third one. I simply told them that Susannah had made a mistake and switched bags. What could they do? They want their stuff in the right hands. They aren't unreasonable."

"How much time they give you?"

Jimmie glanced at Felix, then said easily, "Now don't you start worrying about that. We have plenty of time to find Susannah, plenty of time. Ten whole days."

"Starting when?"

"Last Monday."

Anna Maria Lucia looked aghast. "Ten days, and you don't even know where she is, where she is going, when she will get to that place."

"I've been thinking," Felix said lazily, "if we could rent a plane, and if they are on the way to New York, it might be possible to spot them on the highway. Lots of open space between here and Chicago. They're on Interstate Eighty if they passed through Sacramento, and no doubt they'll stick to it. Can't hide much of anything in the desert country between here and the Rockies, and if they get that far, there's nothing but corn fields for nearly a thousand miles. One little car on the highway shouldn't be that hard to spot."

"Crazy! Crazy!" Anna Maria Lucia cried. "You can't inspect thousands of miles!"

But Jimmie was considering it. He nodded. "Maybe," he said cautiously. "We could estimate their mileage and hop ahead of them, cruise back along the highway until we see them."

"Exactly," Felix said. "And when we find them, we go ahead a hundred miles or so, land and rent a car and be ready to tag along when they pass by. First time they stop, you claim your little bride and we're home free."

"Bride! Bah! Whore! Mistress! Adulteress!"

"We'll need some road maps," Jimmie said. "And the car model, license number, color, all that."

"Salt Lake City," Felix murmured. "We should get a flight to Salt Lake City and rent a Cessna there. They'll pass through sometime tomorrow. We'll get ourselves a grandstand seat along the interstate outside Salt Lake City and wait for them to show."

❖❖❖

Susannah and Brad finished their dinner and savored mugs of coffee over the dying fire. They had started to eat in daylight, a bright dusk actually, and now it was utterly dark. The embers of the campfire seemed to grow brighter and brighter as the light failed, although the fire was all but extinguished. They had driven through Winnemucca, turned off the highway onto a dirt road, which they followed for nearly ten miles to this spot, a level place in a land where level places were very rare. Here they had found pine woods and a dry stream bed. On both sides the mountains rose, barren and stark with jagged rocks and thin woods near seasonal water.

Brad was content; it had been a good day, better than he had anticipated. They had made nearly four hundred miles, and only twenty or thirty had been a mistake, his mistake. She had realized they were heading in the wrong direction and they had turned back at the first chance. That was not bad, he thought. Not bad.

"It's getting awfully cold," she said. "I'm going to get inside my sleeping bag."

"Me too," he said. All day it had been in the low one hundreds through California, through Reno, and now up in the mountains the air felt frosty. He hoped the new cheap sleeping bag would be enough.

They had spread the ground cloth before eating, and he had tied the tarp to make a windbreak and to cover them from dew if nothing else. Now he raked the fire apart, conscientiously spread the embers, covered them with dirt he had left piled next to the fire, and when he was satisfied that nothing remained of it, he got into the other sleeping bag alongside hers.

With the fire gone the darkness was complete, and the silence was more profound than he had ever known. Only an occasional rustle from her sleeping bag, or his own, broke the quiet for a long time, until he began to hear the night creatures that had been frightened by the fire and were only now returning to poke into this area, investigate the strangers.

Susannah listened to wings, at first nearby, then farther and farther away, until they were gone. Something clattered rocks in the dry stream bed, and a distant animal, coyote, she guessed, wailed in the night. Beside her she could hear Brad's even breaths.

After a long time she said in a near whisper, "Are you asleep?"

"No."

"You want to go to sleep though, don't you?"

"Eventually. What do you want to talk about?"

"You. Me. Life. Everything."

Now he heaved himself on one arm and looked toward her. It was too dark to see her outline, anything. "All that's too much for one night," he said.

"Brad, did you ever feel that you were someone else's thing? Someone's creation? You go here and there, do this and that all because that someone wants you to. Maybe he even needs you too, and forces you to do everything you do. And all the time you think you're deciding every second."

"No," Brad said sharply. "That's just you, because of your amnesia. Others don't feel that. You didn't before you were hurt, and you won't after you get well."

"Who am I? Where am I going? And why? Especially why. That's what I'll ask that someone."

"Who?"

"I don't know yet, but I will when the time comes. And I'll be ready to ask because I've given it some thought. Most people won't be ready. Most people won't admit they don't know who they are or what they're doing or why."

"That's nonsense," he said hotly. "And you should know it even if you don't know who you are."

"It's as if I was created a week or so ago; out of the blue, there was this woman without a past. I don't have the whole past reminding me of what I'm supposed to do next. I can't say my mother did this and my father did that, teachers pushed this way, bosses at work pushed that way. None of that exists for me and I can't use it as a crutch. I have to find my own way without excuses, or else I'm someone else's creation and there's a purpose that I haven't been able to discover yet."

"There's no grand purpose," he said angrily. "No one has a grand purpose, why should you?"

"I don't know. Maybe everyone does, but most people are blind to it because they keep looking to the past all the time. Maybe they're just pushed into their purposes without awareness; when they start to wonder about it, they can be distracted by thoughts of injuries done to them, of victories they've won, or think they've won, everything that makes up their past."

"God!" he muttered. "This is so crazy! Do you think that guy pumping gas back in Winnemucca is someone's creation too? And the woman in the little store we stopped at? What about her?"

"Probably."

"And me?"

"Oh yes."

"Then who are the creators? If everyone is created, who's doing it all?"

"A handful of people, maybe. Or maybe God. But since we don't seem to be aimed toward any particular good, I don't think it's God. I think there are a few very powerful people who have learned how to create others to do the things they want done. Fight their wars, sweep their houses, pump gas, write their books, make movies for them, paint pictures . . ."

"You don't believe a word of all that," he said after a pause. "You're kidding me."

"I know. I only believe a small bit of it. I really do think I was created for some purpose."

"Then you're a nut case!" he snapped. Because deep inside where no one else could ever see it he also believed that he had to deny it. It made no sense. If he believed that, he too was a nut case. For a long time there was no rustling noise, no sound of movement. Finally he said, "I thought you wanted to talk."

"Not if it's going to make you mad."

"I'm not mad!"

He didn't know if he heard or imagined a soft chuckle. She was the only person he had ever known who could do that to

142

him, he thought bitterly. Make him mad as hell one minute and puncture the reason for his fury the next.

"You've given me an idea," he said then. "Suppose there *are* spirits, creatures without physical bodies. When they want something done, they have to take over a human, or an animal, or whatever suits their purpose, long enough to do it."

"Not Einstein, or Jesus, or Michelangelo!"

"No, no history maker. Little things, like getting a light on a street corner for whatever reason they would have. The person would come on like a fanatic on the subject and never know quite why."

This time her chuckle was unmistakable. "They're the ones who make someone determined to sow bluegrass in the desert."

"And breed ever smaller horses."

"Or make women wear bustles."

"And men starched shirts and ties."

They both laughed softly and then she said, "Brad, it's been a good day. Thanks. Good night."

He heard the movements of her sleeping bag and then her breathing, sounding more distant now. She had turned over. He thought he could tell when she fell asleep, but he was not sure. Exxon walked across his stomach and settled down between them purring.

16

The blue bag changes hands again.

Mildred Obloski, whose mother called her Mimi, walked up the four flights to her apartment carrying her duffel bag, her purse, and the pretty blue suitcase Mr. DeKalb had given her. She was tired and sleepy. She had had enough hassle from her mother to do her for the year. Her mother wanted her to quit her job at the restaurant here, where she was well paid and not likely to be laid off if the customers kept dwindling, not until the last anyway. Her mother wanted her only daughter to live near her in Chicago, or even Evanston. Her mother did not believe in Mimi's dream of owning her own small restaurant out in the country, near a major highway, where she could have chickens and fresh eggs, buy good country milk and cream, grow her own vegetables. She would hire Leah to be her bookkeeper, she dreamed; and they would close down altogether in August to travel, see Europe.

She opened her door and stared with dismay at the mess in the tiny living room. Leah had strewn clothes everywhere. The windows were open, but the heat was overpowering, and the apartment stank of Leah's perfume.

"Hi," Leah cried, dashing forward to greet her. "Listen, the most fantastic thing happened. Louis asked me to go to Cartagena with him! He's being sent to inspect the restaurant the company's buying. We're leaving in the morning. But I don't have any clothes for Cartagena. Is it very hot, do you suppose? I know some places on the gulf are cool and others are like hell this time of year."

"Louis? And you said yes?"

"You think I'd turn it down? Come on."

Leah was blonde and inclined to plumpness. Her eyes were pretty, big, blue, with heavy lashes, and her skin was wonderful, pink and soft, without blemish. She was twenty-one. They both were twenty-one. They had come to the city together after high school.

"But Louis . . ."

Louis Cordoza was the restaurant manager. Mimi wanted to put strychnine in his soup.

"He's not as bad as the girls pretend," Leah said, picking up a skirt from a chair. "Can I wear this for shopping? Not dinner or anything fancy, but window-shopping."

"I don't know. Leah, think about Louis just a minute. Remember Tillie last year, and just four months ago there was Deborah . . ."

"Yeah, I know. But it takes two to tango, you know. It wasn't all his fault, none of them. Hey, that's a pretty suitcase!"

Mimi let her have it to examine. She had put only one or two things in it since her own duffel bag had already been packed when she got the new blue suitcase. She did not have a key for it.

"Don't you need a passport? Shots?"

Leah giggled. "Louis said he'd fix all that. Ask me no questions honey. Hey, could I use the suitcase? It's just for a few days. We'll be back late Monday night."

"Leah, just let's talk about it a minute. You know what Deborah's doing now, don't you? He set her up. He's a pimp on top of being a slimy toad."

Leah's face lost its baby look for a moment; she looked hard and determined then. "Forget Deborah and Tillie," she said. "I'm not like them. I can take care of myself. You'll see. I tried it this way, and this way stinks. Scrimp and scrounge and save a penny every six months if you're lucky. I'm tired of it, Mimi.

I want out." She flung down the skirt she had been holding. "You'll be in that fucking kitchen until your hair falls out, your teeth fall out, you'll have varicose veins and your skin will stink of garlic. Not me! I want out!"

Mimi picked up her duffel bag and the few things Leah had taken from the blue suitcase. "Keep it as long as you want," she said dully. "Have a good trip."

"Yeah. I will. I'll send you a postcard."

17

Hopscotch

For hours they had driven through the hot barren mountains, ascending into piñon woods, dipping down into juniper and sage country. The wind blew hot and dry, stirring dust in the clumps of sage, making the air hazy. Now the ground was leveling out, the heat increasing; there were no more trees.

"I think what we should do is try to get into the Rockies before night," Brad said, studying the map.

"We have to stop somewhere to shower and wash our clothes," Susannah reminded him.

"Yeah, I'm looking. There's a cut-off just before Salt Lake City. It goes down past what they say is the world's biggest copper mine, then over to Utah. It looks like half a dozen recreation areas in a row on the Utah side. Okay?"

"What time is it?"

"Almost three. Want me to drive awhile?"

"No, I'm just thirsty again. Is there any tea left?"

During their lunch stop she had filled a jug with ice water at a gas station and added a cut-up lemon and instant tea. Neither liked it, but they had nearly emptied the jug and still felt parched.

"Let's pick up foam rubber mats, or inflatable mattresses, or something," she said, trying to work stiffness out of her shoulders by hunching them, then relaxing. She was too sore to talk about it.

"Maybe we should splurge and stop at a motel tonight," Brad said. He was sore and tired and the thought of an air-conditioned room and a shower seemed irresistibly tempting.

For a time they both considered it, and reluctantly decided not to take the chance. "If we have enough money left the last night, when we're close enough to hitchhike the rest of the way if we have to, then let's do it," she said finally.

He sighed and agreed. "The turn-off is near the end of the testing grounds, about twenty miles, I guess. State Road Thirty."

A distant explosion shook the air, the fourth one in the last half-hour.

"I feel as if they're shooting at us," Susannah said. Nothing showed on either side of the road, just the desert that stretched to the horizon, but somewhere out on that desert men with cannons and rockets and mortars were using them. Shooting what? Targets of houses, factories, enemy equipment, ranks of men? She sped up a bit, wanting away from the Wendover Range.

❖❖❖

"Now, Anna Maria Lucia, it was an oversight," Jimmie said patiently. "Felix hasn't flown this way in years, and neither have I. We simply forgot that the airspace is restricted here. This will work just as well."

They were in a rest area off Interstate 80, twenty miles west of Salt Lake City. Felix and Jimmie were seated so that they could scan every car heading east. They had been there for two hours. The hot wind blew incessantly. Anna Maria Lucia watched a couple with three small children unpack picnic supplies and arrange them on a nearby table. They had a jug of something red, thick with ice cubes.

"Here comes a Corvair," Jimmie said quietly. Felix raised his binoculars and looked at the automobile. Wrong color, wrong license. He swung the glasses around as if watching a bird, then put them down again. Anna Maria Lucia watched a small child deliberately pour out the iced red drink on an ant hill. She would have moistened her lips, but her tongue was too dry.

"We should have brought something to put water in," she

said. The other two children were at the fountain splashing each other. Tiredly, she got up and went to it for yet another drink of the salty-tasting water.

"Another one," Jimmie said. Felix looked briefly, put the glasses down. They both continued to watch. The wind blew.

◈◈◈

Brad pointed. "There it is. Are you ready for the world's biggest open copper mine?" He was driving now.

"It's obscene! I can't even see the top of the smoke stack!"

"Where do we turn next?"

"Onto State Seventy-three. It's not very far. We cross Interstate Seventy and go up One Eighty-nine to the park areas. I can hardly wait for a shower. I'm gritty all over."

◈◈◈

"Jimmie, they are not coming this way. They take another road. Or they're climbing mountains, or swimming, or fishing. They are not coming!"

"Now, Anna Maria Lucia, we know they may not come this way. They may not even be going to New York, but if they are going to New York and if they passed through Sacramento, then you can rest assured that they are coming this way, and when they do, we'll see them. There's no way any car can head east through this area without our seeing it sooner or later."

"And what if they don't come today? What if they stop for sightseeing, or have automobile breakdown? Maybe they stop to fix it. Then what?"

"I figure sooner or later they'll pass this point. We'll give it another day, and then hop over to Cheyenne. I know they can't slip past us at Cheyenne."

"I am dirty, and I think I am sick also. My skin is coming off."

"It's the aridity, Anna Maria Lucia. This is desert country and the humidity is very low. That means you lose more moisture from your skin than you're used to, but it doesn't indicate anything's really wrong . . . There's another one, Felix."

149

Felix looked, put the glasses down, and stared without expression at the shimmering highway.

◆◆◆

"Good shower?"

"Heavenly. I feel like a new person. Where's Exxon?"

"I had to turn him loose for a while. He was going nuts. The heat's getting to him, I think. Look, let's try for the mountains before we stop for the day. At least as far as Evanston, and if it's still hot there, up higher. Okay?"

"Oh yes. Did you wash your clothes? I think they'll dry in a few minutes just draped on the back seat."

"Yeah, my stuff's in the car already. What we want now is a grocery store, and a store that handles mattress pads, and then back on the road."

"Exxon! Come on, boy!" She put her fingers to her mouth and whistled shrilly and Exxon bounded into view looking pleased with himself.

"Will you teach me how to do that?" Brad asked, as he started the car again.

She laughed.

◆◆◆

"Look at my face! I must be having the fever. I am sick."

"No, that's just a little windburn."

"Jimmie, just please tell me what we do if you don't see the car on this road?"

"Now look, Anna Maria Lucia. I told you not to worry about this little setback. We'll work things out. We'll give them three days and if we haven't spotted them by Sunday, we'll hop a flight to New York and wait for them there."

"Jimmie, it is to worry. What if you find her and she say I am sorry, but I don't remember? Then what, Jimmie?"

"We're working on that, Anna Maria Lucia. Felix and I are working on that."

◆◆◆

"Why are your eyes closed?" Brad asked. "Are you too tired to keep going? Want to stop?"

"Oh, no, it's not that. I'm tired, all right, but I want to stop where it's cooler. It's just that I don't think I can take in any more scenery today. It's so beautiful. When I'm driving, I see it but it doesn't overwhelm me because I'm concentrating on the road, the car, all that. But when you're driving, I begin to feel almost swallowed up by it all."

"I'm glad we're doing this," he said happily. "I've never driven across the country before. I never thought I had enough time for it."

"You're making memories," she said softly. "That's nice, to make good memories. Maybe I've traveled this road a dozen times, a hundred times. Maybe I was a truck driver and this was my route."

"Or a mule driver," he said, trying for a light tone, not quite making it. She would forget all this, he thought with regret. The whole trip, whistling for the fool cat, drying her laundry in the back seat, cooking over a campfire . . . Talking to him for hours.

"Anyway," he said, "you don't set out deliberately to make memories. That's a by-product."

"I know. And that's a mistake. You should keep in mind that memory is all you'll have eventually."

"That makes you live for the future so that you can look back on the past and have a good memory," he said. "It makes me dizzy to think too hard about it."

"You would have to learn it so well that it became automatic, like typing, or riding a bicycle. I don't think it would be wise to do it deliberately and consciously. Classes could start in kindergarten and continue through high school. Tests could be devised to see if it's taking. There would come a time when you would unconsciously redirect your own activities if you knew they would make a bad taste in your mouth in ten years, or twenty years. And that would make every day really good in present time."

"And what about those times when you know a bad day is coming, as inevitably as the months roll around? Maybe we should take pills to erase them from memory as soon as they happen?"

She shook her head. "I don't think so. You'd have to have a few bad memories just to make you appreciate how good the best ones are. And you have to remember that what makes for a bad memory for one person may very well be one of the best for someone else. You would learn to accept that. If you have a bad day and lose a game, someone else wins it. Good and bad. Maybe with enough training we could even rejoice in someone else's good memories and ignore our own bad ones."

His hands were tight on the wheel. They were no longer talking about an abstract, rather silly idea. They were talking about the days ahead, rolling inevitably toward them the way the seasons roll around, without regard for the readiness of those who will live through them. It could not be both ways, he thought dully. Her good day, her day of recovery, would be his worst day.

When he glanced at her, she had turned her face away, and was looking out the side window. She was too stiff, too tense to be enjoying scenery. He wanted to touch her, to say it was all right, but he found he could not bring himself to do it. It was not all right and could never be all right again.

He stared ahead and drove, and the silence persisted. Forty miles past Evanston, in a grove of cottonwood trees, they made camp. Brad cooked their meal while she arranged the mattresses and sleeping bags.

They crawled into the bags as soon as it was dark, and each one pretended to think the other was asleep long before either drifted off.

❖❖❖

"They could have gone through Salt Lake City during the night," Felix said slowly, watching the road. "I think we'd better take that flight to Cheyenne at two."

"Well, they could have, but they have to sleep sometime. You check those miles, old buddy?"

"Yep. If they went through in the evening they could clear Cheyenne this afternoon."

"What flight is that?"

"Frontier. It's a DC-Three."

Jimmie nodded and turned to Anna Maria Lucia who was starting to unwrap her sandwich. Today they had brought their lunches with them, and a six-pack of beer.

"Ah, Anna Maria Lucia, I don't think I would eat much if we're getting that Frontier plane. I think Felix is right and we should consider this spot unlikely. But out of Cheyenne, why that's different. There's nothing east of Cheyenne but level prairie. You can see ten miles in every direction."

"Why you say I should eat nothing, Jimmie? We have time. I finish in the car while we drive to airport."

"You see, Anna Maria Lucia, in the middle of the summer, like now, there's a lot of heat rising from the desert country. And also, there's a fair amount of cold air up on the mountains. There are glaciers on those mountains, Anna Maria Lucia; that snow stays there summer and winter, and it chills the air quite a lot. Chills it way down. Now it's a law of nature, Anna Maria Lucia, that cold air sinks while hot air rises and in most places that's all right because the atmosphere cushions the air masses, clouds form and you might get a shower or two. But out here, there isn't enough moisture in the air to have that effect, and what happens is that the hot air rises pretty high and pretty fast, and that creates a low pressure area near the ground, and that's another thing that nature hurries to take care of. Yes sir, nature just can't abide emptiness. And there's all that cold air rolling down the slopes, you see. So it rolls faster and faster, trying to fill that near-vacuum, and the hot air is racing upward and it creates a little bit of turbulence sometimes. Nothing dangerous, you understand, but you feel it if you're flying over the mountains and if you aren't up pretty high, and especially in a small-ish plane. You do tend to feel some of those forces of nature."

"You mean I get sick?"

"Well, probably not. Not everyone does, you know. But I would wait until we hit Cheyenne to eat, if I were you, that is."

❖❖❖

"I think what I'll be when I grow up," Susannah said, "is a hermit, and live in these mountains. Or some mountains. So far from the road that you'd have to walk in three days to find me."

"Good thinking," Brad agreed. "You pick a mountaintop and I'll take a peak opposite it. We can signal each other from time to time."

They were in deep woods high on Medicine Bow Mountain, an hour's drive from Cheyenne. They had eaten lunch, had splashed in an ice-water stream that was only two feet across, and now they were waiting for Exxon to tire from his frantic chases after quick silver ground squirrels and chipmunks.

It was so quiet here that the sound of a plane was an affront. It was so low that if they had been on a ridge, Brad thought, they would have been able to look in the windows, wave to the passengers making their descent into Cheyenne. The noise faded. He put his fingers to his mouth and blew. There was a rush of air, but no whistle.

"You still aren't holding your tongue right. Look, like this." She used her forefinger and her little finger; her tongue was curled a bit.

He tried again, then shook his head. "I give up. How did you learn?"

"I don't think anyone taught me. I just do it."

He nodded. They were pretending that she could remember her family, growing up in Dreamland, Ohio, going to school at Ohio State.

"How are we doing for money?" she asked after a while.

"Not too bad. We didn't count on having to pay park fees, but we're not hurting yet."

"I was thinking, it's so nice and cool up here, maybe we could just stay here and rest, make something to eat later, maybe even sleep a little, and then drive on after dark. The radio says it's one hundred eight in Cheyenne. I hate to think of driving out over the prairie when it's so hot."

"We could drive from ten until one or even two," he said. "It might be kind of nice driving at night for a change. But what's that got to do with money?"

"Oh, if we're staying in our budget, maybe we could stop in Cheyenne for an ice cream cone."

"A sundae," he said. "Double-dip sundae."

"Bittersweet chocolate topping."

"Caramel, with pecans."

◆◆◆

"Jimmie, what are you doing? Stop!"

"Remember our little discussion back at Salt Lake City, Anna Maria Lucia? I explained turbulence . . ."

"Stop the plane! I want out! Jimmie!"

"I think we can go in now," Felix said. "They aren't on Interstate Eighty. They must still be in the mountains. Let's pick a good lookout spot first and then turn in the plane."

"Jimmie! Please, dear God, please let me out!"

"It might help if you put your head down between your knees, Anna Maria Lucia. I'm taking her in now. It won't be long. It's perfectly safe, understand, and even predictable at this time of year. I've seen turbulence much worse than this. Sometimes you can't even tell if you're going up and down or side to side; they're all mixed up together."

"I want out! Please, I want to get out now."

"There's a fine place, Jimmie. Little cafe, it looks like. Good view of the highway three, four miles. It's far enough from Cheyenne not to mix up local traffic with the real travelers."

Jimmie nodded. "Here we go in now, Anna Maria Lucia. Just relax now and don't worry. It might get a little bumpy as we approach the mountains again, but everything's under control . . ."

She groaned feebly.

"You want to take her in, old buddy? She's a sweet little machine, handles real well."

Jimmie offered generously, and Felix accepted. The plane dipped, then shot upward as he got the feel of it. Anna Maria Lucia started to pray audibly for death.

◈◈◈

"We have bread and cheese for a snack when we stop," Susannah said. "Can you think of anything else we'll need? I expect nothing's going to be open this time of night."

"All set, I guess. Aren't you going to finish your sundae?" He had finished his and scraped the dish.

"No. Too much. You want the rest?"

He finished hers, drank his water, and they were ready to start driving again. Exxon greeted their return to the car with a pitiful meow that became a screech.

"All right," Susannah said. "But you have to be tied this time. We can't wait an hour for you to decide to come back." She fastened the twenty-foot length of cord to his collar as she spoke, and then let him out. They had stopped next to a small city park in Cheyenne. The cat loped away from her almost to the length of the tether, then began to walk, fully expecting her to follow, to keep any tension from threatening him. She laughed softly and trailed after him into the park. He vanished among bushes.

"Why so long?" Brad remembered asking, when she told him twenty feet of rope or twine.

"Cats have too much dignity to do their business on a short line. Exxon would rather die, I'm sure. This way we can both pretend he's free."

Brad tidied up the car while Susannah saw to the cat. He inspected the tires by kicking each in turn, wiped the rear lights with his bare hand, and then had to find the paper towel in the trunk to clean his hand. Everything was in order; he walked into the park a step or two looking for Susannah.

And on the sidewalk two men and a woman passed by. The

woman was talking in a low rapid monologue.

"That restaurant! Bah! And tomorrow you fly back and forth across the prairie all day! For what? No more planes for me. You take me out to sunburn and windburn and I get seasick and eat so much bad food I may be poisoned . . ."

Her voice and their footsteps faded as Susannah joined Brad. "He's protesting, but we're coming in now. I think he wants to hunt chipmunks. Poor Exxon, we keep enticing him with all these good things and telling him, just look and come along."

"Come on, you brute. You can prowl all night after we stop. You want to drive, or want me to?"

"I'll drive. I like to drive at night." She was winding up the long rope, reeling in the reluctant cat. They all went to the car and arranged themselves and she drove out of town.

"Do you know where we are?" Susannah asked, yawning. It was seven and already hot. Breakfast was over, their gear stowed away.

"Past North Platte, that's all I know. Wish we had slept later. We'll both probably be dead by afternoon."

"Then let's stop the way we did yesterday. If we can find a place that even pretends to be cool. Driving at night is the best way in this weather."

"Okay, might as well start, I guess."

"See, Anna Maria Lucia, calm as your living room. And didn't I tell you, you can see for twenty or thirty miles. We'll spot them today for sure."

She muttered a curse and stared morosely out the side window.

"What we'll do is fly clear over to Omaha and then make a search of the whole stretch of road on the way back. We'll see them, you can count on that. Can you imagine anything moving down there without our seeing it?"

Down there, covering the high plains of Nebraska, were endless corn fields and straight white roads, with rare farmhouses shaded with trees, and fewer rest areas with groves. Even the filling stations were exposed, the cars in them clearly visible. They could see farm equipment and people, cattle, even chickens.

Jimmie hummed softly as he made a sweeping turn west of Omaha and started the patrol of the highway.

◆◆◆

"What's wrong with it?" Susannah asked, looking at the red light on the dash.

"Not sure. Maybe it's a water line going out. I filled the radiator yesterday. Look at the map, will you, and see if there's a town ahead soon?"

She studied it a moment. "Kearney, about five or ten miles. Can we make it that far?"

"Yeah, I think so. The light just came on." He slowed down and they watched the light until they reached the town of Kearney, where they pulled into the first gas station.

"Might as well put her in the garage," the mechanic said. "No use staying out in the sun if you don't have to."

◆◆◆

"I think we didn't spot them because they haven't really cleared the mountains yet. Bet they stayed up where it was cool last night, what I would have done in their place."

"Jimmie, let's go to New York now and wait for them. There is too much road, too many cars, too many other ways they go just the same as this way."

"But, Anna Maria Lucia, if they don't show up in New York until Tuesday, or maybe Wednesday, you see, that'll be just a little bit late for our purposes. We have a date down in Miami on Wednesday afternoon."

"I've been thinking, old friend," Felix said slowly, "it's a shame I've never traveled very much in Central America or South

America. I hear that Costa Rica is a lovely little country. Friendly, not too expensive."

"There's one," Jimmie said, nodding toward the road about ten miles distant. "Looks familiar somehow."

Felix studied it with the binoculars and said, "We saw it yesterday. We're counting the same cars again, old buddy."

"Well, that means they couldn't very well have gone beyond about here, isn't that right? Let's just fly back to Cheyenne to make sure we didn't miss them on the road, and then back over here to Grand Island and put her down and get a car, same as yesterday."

"And the day before and the day before that," Anna Maria Lucia muttered.

"Well yes, but their chances are lessening every day, you know. We'll spot them today, you can count on that."

"You folks heading for Lincoln?" the mechanic asked, wiping his hands.

"Chicago," Brad said.

"You'll miss it then, I guess. If you're in a hurry, I'd advise you to get off the interstate. It's going to be as busy as a hound dog that wallowed in a flea hive. County Fair, Fourth of July celebration at Lincoln. It'll bring folks in for miles. And most of them will be on the interstate. Once you get an interstate, folks forget other perfectly good roads that were fine before."

Brad paid him for a water hose and a fan belt that had almost melted in half.

"Better change your minds and see the celebration," the mechanic said. He stopped as a plane flew over, very low, buzzing like a toy. "Bet he's warming up for the airshow. Going to have the Blue Angels, and old biplanes, everything. I'm closing at eleven to go over myself." He gave them change and Brad and Susannah got into the car. Susannah opened the map to see if there was an alternate route they could take.

"Up U.S. Thirty," she said. "It doesn't seem any longer than the interstate, and it will take us north of Des Moines, not through it. What do you think?"

"Let's. Look, it follows the river. There may even be trees we can cool off under."

They waved to the attendant, pulled out of the garage, and turned to get onto U.S. 30, heading north toward Grand Island.

❖❖❖

"How you know they won't be on that road?" Anna Maria Lucia asked as Jimmie, driving south toward the interstate, crossed over U.S. 30.

Jimmie laughed and patted her thigh. "Some things you just don't understand about Americans, Anna Maria Lucia. We like nice wide highways without any bumps, without any towns to slow us down every five or six miles, without any traffic lights. This is a big country, Anna Maria Lucia, and it's the interstates that have made it accessible to everyone who has a car. Used to take two weeks to drive coast to coast and now you can do it in five or six days, in comfort and safety. Those other roads, why they're for the locals to go shopping on, or to church, or to visit each other, but when they really want to travel, they head for the interstate same as anyone else. That's what they're for, to travel."

❖❖❖

"We have a hundred thirty-five dollars," Susannah said. "And we'll need to buy gas again after a while, and on Sunday and Monday. Say seventy dollars for gas. That still leaves us enough, doesn't it?"

"If we don't have any more mechanical problems," he said, after thinking about it a moment. "We're nearly out of everything to eat though."

"I know." She had the map open on her legs and looked at it again. "There's a big lake and park north of Des Moines. I guess we could stay there until dark again tonight. I think it's hotter than yesterday." It was ten-thirty and one hundred degrees.

❖❖❖

"Why are so many cars on the road now?" Anna Maria Lucia asked. The traffic had grown heavier and heavier in the hour they had been in the rest area.

"Well now, Anna Maria Lucia, I have to tell you that I honestly don't know."

"Bah! How you spot one bee in a hive? Jimmie, you have to decide what you do if she say she lose the suitcase, or doesn't remember."

"We talked about that a little bit last night, Felix and I, and we are of a mind about it. We reached a consensus of opinion concerning that very problem. I say to her, Susannah, don't you know me? I'm your husband. I called a doctor in Miami and he's waiting to see you right now. And we get her on a plane and go to Miami and introduce her to our ah, associates there."

"I think we should make reservations to go to Costa Rica," Anna Maria Lucia said darkly.

"Well, you see, we discussed that at some length and we agreed that on reflection Costa Rica is not quite ah, far enough away."

"Then Sri Lanka, or Tibet! Jimmie, they don't care if you bring little Susannah for to excuse yourself! What do they care for Susannah?"

Felix said soothingly, "Now, Anna Maria Lucia, don't get excited. We're aware of the problem, you understand. We're handling it. We are taking care of things. But you see, no place is remote enough or hard enough not to trace people to, if you're determined. And we have to take Susannah to them, you know, because she's all we have."

"You idiot! You don't have her!"

"Now, now, Anna Maria Lucia. We will. Before the day ends we'll have her. Or tomorrow at the latest."

Brad stirred sleepily but did not open his eyes. He heard it again, a small voice whispering nearby. Now he looked and saw a little girl squatting down near Susannah's head, peering at her intently. They were in the shade of an oak tree several hundred yards from the lake where boaters and swimmers were setting up a din. The little girl was no more than five; he started to shoo her away, but Susannah opened her eyes then and smiled at the child.

"I said are you sleeping?" the girl asked.

"No. I'm resting."

"My mommy's sleeping, and daddy too. My name's Lisa. What's your name?"

18

"I am a fairy princess."

My name is Thalia," she said softly. "Because you have golden hair I am allowed to tell you this. I am a fairy princess."

The little girl laughed with delight. "Your hair is golden too."

"Of course. All fairy princesses have golden hair. The sun kissed each of us when we were born."

"Did the sun kiss me too?"

"Oh no! If the sun kisses human babies they die. But he smiled at you and made your hair gold. Tell me what you're afraid of and I will fix it for you."

Brad caught his breath, wanting to stop her, but the look of terror that crossed the child's face stilled him.

"Thunder," Lisa whispered.

"I suspected that," Susannah said thoughtfully. "That's my sister Hulda's work, you know. We live in the clouds and every morning when we get up we shake our clouds to fluff them up again, and sprinkle the grass with dew. Sometimes when the corn needs water, we shake our beds much harder. And when we have a dance or a party or a celebration and many of us get together, then a lot of water is shaken loose. In the winter we like to play with the snowflakes, just as you do. But our games are different. We like to ride the snowflakes to earth; sometimes we race, but I like it better when we make flakes large enough to sit on and drift down slowly, like this." She held up her hand and rocked it slightly, lowering it gracefully.

"I've never seen anyone on a snowflake."

"Of course not. No one can see fairies, unless the fairies let them, like now."

"Who makes the thunder?"

"Oh yes, the thunder. One of my sisters is very old and sour and mean. It makes her cross when she sees the rest of us playing and having fun, and she comes in stamping her feet and screaming at us and beating the clouds with a long stick that she carries. We're not afraid of her because you can't hurt a fairy, not even a fairy can hurt another fairy. But we don't like the noise she makes and we all scatter far away until she gets over her tantrum. You can't see her up there banging on the clouds with her stick, but you can hear her. The noise she makes is the thunder you hear. She has a green nose, about this long." She held out her hand from her face. "It's pointed like a parsnip. You know why she's so sour all the time?"

Lisa shook her head.

"I don't know for sure, but I think it's because she eats too many grasshoppers."

"Yuch!"

"That's how I feel about grasshoppers, but Hulda began to eat them when she was very little, about your age, and now it's a habit that she can't stop. And I'm certain they make her very sour and mean. Her legs are getting skinny too. I'll tell you what I think is going to happen to her. I think she's going to turn into a grasshopper. In about ten thousand years or so, she'll be just like them. And that will be her punishment for all the noise she makes when she bangs on the clouds with her stick."

"Can she hit me with her stick?"

"Goodness no! She's not allowed to leave the clouds ever! No fairy with a green nose would be allowed to come down here. It would give fairies a very bad name. That's another thing that makes her mad, that she can't come down once in a while."

"He isn't a fairy, is he?" Lisa pointed to Brad.

"Of course not. Look at his hair! Dark brown. The sun didn't kiss him, or even smile at him. He's my servant when I come here. He carries my things for me and brings me ice cream. That's why I like to come down, for ice cream. We don't have that in the clouds."

"*Lisa!*"

The child jumped to her feet and looked down the slope toward the lake. Hurriedly she asked, "Do the fairies make the rainbows?"

"Someone told you! They are sliding boards from the clouds to earth."

"I thought so," Lisa said, and turned and ran down the hill. Susannah lay down again and yawned.

"Go to sleep, princess," Brad whispered. "You've had a very busy day."

He watched her for a long time and he almost believed she was truly a sun-kissed fairy princess. A wave of such tenderness bathed him that he felt tears smarting in his eyes and he too lay back with his hands under his head, his eyes tightly closed.

"Are you the nut that's been telling my kid all that pagan bullshit?"

Brad jerked upright; he had not been asleep. Susannah sat up slower, blinking in confusion. Brad found himself on his feet standing between the large man and Susannah.

"I don't know who you are or why you're here, but I'll tell you this, mister, in this part of the country there's no place for that kind of heathen nonsense. You'd better just hightail it back to where you come from." He was no more than thirty-five, sunburned a dark mahogany, with deep squint lines. His mouth was tight and hard. He was wearing shorts and a tank top and was very muscular.

"Your kid could have fallen in the lake, wandering around all by herself the way she was. Why weren't you keeping an eye on her?" Brad demanded.

"If she did, it'd be the Lord's will," the man said slowly, menacingly. "He protected her."

"And she helped," Brad said, indicating Susannah. "She told

the child a story and kept her amused for a few minutes. No harm done."

"She told her pagan beliefs. Witchcraft stuff! We don't hold with that here." He took a step forward, his fists balled. "You just roll up them sleeping bags and get out of here! This is a family park, not a place for vagabond hippies."

"This is a public park! We're not going anywhere!"

"Mister, you're getting out or I'm going to put the fear of the Lord in you."

Susannah had stood up now. She did not know what she had told the child, but she did know that this man was going to beat up Brad. "I didn't hurt the child," she said, stepping around Brad. "If I offended you, I'm sorry. Now you leave us alone."

"Keep out of the way," he said, watching Brad.

"Listen to me," she said clearly, although now she was speaking in a near whisper. "You talk about your Lord, but he's not here now, and I am. If you don't go back to your family, I'll put a curse on you, on your land, your crops, your livestock, your work. For five years everything you touch will turn to dust!" She raised her hand and pointed at him. "Now, go back to your family!"

He stared at her for a moment, then said, "I just come up to tell you not to go telling our kids your pagan beliefs. That's all I wanted to do." He turned and strode down the hill.

"Look at you!" Susannah said to Brad. "You were going to fight that gorilla! He would have killed you!"

"We wouldn't have fought."

"Yes, you would. He's so afraid. He would fight to try to relieve his fear. Let's go somewhere else and make our dinner."

"He'll think we're running away."

"Do you care what he thinks?"

Looking at her, he knew he did not care. Sun-kissed princess, he thought, and when she started to roll up her sleeping bag, he did it and the other one and picked up both. "I'll carry them," he said. "The little girl shouldn't see you carrying anything, and I bet she's watching."

They ate, and before they were finished cleaning up afterward, the fireworks started. They had found their car blocked by others, and there was nothing to do but watch the show. It was nearly eleven before they were back on the highway.

◈◈◈

The corn stretched out forever, black on both sides of the road, higher than the Corvair. The night was sultry and heavy with approaching rain that hit at twelve-thirty. There was no place to stop. They pulled off into one of the rest areas and studied the map. Davenport, Iowa, they decided. They would have to keep on to Davenport and then find a motel. The rain beat down on the windshield, thunder rocked the land, and lightning danced erratically. Brad hoped they were not in for a tornado; he knew this was tornado weather. The car radio brought in static, country music, and more static. He turned it on and off again and again. At one-thirty they found a motel with a vacancy; it cost thirty-two dollars; neither cared. Exxon hissed at the rain, but balked at going inside, and finally they left him out, untethered, to fend for himself, and they entered, took off their shoes and collapsed onto the two beds. Belatedly, Brad thought he should not have parked under a tree during a storm. He did not get up to move the car.

◈◈◈

"Now, Anna Maria Lucia, you have to admit this is a pretty day, a beautiful day. We're going to fly up over Iowa, into Illinois a couple of times. They're bound to be on the road on such a beautiful morning. Best driving day they've had so far, I'd say."

The storm front had passed through; the morning was cool and crisp with a light northerly breeze.

"And then we go to New York?"

"Yes, indeed. But we'll find them before noon, well before noon, I'd guess. Isn't that your estimate, Felix?"

"They're down there, driving along, enjoying the cool air,"

Felix said, scanning the road with the binoculars. "And we'll see them this time. We know they are between Chicago and Des Moines. Stands to reason they're between those two points. I've added miles and figured miles per hour and I know that's right, Anna Maria Lucia. We'll find them this morning, before noon. I guarantee it."

"Oh, shut up!" Anna Maria Lucia snapped.

❖❖❖

"I feel wonderful!" Susannah cried, driving again. "What a marvelous thing sleep is in a cool room!"

Brad laughed. He felt equally good. It was after twelve and they were just getting on the road. They had slept eleven hours. Two more days, he thought. He would have two more days with her. They never talked about what next after they reached New York and his father. When the thought intruded, he tried to push it out again, like now. He had to write down the little fantasy she had told the child. "I wonder if little Lisa got up to watch the storm last night. Bet she tried to see Hulda beating the clouds. Bet she wasn't a bit scared."

He had told Susannah the story and she had been shocked that she had told such a thing to a child. "She couldn't have believed in it," she said rather anxiously.

"Belief is too strong a word. I didn't believe the fairy tales I read when I was a kid, but they helped somehow. A little kid like that can't cope with the world without some fantasy. Your story didn't convince her that there are fairies, I guess, but you gave her something to peg storms to, something she can grasp and handle and examine, and even feel superior to. That's not a bad thing to give a helpless little kid."

He had brought out his notebook to write down the story and for a long time neither spoke, and on the sides of the road the corn marched in endless rows.

Later, when he drove, she would bring her diary up to date. More and more often she was writing out her fears about that other forgotten life. It became more remote every day, less wanted. This life seemed normal; Brad was her . . . she never could finish in her mind what he was to her. Friend was not right. Lover certainly not right. Somehow he was more than what either of those words expressed alone or in combination, although there had been no word of love between them, not a touch, not even a glance. She knew him better than anyone else on earth, and in a blink of a second, she could forget him. She did not dare examine her feelings toward him, shied away from thinking about their arrival in New York and the new beginning that was certain to come from it. She didn't want this trip to end, this easy comradeship with this man she had known such a short time and knew so well.

Leah Duval loved Cartagena. It was so close to home and so alien, she thought happily, strolling down the street of motels and shops. Music came from everywhere: every clothing shop, every video-tape shop, the laundromat, even a mall had a three-piece band playing, surrounded by bobbing, dancing, toe-tapping shoppers and clerks. And people sang to the music along with the professional musicians. The sidewalks were uptilted here and there, nothing was clean, the heat was intense, and she had never been so happy. She understood not a word being spoken, but she smiled, and the people smiled back at her.

Louis hated it. Especially the flies. No one had told him there would be flies everywhere. There had been a fly in the marmalade that morning.

"We've got to get back to the hotel," he said, jostling an Indian man who didn't move quickly enough out of the way. No manners here, Louis thought; these people had no rules. They got in the way and stayed there, and no one moved as fast as he was used to. He wondered that they ever got anything done, and looking about at the unkempt street, the horn-blowing, stalled traffic, the potholes and ruined sidewalks, he added that nothing did get done, and no wonder about it. Bunch of lazy devils, mixed blood did it, no one knew where the

Indian left off and the black began, or the Spanish, or whatever the hell mix they were. Every street corner had tables spread with junk, and Leah wanted to stop at them all. Toothpaste, straw hats, wind-up toys, woven shawls, and everywhere Marlboro cigarettes. Smuggled cigarettes sold openly, he thought with contempt.

"Look," Leah said, pointing. "There's some more of those wall hangings we saw last night. I want to buy one. Let's go over there."

"We'd better not stop," Louis said, dragging on her arm. "Heinrich is coming over for drinks any minute now."

"Heinrich!" she said with a sniff. "What a pig! He'll be late anyway. It won't take a minute."

"Heinrich is a very important man in this town," Louis said grimly, his fingers now biting hard into her arm. "I said come on. He'll be my boss here, and when he moves up, I'll have his job. He's important."

"You're hurting me. Let go!"

"No more stopping at every junk stand on the street!"

"You go on and have your drinks with him. I'll be there in a few minutes. He wants to talk business with you. I'd just be in the way."

"He wants you to be good to him," Louis said, practically dragging her along. "And I want you to be good to him."

"He wants to go to bed with me," she said sullenly. "Did you know that's what he wants?"

"I want you to treat him right," Louis said. "He's important to me."

"No!" Now she stopped cooperating altogether and they came to a halt. "I won't go to bed with that fat pig! Louis, you wouldn't want me to do that!"

"Why do you think I brought you along? Heinrich likes blonde American girls with big tits, that's why! Now come on!"

"No way, Louis! You bum! I'm paying my way fair and square with you, doing whatever you want, but I don't intend to take on your drinking pals. Forget it!"

"Then you walk home, you little bitch!" Furiously he stamped off, pushing people aside right and left.

Leah stopped uncertainly; he had the passports, her clothes, everything but the purse she carried and about seventy dollars she had brought. Let him cool off, she thought fearfully, and then apologize or something, long enough to get her hands on the passport and her ticket home. She had not yet moved when she heard a voice at her side:

"Miss, is anything wrong? I was at a table across the way and noticed when your father marched off mad."

She turned and saw a lanky red-haired man. Thirty, she thought, green eyes, mustache. She nodded then. "He's not my father and he's pretty sore at me."

The man was staring at her with amazement. "Say something else," he demanded.

"What? What's the matter with you? What did I do?"

"I'll be a son of a bitch! Illinois. Right? You're from Illinois." She nodded. "Kankakee."

"Joliet. Shake." They shook hands, then he said, "Let's have a rum and coke, the only decent drink you can get here, by the way. The only thing that comes out anything like the way you'd expect it to, I mean. Come on, Kankakee. A drink. I'm Andy MacMannus, by the way, the director of the Binational Center here. Only because the State Department couldn't find anyone else insane enough to want to stay for more than two weeks."

By the time they got back to her hotel that night, Louis was gone; he had taken all the luggage including her blue bag. He had not even left a note.

"Don't you worry about it," Andy said. "You're in the right hands for a crisis in Cartagena."

She suspected he was right.

19

A *Berryman Associates, Inc., production*

Now, remember, Anna Maria Lucia, we agreed that I'll do the talking. It's the same situation that it was with Mrs. Murphy. Felix is my brother and you're his wife. You've come along to console me in my loss, even though we all expect it to be a temporary loss."

They were outside the door of Michael Berryman's twenty-eighth-floor apartment. They had been announced by the front desk security guard who had checked Jimmie's identification carefully before calling up Berryman. Jimmie pushed the button again. Not a whisper seeped through the heavy door.

"And maybe nobody does talking," Anna Maria Lucia muttered.

"He's home. Maybe he's old and slow and his help are all off on Sunday."

"Maybe he change his mind and does not want to see us."

"I talked to him myself remember, and he was very interested in seeing us. Intrigued by the idea that his son may be a kidnapper, I should suspect. He was fairly chortling with glee," Jimmie said, pleased with the expression.

"He comes," Anna Maria Lucia said, pointing to the doorknob, which turned, stopped, turned again; finally the door opened a few inches, held there by a chain.

"Captain Rivers?" A woman examined them through the opening. Little of her could be seen.

172

"Yes, ma'am. And my brother and Mrs. Rivers."

"Yes. Well, you might as well come in then." She released the chain and opened the door fully to admit them. She was sixty, with gray hair and gray eyes, dressed in a flame-colored caftan.

"I'm Sylvia Brasser. He's in here." As she spoke she led them through a foyer into a living room with a glass wall. The view beyond was of Central Park. There was a telescope set up at the window. The room was furnished in understated Danish modern sofas and chairs, tables, coffee tables. Every level surface was covered with books, magazines, manuscripts, sketchbooks, drawings. On the floor were many boxes of Polaroid prints in a jumble.

"You've caught us at a bad time," said a voice from an open doorway into a connecting room. The man entered. "I'm Berryman."

He was in his late sixties, a slender man with longish, dark hair touched lightly with gray. He wore heavy glasses, dark, neatly pressed slacks and a shortsleeved shirt hanging out loose.

Jimmie made the introductions and they were invited to sit down, while their host went to stand before the window where he appeared to them in silhouette.

"Now tell me about my son and your wife, captain," Mike Berryman said in an amused voice.

"I'm not certain that's quite the way to think of it, sir. You see, my wife has amnesia and from all the eyewitness statements, and the police reports, the evidence appears conclusive that your son is responsible for it, he hit her with his car."

"My, my. Brad is losing control. First he ran over her and then ran off with her?"

"Well, sir, let me explain." Jimmie continued to explain for a long time.

Berryman finally stopped him by leaving the room. He came back quickly, before the three guests could do more than exchange worried glances. When he returned, he was carrying a Polaroid camera.

"Captain, I wonder if you would be so good as to allow me

to take a few pictures of you?" He didn't wait for a response, but began to slide a film pack inside the camera and check the flashbar. "Over there, by the door, just entering the room. If you will."

Jimmie looked at Felix helplessly. Felix shrugged and leaned back in his chair to watch. Anna Maria Lucia was obviously bewildered.

"And your brother, too. Mr. Felix? One or two of you together. Would you mind?" He waved to Felix to join Jimmie. "Not like that. Slightly behind him and to one side. Here, allow me . . ." He positioned them, stepped backward six or seven feet, and clicked the button. The picture slid out. He caught it and put it in his pocket without a glance, snapped another one. "Now if you'll act as if you're just arriving, enter slowly, look around at the mess . . ." He snapped again, then again. "Good, very good. Keep moving to the couch and sit down. Excellent!" He finished the pack and put the camera down, resumed his place by the window wall.

"Exactly what do you want of me, captain? Your wife has not been abducted against her will. My son did not drive over her on purpose. And apparently wherever they are, it is by mutual consent. I fail to see what possible role I might play in this little drama."

"Well now, sir, mutual consent is a tricky phrase, especially if one of the parties is psychologically incapable of making a sound judgment, based on past experiences and training. I mean, if Susannah signed a contract now, no court in the world would hold her to it when she recovers her memory. When that happens, she'll forget everything in the middle, I mean. All we want from you, sir, is a phone call when they get here. If they even decide to come to you. And I'd like to leave a couple of other numbers with you, if you want to confirm my statements. There's Mrs. Murphy, who initiated the search for Susannah's identity. A remarkable woman of compassion, sir. And her attorney, who verified my claim on Susannah."

"Amnesia with confabulation," Berryman said dreamily.

"What a lovely idea. Sylvie, call Clay and tell him to round up whatever he has on the subject. A tame psychiatrist," he said by way of explanation. He started for the door to the adjacent room. "Leave the numbers with Sylvie." He left without another word, or a glance back at them.

❖❖❖

Sylvia had shown the guests out and now entered Mike Berryman's studio, which was a bigger mess than the living room. In here every wall was covered with paintings of the various characters from his books. There was Rouse Mouse with a sword, Hoy Boy on the prow of a pirate ship, Pinkie Wink in a chariot drawn through the air by butterflies, Muck Duck dripping goo, Billyup Willyup, Wish Fish, Juice Goose, Limp Chimp . . . There was a long work table laden with notebooks, drawings, artbooks, portfolios. There were stuffed animals here and there, a group of them in a small circle as if in conference, and all these too were from his books. Limp Chimp was draped over a chair arm. At opposite ends of the room were two desks, one piled with yellow sheets and more notebooks, the other tidy, with two wire baskets, incoming and outgoing mail. That was Sylvia's desk. Each had a typewriter.

"Mike, are they coming here? Brad and the girl?" Sylvia asked.

"Damned if I know," Mike said. He was studying the pictures he had made of the airline captain. "Isn't he perfect!"

"Perfect stuffed shirt," Sylvia said.

"Exactly. Pompous ass. Did you call Clay yet?"

"On my way. How about that Mrs. Murphy in San Francisco?"

He nodded absently, engrossed in the pictures. She went to her desk to make the calls, and when she finished, he was pawing through papers on his desk.

"You've been through all that stuff a thousand times."

"But there's something somewhere for the captain. I almost remember a note I made years ago."

"Mike, relax, will you? So one year goes by without a new book. It's no big deal."

"I have until August first," he said grimly. "That's plenty of time."

"Plenty of time if you're already working on something. Not plenty of time to find something to work on and finish."

"It's enough time, if you'd get off your butt and help me find that note!"

"You've been through those notebooks and through them. Nothing appeals to you, remember? Nothing is fresh anymore. Nothing exciting. So relax and go with it. They'll buy last year's book and never know the difference."

"Little bastards don't know up from down," he muttered. "That's beside the point." A stack of papers began to slide toward the edge of the desk. He made a halfhearted lunge at them, missed, and stood watching as they fell. "Shit!" Abruptly he sat down behind his desk. "Did you make those calls yet?"

"Yes. Mrs. Murphy sounds like a doll. She repeated pretty much what the captain said about the girl. Mrs. Murphy thinks they could be on their way here. She said someone robbed Brad's apartment, and gangsters are mixed up with Susannah somehow. That's about all she knows. And Clay says he'll drop by with some articles tomorrow after office hours. We can feed him a martini, he says." She sighed. "Isn't it just like Brad to get involved with another man's wife? And her with amnesia yet! What next?"

"Never did anything right in his life," Mike Berryman said sourly. He brightened. "But at least they're coming here. He hates my guts, but he knows this is his final refuge, the only place where he can find help for himself and the woman he loves. He's turning at last to his old man, olive branch in hand . . ." He narrowed his eyes, staring at a spot just past Sylvia's head. "Don't you make him mad this time," he said. "He's coming here for help, and by God I intend to help him. And her too if that's what he wants. What do you suppose Mrs. Murphy meant by gangsters being interested in her?"

"I suppose it means trouble," Sylvia said tartly. "Also we don't know what he thinks about her; all we know is that he ran her down. And I'm telling you that if you get that silly camera out in front of him, he'll more than likely bolt again and never come back next time. Treat them like people, for God's sake, not specimens sent by God for your private study."

That reminded him of the captain's pictures and he spread them out on top of the papers on his desk. Sylvia went back to her work answering his correspondence.

❖❖❖

"Are you asleep?" Brad asked.

"No."

"Nice night, isn't it?"

"Beautiful."

It was very dark under the trees where they had stopped for the night. Not far away to the north was Lake Erie and still closer was the interstate highway with its ceaseless traffic. Now and again the ground rumbled as a tractor trailer sped through the countryside.

"What a difference from our other camps," Brad said after a pause.

"Like another world altogether."

The pause lengthened this time. Neither moved. "I've been thinking," Brad said finally, "what we can do is find a small apartment in New York, rent it, change our names . . ."

She laughed. "From Jane Doe to Mary Smith, right?"

"I mean I'll change my name, so they can't trace you through me."

"Brad, stop. We can't do that."

"I didn't mean . . . It would be the same way it was in San Francisco. You'd have your room and I'd have mine. I wasn't suggesting . . ."

"I know. But we can't do that anyway." Her voice was very low and subdued. "It wouldn't be fair to either of us. Marlene must have heard from someone by now. Whoever it is will come and get me and I'll go home and you'll get back to your dissertation and a normal life again." Her voice trailed off.

In a little while Brad got up and went over to the fire to stir it into life.

"What are you doing?"

"Did I wake you up? I'm sorry. I'm not sleepy yet. I thought I might have a cup of coffee or something."

She joined him. "Neither am I. Make it two cups."

When they had their mugs of coffee, they sat opposite each other with the fire between them.

"Tell me more about your father," she said.

"Okay. Might as well prepare you, I guess. And there's Sylvia. I forgot to tell you about Sylvia. She's about sixty, give or take a few years. She's been with him always, I have no idea when she first started working for him. She was there from my earliest memories. Smart woman. At first she did secretarial work, did his typing, correspondence, and now she does everything else too. She lives in the apartment. But they've never been lovers." He poured himself more coffee, offered more to her; she shook her head. "It just occurred to me that he must be lonely. I don't think he's ever had a woman he cared about. Not even my mother. He wanted a kid, that's all that amounted to. She was a lot younger than he was, and, predictably, found someone else who wanted her. I didn't blame her, still don't blame her. But I never thought of it from his side. I'm sure now that for him it was a business arrangement, a marriage of convenience. And there's been no steady woman since then."

"He must have many friends."

"Oh sure. He stays busy, travels a lot. I think he just does one lousy book a year now, but there are TV appearances, and he's a consultant for all those rotten TV specials, you know the Christmas junk and Easter shows. And someone has to look after all the other spin-offs — the comic strip, the shirts, kiddie furniture, toys . . . Friends, business, acquaintances. I guess it all keeps him busy, but there's been no one person in his life as far as I know."

They both realized he was talking about himself. "My father is an orthodontist," Susannah said confidentially. "All day, year after year, he's in kids' mouths up to his elbows. Putting braces on, taking them off. He used to watch me chew at the table until I got so paranoid, I went on a liquid diet and lost forty-nine pounds. Since I only weighed one hundred at the time, that was disastrous, as you can imagine. He used to snatch an apple from my hand, just to inspect the teeth marks, to make sure my bite was okay."

Brad laughed softly. "God," he said, "it's been a good day! It's been a good week! A good two weeks! Thank you, whoever you are."

"You started to tell me about your summer camp experience a few days ago and never finished. What happened?"

"Oh, that was the year I was struck by the hand of God, who said in a loud voice: 'Thou shalt not participate in competitive sports!'"

He told her about it. That summer he had broken his leg and his arm in two separate accidents. "So I can't do anything but walk and swim," he finished happily.

"I, on the other hand, am expert in racquet ball, tennis, mountain climbing, and ice hockey. Also gymnastics."

They talked and laughed and talked some more far into the night. Their last night together, their last night on the road, they both seemed to sense should not be wasted in sleeping.

20

Stat Cat

"**M**_ama mia!_" Anna Maria Lucia breathed into the phone, her eyes shut tightly. "_No, no. Avanti!_" She listened some more, shaking her head from time to time. Finally she said, "_Grazie, Mama. Grazie . . . No. No . . . Arrivederci, Mama._"

She hung up and for a long time did not move from the bed where she was sitting.

"Well?" Jimmie asked. "Has she managed to call off cousin Rudy?"

"Rudy? Oh, Rudy! Jimmie, listen to me this minute. Those little jewels, you know what they are? The blessed jewels of power! Blessed and cursed! They have the curse on them, Jimmie!"

"Now, Anna Maria Lucia —"

"No! You must listen! Before I forget I must tell you the curse!" She closed her eyes to recite: " 'These are the stones of power, with power bestowed. Let only him who ascends the throne touch them. To all else they bring but grief: to the infidel comes evil, to all who handle them, change, a thousand-fold. Those whose hearts are pure alone will escape this curse.' "
She opened her eyes and took a deep breath. "I think that's all. When my mama say it, it is poetry, terrible and beautiful. It is true, Jimmie. You handle them and now you are forced to go hippity hipping all over the country. Poor Susannah handle them

and she is lost, maybe forever from herself. We don't touch them no more, Jimmie. Please say nobody touch them no more."

"Honey, you're so doggone cute when you come on like that. Curses! But seriously, Anna Maria Lucia, you shouldn't have told your mama about the jewels. You said you wouldn't tell her anything else. It's dangerous if too many people know about this little business venture we're engaged in. And you never did tell me if cousin Rudy is still after Susannah."

"Cousin Rudy," she said with a sniff, "he no longer interested in poor little Susannah. He say he don't believe in curse, but he believe in two groups of crazies who both want the jewels. The Shah's followers who steal them for to sell, and the Inman's followers who want them back. They all the same, crazy. His friends don't want the trouble. They say no mess it, turn off, drop out. Cousin Rudy, he go back to Los Angeles. The family don't know nothing no more about nothing."

"Well now, isn't that just fine." Jimmie and Felix smiled at each other in relief.

Mike Berryman was going through the files, just to make certain there was not a character he had forgotten, a throwaway spear carrier who might do for a new book. Sylvia was at her desk, working, taking phone calls, feigning unawareness of his activities. Now she hung up the phone and looked at him speculatively.

"Another person wants to talk to you about Brad and his mysterious traveling companion," she said. "A Miss Donna Murphy, daughter of the compassionate Mrs. Murphy."

"Tell her I'm working, too busy," he snapped.

"I told her to come at five-thirty."

"You know," he said, "you can be replaced. I don't have to put up with this."

"Not since we incorporated," she said complacently, and swiveled back to pick up the phone that had started to ring again. "No, I'm sorry, he's out of town and won't be back for

181

several weeks . . . I'm afraid so . . . I'll have him call you then."
She did not bother to tell him who that one was, nor did she
make a note of it. She opened another letter and he pulled
another file drawer all the way out.

◇◇◇

Donna arrived promptly at five-thirty. She looked around the
unkempt room making a wonderful effort to keep her expression serene. She was startled to see how much Brad looked like
his father. She had seen Mike Berryman once briefly at the
bookstore in San Francisco, but it had been at a distance, and
he had been dressed as if hired to advertise Savile Row's best
tailors.

She shook his hand vigorously and accepted a seat on the
couch that was two-thirds covered with papers. "Mr. Berryman,"
she began at once, "I don't want to take up much of your time.
I appreciate how busy you must be. But you see, I am very
worried about Brad."

"You said you're a friend of his?" Mike asked.

"Well, perhaps more than a friend," she said delicately. "And
now he's off on this schoolboy adventure with a woman he
doesn't even know. He's playing Huck Finn, cruising down the
interstate highways."

"That doesn't sound too bad," Mike murmured.

"No, not the cruising, but the stopping may be terribly hard.
That's what concerns me, the stopping, and what will happen
to him then."

"Miss Murphy, we've heard a couple of different accounts
about what's going on here. Would you give your version, just
to keep the confusion level at a high pitch?" Mike studied her
as he spoke, decided he did not want any pictures. He leaned
back and waited.

Her version differed only in details. Her description of Brad
was interesting, he thought.

"He is so gentle, so naive, susceptible to romanticism in any
form. She appealed to his conscience, of course, made him feel

personally responsible for what was actually an act of fate, something out of his hands entirely. But he felt his responsibility toward her, enough to abandon his brilliant research. He is a brilliant scholar, of course. He'll be very famous . . ."

"How famous can anyone be in twelfth-century literature?" Mike asked with honest curiosity. "Famous to whom? A handful of other scholars in that field?"

Donna felt confused. She had assumed that since Brad's father was financing his education, he also approved of it. Cautiously she said, "Brad thinks it very important to have continuing scholarship in every area." She was looking for a place to put her glass down, there was no surface free of clutter. "Of course, I feel that living in the present is equally important. Writing for today's generation is immensely vital. Your writing, for example, shaping the way our children regard the world and their place in it is important. It's as if you're reaching out a hand for a small child to grasp, helping him through a difficult period. The very young have a difficult time, I'm sure."

"Do you have children?"

"No. I expect to eventually . . ."

"You said 'our children' but you mean other people's children. Do you teach, work in a day care center, live in an extended family that has a lot of kids around? Anything like that?"

"I work in a brokerage firm and live with my mother," she said stiffly.

"Ah. You're speaking in abstract terms, not because you're familiar with the effect of my books on children. I was curious. Go on."

She had forgotten what she meant to say next. She stood up, still holding her glass. "I'm staying in town for the next few days. When Brad shows up, please have your secretary give me a call. I'm afraid it will be devastating to him, having her husband arrive to claim her. He'll need help."

"Tea and sympathy," Mike murmured and crossed the room to take the glass from her. "Yes, my dear, you'll hear when he comes, if he comes."

"We'll throw a party," Sylvia said, after showing Donna out. "The three stooges, brittle Miss Murphy, who else?"

"Now, Sylvie, what else could I tell her? She's concerned. She cares for him."

"Uh huh. Brokerage firm! I'm going to tell Geneva to make sure there's sandwich stuff in the fridge, just in case they do come tonight."

◆◆◆

The traffic was thinner than Brad remembered; in his mind was a picture of endless, stalled cars, each one blowing a horn while fumes rose in visible clouds over them.

"It's just a block or two," he said. "We'll take as much stuff in as we can manage and let someone go park the car for us. Tomorrow we can finish cleaning out our gear. Okay?"

"I don't think you can park in New York." She felt a bit afraid of the traffic, the maze of streets, the noise.

"There are places," he said vaguely. He had no idea where those places were; when he had lived in New York before he had not owned a car, and his father had not owned a car for years. They were on Park Avenue West, crawling along; he had forgotten how alike the apartment buildings were, with their uniformed doormen, the open lobby doors, the potted plants, canopies.

"Here we are," he said, braking suddenly, pulling in sharply toward the curb. "You carry Exxon, I'll bring in what I can."

The doorman had come to the car, waiting to open it as soon as it was unlocked. Brad leaned down and called, "Hello, Mr. Jenkins. How are you?" He unlocked the door and Mr. Jenkins opened it for Susannah.

"Mr. Berryman, ah, I mean Mr. Hale," he said, pleased. "How nice to see you again."

"We've been camping," Brad said, tugging out the cat box they had bought that day, and the bag of litter, the cat food. He pulled out their spare clothes tied up in a shirt, and went inside with his burden. "Be back for a few more things," he said. "Don't bother with them, Mr. Jenkins. I have to sort through them."

"Yes sir," Mr. Jenkins said, revealing only pleasure at seeing the younger Berryman and his strange cargo.

Brad dumped the miscellaneous items on the marble floor in front of the security desk. "Please call up two-eight-oh-one and tell Mr. Berryman Bradford Hale is here," he said. "I have a few more things to get from the car." He started for the door and froze when he heard the security man ask Susannah:

"Your name, Miss? We're not allowed to admit anyone to the building without registering them."

"Of course," she said agreeably. "I'm Virginia Dennis. From Boston."

"You want to see Mr. Berryman, too?"

"That's right. We have to talk to him about his titles. You see, I was working in the library in Boston when I found this man hiding in the stacks." She pointed to Brad. "At first I was tempted to turn him in, but he intrigued me. He had been living there for months, smuggling in food, leaving only long enough to change his clothes. He was looking up secret data that will very likely save the entire world once it's understood."

Brad tried to nudge her aside. He smiled weakly at the security guard who had motioned his partner away from his post before a cluster of television screens. "She's playing a joke on me," Brad said. "Just call my father."

"What he had discovered was remarkable," Susannah went on, ignoring Brad, leaning forward to talk to the guard in a confidential manner. "There are messages in book titles. Not all of them, of course, but some of them are secret messages. For example, from *Huckleberry Finn* you get *rebel*. You just lift it out and reverse it, you see. And *Madame Bovary* gives you *mad damn ovary*. That's a sounds-like message. They count, too."

Both guards were watching her, one with his finger on the dial of the house phone, the other unmoving behind the desk, one hand on a gun in the drawer that he had opened on their arrival.

"For God's sake!" Brad yelled. "Make the phone call!"

"And *Alice in Wonderland* is an important message," Susannah went on. "You get *a loner in wild dance.* That's rich in significance, once we figure it out."

The guard dialed and Sylvia answered. "Mr. Bradford Hale and Miss Virginia Dennis to see Mr. Berryman," he said.

"Fine," Sylvia said. "We've been expecting them. Send them up."

"Miss Brasser, would you mind checking them out on the screen first?" he asked, keeping a close watch on Susannah.

She was saying, "Acrostics work. There's nothing wrong in unscrambling the letters if that's what it takes. Like *A Catcher in the Rye* could mean *their N.Y. ache trace.*"

"Of course, that's Brad. What in the world is going on down there?" Sylvia demanded.

"Sorry, ma'am," the guard said. "We'll let them come up."

"And sometimes you have to go to a foreign language, if it's appropriate. *Don Quixote* puzzled him for a long time, but he sensed that it had meaning. And finally he found it: *¡No que exito!*" She frowned slightly and shifted the cat in her arms. "That could be one of the most important ones." Exxon meowed unhappily and she scratched his head. "You can't always count on them to be direct messages, sometimes they exist simply to lead to something else. For instance, *A Tale of Two Cities* gave him *it, a storied wet foe,* and that didn't mean anything until he realized it was a pointer clue. What it led to was *Moby Dick,* and that gave him *mock by id.* You have to agree that that one is meaningful."

"Come on," Brad said, trying to carry sleeping bags and cat litter, cat box, clothes and notebooks, stuff Mr. Jenkins had brought in despite being told not to. Brad kept dropping things until Mr. Jenkins came to his aid and helped get everything into the elevator. "We'll manage at the other end," Brad said gratefully. "Thanks. She's playing a trick on me," he repeated louder for the benefit of the security men.

As soon as the door slid shut, he said, "Listen, don't tell anyone else any of that stuff right away. Promise?"

"But we have to tell him his titles won't work. They don't have messages. Nothing of his matches *Pride and Prejudice.* That's *pen, drip dread juice.*"

"I know, but we have to play it cool for now. Later, after he knows you better, then we'll tell him. Why don't you lean back and close your eyes for a minute. You look tired."

She smiled at him. "I am rather tired." She rested her head on the wall and closed her eyes.

At the security desk the two guards exchanged looks as they both watched the television scene of the elevator interior where the woman was apparently sleeping standing up.

When the elevator stopped, Brad touched her arm. "We're here," he said.

She blinked in confusion at finding herself in an elevator. In dismay she asked, "Again? I did it again?"

"It was wonderful," he said, grinning now that it was over. "Wait till I tell you." He pushed the hold button and steered her across the hall where he pounded on the door of 2801. "He hates the bell," he said. "Always did."

Sylvia threw open the door and reached out to hug Brad. "I'm so glad to see you! You look tired, but wonderful."

"And this is Miss Dennis?" his father asked, coming up behind Sylvia. The two men did not touch.

"Hello, Dad. No, she isn't Virginia Dennis. I'll explain in a minute. I've got to get our stuff off the elevator."

He hurried out, leaving Susannah who was still holding Exxon.

Mike Berryman stared, then turned and raced off. He returned with the Polaroid and hurriedly took a picture of Susannah and the cat. At the same time Brad came in with a load of stuff.

"Good God!" he muttered. "Sylvia, make him stop." He went out for the rest of the things.

"Mike, for heaven's . . ."

"I've got it! Sylvie, I've got it! *Stat Cat!* Whoopee!" He let out a wild Tarzan yell.

Exxon had been growing increasingly nervous all day. Too

much traffic, too few stops in interesting places, too much riding, and now being held too tightly, and having a stranger scream like a thing out of nightmares. Exxon stiffened, then leaped from Susannah's arms and raced to the open door, out through the hall, passing Brad on his way in. The cat made it into the elevator just as the door slid shut. Susannah sped after him and stabbed the button trying to catch the car before it started its descent. She was too late.

"Sylvie, get on the phone and tell them to catch that cat!" Mike ran after Brad who was getting into the next elevator with Susannah.

The security men watched in fascination as Mr. Hale, his crazy girl friend, and his father rode down; Mr. Berryman kept his finger on the down button all the way. The puzzled men could see nothing on the other elevator. Their scan was not made to cover the floor and the corners, and it was in one of the corners on the floor that Exxon crouched, panic-stricken at the uncertain floor, the caged-in space.

In the lobby Mr. Jenkins was just putting down the phone when the elevator arrived. He watched the door open, braced himself to intercept the cat, and then prudently stepped out of the way as the crazed beast streaked past him.

Mike Berryman and Brad hesitated long enough to ask Mr. Jenkins which way the cat had gone, but Susannah ran outside, and across the street, dodging cars automatically. She knew where Exxon had gone. Under the bushes, away from cars and screaming strangers. By the time Mike and Brad had crossed the street and entered the park, she was out of sight.

"We've got to find her," Brad said, panting. His father was hardly winded. He ran a mile every day in the park.

"If we don't, she'll come back eventually, won't she?"

"Maybe. Sometimes she forgets things."

"Ah yes, the amnesia. Does she forget you?"

"More and more she's including me in her fantasies, the confabulations she tells. I think that's a good sign, but if I'm not around, she could forget me too."

"Well, aside from that, it's going to be dark in an hour or so. She certainly must not be running around in the park then."

"We'd better split up," Brad said, suddenly very frightened. "Maybe one of us can find a cop to tell, have them keep an eye out for her."

His father nodded and veered to the right. Brad trotted away. He couldn't even call her, he thought miserably. She never answered to Jane Doe unless the speaker was looking at her directly, obviously meaning her. Instead he started to call the cat: "Exxon! Here Exxon!"

Susannah realized that footsteps were echoing her own, and she did not know how long she had been hearing them. She wished they would go away. Exxon might not come out of hiding if a crowd was pursuing him. She ran faster.

Brad was running at half speed, stopping altogether to call the cat from time to time, listening to see if her voice also called Exxon. He groaned when he saw his father coming toward him. He had run in a circle apparently.

"I talked to some park patrolmen," his father said, joining him. "They'll be watching, but I have to tell you they thought I was a nut case. I don't know her name, or even a description, except pretty, short blonde hair."

"Yeah, I know," Brad said. "It's been like that with me for a couple of weeks now." He called the cat again.

"You think she'll come when she hears you?"

"She'll find the damn cat, and if I have it, she'll find me," he said.

His father nodded.

Suddenly Brad stopped. "Listen," he said. It came again, a piercing whistle. "That's her!" He raced off to the right. His father came after him more slowly.

She had heard the footsteps closer, then farther away when she picked up speed, but now they were coming in close once more. It was dusk, and the many people in the park earlier seemed to have vanished. Even the paths were empty of pedestrian traffic, and no children were throwing Frisbees, or batting softballs. Surely Exxon would not have run this far, she thought. She realized that she had no idea where she was, how far into the park she had run, or where the park ended. Again, she whistled for the cat, then once more. Behind her the footsteps faltered, resumed. For the first time she thought there was more than one person, maybe two, or even three back there. Then from the corner of her eye she saw a motion close to the ground, and she slowed and called, "Exxon, come on, boy!"

He crouched in the shadow of a bush, and backed off when two strangers appeared, running. Susannah turned to face them. "You've scared him off again!" she cried. "He may not come out for another hour now. Go away!"

They stopped, two youths under twenty, dark-haired, dark-eyed. "What you looking for, babe?" one of them asked.

Since they were moving apart so that she could not see them at the same time, she turned her back on both of them. "Exxon," she said. "He's in there somewhere."

"Oh wow!" one cried. "Get on out of there, Exxon, you old devil!"

"Don't do that!" she called angrily. "You'll just make him go in deeper."

"Go in deeper! That's the stuff!"

"Are you ready, Teddy?"

When Brad approached the trio, the two young men were on her right and left, the bushes before her, leaving her no place to run. They were all facing away from him, and he suspected that the man on the left had a knife. His attitude was that of someone with a knife out. Brad reached down for a stone. He got closer before he threw it hard at the one on the left, and rushed toward the other one. Susannah turned and screamed as Brad knocked the youth down with the force of his rush. The other one was advancing waving the knife back and forth, cursing.

"Officers, here they are! I found them! This way!" Mike yelled, running toward the group. Brad was rolling in the dirt with one of the men, the other was waiting for a chance to move in. At Mike's shout, the one with the knife fled, and the other one rolled out from under Brad, scrambled to his feet and also ran.

"Where are the cops?" Brad yelled. "Catch them!"

"No cops," Mike said. "We'd better get the hell out of here before they realize that."

Susannah looked bewildered and very frightened. "Did he hurt you very much?"

"It's all right," he said, breathing hard.

"You are hurt, though. He could have killed you!"

Exxon stalked out from the bushes with his crooked tail rigid, quivering with displeasure. Susannah scooped him up and held him very tightly, her gaze on Brad all the while.

"Let's get," Mike said. "We can cut through right there and be out on the sidewalk in a minute. But let's do it now."

He kept looking at his son as they walked back toward the apartment, and he knew the meaning of the phrase "bursting with pride" for the first time in his life.

21

Together at last

"Get Max over here!" Mike called to Sylvia before he even closed the apartment door. "You kids need to wash up a little and then eat something," he said. He was watching Exxon as a man in midocean might watch a life raft bobbing just out of reach. "Come on, I'll show you your rooms."

Susannah continued to carry Exxon, almost afraid he would find another exit from the apartment, but more because she could not hold Brad. He had not been hurt, but he was filthy, with dirty sweat on his cheek and arms.

"I put some clean things in the room for you to use until you can get your own clothes washed," Sylvia said. "Brad, I'm afraid you'll have to put up with a bed in the library." She was in the living room with Geneva, the cook, who now rushed over to hug Brad with unabashed affection. To Mike she said, "Max is on the way. I already called him."

Max Klinerman drew the comic strips of Rouse Mouse, and did the finished illustrations for the books, working from Mike's rough sketches. He was the third officer of Berryman Associates, Inc.

Mike saw Susannah and Brad to their rooms and went looking first for his camera, then for Exxon, who was stalking about the apartment, sniffing at everything. Mike began to trail him, snapping picture after picture, muttering softly to himself. On the floor in the living room, sorting through a stack of note-books, Sylvia began to hum happily.

Susannah wakened early, started to get up, remembered that today they were not traveling, and went back to sleep. The next time she woke up, it was nearly ten. She found Mike having breakfast in the dining room.

"Brad's still sleeping," Mike said, after their good mornings. "What do you want? Eggs, bacon, ham . . . ?"

"I'm starved," she said. "Anything."

He went to the kitchen door and spoke to Geneva, brought back the coffeepot, and poured some for her.

"That's a remarkable cat," he said then. "Brad's?"

"I don't think so," she said after a slight pause. "I think he owns the apartment Brad lives in."

Mike nodded, not at all surprised.

She drank coffee and he offered her a piece of his toast, which she accepted and jellied and began to eat.

When she looked up, he was studying her closely. "Do you know me?" she asked, putting down the piece of toast, suddenly tense. "The way you're looking at me . . . Are you the one who created me?"

He shook his head. "No, for both questions. But you remind me of someone I used to know, long before you were born. I'm sorry, I didn't mean to embarrass you. We never did get around to names last night. What do you call yourself?"

"Marash," she said in a low intense voice. "I have been sent here to tell you things. I am a Gypsy from Rumania where my family has lived for three thousand years. I am the seventh daughter of a seventh daughter. To us is given the gift of vision."

Mike felt skewered by the intensity of her stare. It seemed to penetrate far below the surface of his face, the surface of his eyes. "What things?" he whispered.

"I see a woman in a long gray skirt walking beside a man who is leading a horse and wagon through dense woods.

They are going down a hillside on a trail hardly wide enough for the wagon. Now they are in a valley and the woman walks alone into the small area that is cleared of trees, where their house has been built of logs. It is an area spotlighted by the sun, which can penetrate the darkness only a few hours each day as it rises over the great trees and then sinks behind them once more. She looks at the trees all around, then lifts her face to the sun. There are tears on her cheeks; she is afraid of the gloom of the woods, afraid of the isolation of their homestead. This woman carries the seed that will come to haunt you."

Mike was frozen in his chair. When Susannah stopped, he said hoarsely, "Go on. Tell me what else you see."

"There are sons who inherit the evil the woman has in her blood. She thinks it is a curse, but now we know it is a genetic disease that she passes to her sons. Her daughters pass it to their sons, and so it is through the years. At puberty many of the male children change, become like ravening beasts and finally turn on their mothers, their sisters..." She stopped again and shook her head violently. "Ah, now it changes. There is a young man, you, planting corn in that valley. The trees are removed far around, the valley is cleared. You are happy, working with a smile on your lips, singing. You watch a tall woman draw water at a pump and your song stops because you love her too much to make a sound..." Susannah's voice changed, became conversational. "You show her a manuscript and she reads it and becomes angry. She sends you away. Many travels, many foreign countries. You begin to fear children and say you don't know why. But you know, you always knew. You make pictures and write books, not to please them but to reveal their monstrous nature, to expose them to the world. It is always children fighting authority, fighting their parents, everything that is civilized and safe. You know them and they respond to your truth, but your real hatred is not for children. The hatred and contempt are for yourself because you had no power to act a long time ago; you were afraid to act; it was her fear of a male child that destroyed you."

194

Sometime during her monologue Mike had stood up, his face pale, hands trembling. He dropped his coffee cup and watched as coffee splashed over the tabletop, pieces of china scattered. It seemed in slow motion. Wordlessly he walked from the dining room, passing Sylvia and Brad who were rigid at the open door. Sylvia followed him and Brad entered the dining room and sat down by Susannah, taking her hand and holding it.

"You won't remember this," he said softly, "but I have to tell you. I love you."

She nodded and turned her piercing gaze to him, but Brad shook his head. "No, don't tell me anything. Just relax, rest a minute until Geneva brings your breakfast." He released her hand.

She closed her eyes a moment, then opened them to see her coffee cup emerging from a blur, taking shape gradually. When it was solid again, she looked across the table at Brad who was picking up pieces of china.

"What happened? What did I do?"

"Nothing," he said. "It's okay. Don't worry about it." He continued to pick up the pieces.

"Your father was sitting there. I said something terrible to him, didn't I? He broke his cup because of what I said." She stood up uncertainly.

"Well, you startled him," Brad admitted.

She walked to the door. "I'll be back in a minute."

Geneva entered through the kitchen door at that moment. "My, had a little accident, did we? Never you mind that, Brad. I'll get it cleaned up. Why don't I just set the little table by the living room window for you and your friend. Won't take a minute."

"Fine," he muttered and rushed out to see where Susannah had gone. Her door was closing. Helplessly he went to the living room to wait for her and found his father looking out the window.

"Dad," he started, "she doesn't know. She doesn't even remember afterward."

195

"I understand," Mike said. "You care for her, don't you?"

Brad nodded miserably, said, "I care."

"If you care enough, keep her," his father said, turning to face him. "Don't let her get away. I did, and I've spent a lifetime regretting it. Everything she said, it was all true. I never finished that manuscript she talked about. Sarah was horrified by it, too much sex, too passionate, too brutal, too real, I guess. It was probably very bad, but it had passion. It did have passion. I never touched it after that or anything remotely like it. But, after reading it, she knew what I felt and she sent me away. She was married, older than I was, and she was cursed. That's what she thought, she was cursed. She told me to clear out and I did."

"It was all true? Even the genetic disease?"

"True. Premature sexual maturation, caused by a chromosomal link that makes the kid around eleven or twelve suddenly become sexually mature and more than slightly crazy. The secret curse of the family that no one ever talked about and everyone eventually knew. Sarah found out after she was married, and she left her husband, afraid of pregnancy, afraid of male children. She had two sisters and none of them had a child. They were determined to end the curse and I guess they did. When she knew how I felt, she chased me, too. And I put my tail between my legs and went. I thought it was because I was too young, because I was foolish, because I was a rotten farmer and wanted to write. I left."

"Dad, I'm sorry. I'm sorry all this came up now because of . . . her. I don't know how she knew any of that stuff. She couldn't have known. She was guessing, playing games. I'm sorry," he said again.

"Don't be. She's the only person I've ever met who actually knew what my children's books are about. I don't know when she read them, or why she remembers them, but she knows what they mean. She dips down to a place where she can see the truth; that's scary. The truth is so rare that when we see it we panic." He straightened his shoulders and moved toward the study door. "And now I'm working on a new book for the little bastards. Another day, another nickel, another dose of rebellion and resentment coming to the surface in pretty colors and funny pictures. This one's called Stat Cat, about a buttoned-down, uptight, long-talking, grant-getting scientist whose experiments in trying to get a photostatic copy of a cat keep failing, until one night his machine runs off a cat all by itself, made up of bits and pieces of all the cats the scientist used from the start. It's Stat Cat, of course, ready to tell the whole fucking world to go to hell."

He looked into the study and bellowed, "Sylvie, get Emma on the phone and tell her I have the title and we'll have the cover sketch by afternoon. I'll send it over by messenger."

After his father left, Brad stood unmoving for a long time. She dipped down to a place where she could see the truth, that was right. Her stories were always what the listener wanted or needed. She had an uncanny vision that let her pierce the superfluities of the listener, see into the core of the person she was telling a story to. She had roused him from apathy and inertia; the story she had told that awful woman at the fashion show, the one to the little girl at the lake, they had been just right. Even the security men in the lobby, their story had been right too in a strange way. He wondered uneasily what she would have told him as Marash the seer. The trouble, he thought then, was that you don't always want what you need, or need what you want.

◆◆◆

Susannah hung up the phone and took a deep breath. She felt only confusion. At the very last moment she had said, "Marlene, don't call Ji . . . my husband, yet, please. Wait until ten or eleven New York time, tonight. Is that all right?"

Why had she done that? It wasn't fair to him, or to herself. It wasn't fair to anyone to put it off a minute longer than necessary. She was hurting people on all sides and, knowing that, she still wanted more time. She tried to imagine her husband, Jimmie Rivers, pacing a hotel room waiting to hear that she had been found, haggard with worry about her disappearance. Nothing came. She said the name over to herself: Jimmie Rivers. Nothing went with it. A stranger. She had loved him enough to marry him, and presumably he still loved her; yet he was a stranger whose name meant nothing.

What if, when he appeared, it all came back to her in a flash? What if in that one instant, less than an instant, Brad became that kind of stranger? She looked at the diary she had been keeping and knew it would not help. Words, only words without meaning, just as the name of her husband had no meaning. Her own name, Susannah, had no meaning. Words. Empty words. Tonight Jimmie Rivers would know she was in New York and he would come for her and the dream would end. Whose dream? she asked herself. Who was dreaming this insane dream? And why didn't the dreamer wake up and release her?

There was a tap on her door and Brad called out, "Breakfast's ready. Come and get it!"

She took a deep breath. Ten or eleven more hours of dreaming, she thought, and went out to join him before the picture window overlooking Central Park. From the study they could hear the work in progress:

"Goddamn it, Max, it's not supposed to be orange!"

"It has to be orange! That stupid cat is orange!"

"Brown! With a touch of red-gold!"

"Bullshit! Let's go have a look. You too, come on, I want to prove to you once and for all that you're wrong. Where's that fucker?"

All three marched out from the study in search of Exxon, who had found a hiding place in the library, high on a shelf where he had pushed books out of the way. Some lay on the floor, some had hit a table.

Brad looked grim and studiously watched the trees in the park. Susannah giggled and covered it with her napkin. "Is that how they always work?"

"Ever since I can remember."

The voices were coming back. Exxon led the group into the

living room. "That light was piss poor in there. Like a tomb. Sylvie, I told you to get an electrician up here and put in some decent lights!"

"You did not! You never thought of those lights until this second. Look at him in the sunlight over there!"

Exxon had found a sunny window ledge.

"Red-gold! I told you, you blind moron!"

"Orange!"

They headed back into the study and now Susannah's giggles became outright laughter. Brad joined her after a moment.

"Let's do the whole tourist bit today," Brad said, pushing his plate back. "The Statue of Liberty, Empire State Building, a boat ride around Manhattan, everything."

"Oh yes! I'd like that. Will Exxon be safe here? They won't dismember him or anything to prove a point?"

"Are you kidding? That fool cat is pure red-gold at this time in his sinful life. Let's go."

Overnight someone, probably Geneva, had washed their jeans and shirts, everything. They were both rested and fed, and within minutes they were in the elevator.

In the lobby, the security men on the day shift became alert when they saw who was coming down. They had heard about Mr. Hale's crazy girl friend.

"Good morning, Mr. Hale, Miss Dennis," one of them said as the pair passed the desk.

Brad said good morning, and began to laugh. Susannah looked wary.

She wasn't the nut case, the guards agreed. They could hear their voices as they went through the lobby and to the street:

"It isn't funny!"

"But it was! You were wonderful!"

◆◆◆

At two-thirty the messenger came and took away the cover painting for delivery to Mike's editor. Sylvia turned on the answering machine they always used when they were working.

She listened to the messages, then joined Mike and Max in the dining room for lunch.

"Captain Jimmie called three times," she said helping herself to crab salad. "And Donna Murphy called once."

"Where are the kids?"

"Sightseeing. Remember, Brad stuck his head in and said they were off for the day?"

"I don't remember. I doubt that he mentioned it, and it's an insane idea. What if they get separated? What if he gets mugged and she wanders around all day, has no place to sleep tonight? She's too vulnerable. She doesn't know enough to be afraid of anyone or anything. Where did they go?"

"I don't know. Mike, relax. They've been together for two weeks now and he hasn't let anything happen to her."

"You didn't see what almost happened in the park," he said grimly.

Max looked from one to the other as he ate. Now he said, "I don't get it, Mike. You said her husband's in town looking for her. Give him a call, for Christ sake, and let the poor kid go home where she belongs."

Mike glowered at him. "She isn't going anywhere with that hotshot. She's staying with Brad."

"Mike!" Sylvia cried. "You're crazy! You can't treat her like a stray that followed your son home from school."

"That's what she is, though. He wants her, and you only have to watch them one second to know that's what she wants. She stays right here. Let that son of a bitch captain try to get her away!"

"You're going too far!" Sylvia said dangerously. "You'll be charged with a criminal offense, kidnapping or something."

"Did I hold a gun to her head and make her come here? Is she locked in her room all day? What I'm going to do is suggest to Brad that he's been working too hard for too many years. What he needs is a long cruise, a vacation at sea, and he should take her with him."

"She isn't your property, for God's sake! She's a sick little

200

girl who should be cured as soon as possible. Her husband is the one to take care of her. Have you thought how much it's going to hurt Brad when she comes out of this? The longer you put it off, the harder it will be for him. Think of him!"

"I'm thinking of him. How much time has he spent with me in the last ten years, Sylvie? Fifteen minutes a year, that's how much. One little duty call once a year and fifteen minutes later he has to run, business to take care of, sorry and all that. And now he's here. He talks to me. He looks at me as if I were a human being, not a monster. And how long since I did a new book? Really new. Three years, that's how long. Two years in a row it's been old tired ideas dragged out and dusted off and used because there wasn't anything else. And now I have a great idea! The best in fifteen years! And you know why these two little miracles came about? Because of her! She brought my boy back to me, and she brought me a new start. You know what it would have done to me if I had dried up now? Stroke time, Sylvie, or heart attack time, or my liver would have fallen out, or something else terrible would have happened. She said to me that she knows why I write these kinds of books and she said it was all right. Not just all right, by God, there's a need for them, for me! Who else ever could have done that for me? No one, that's who! We keep her, Sylvie! Keep that damn machine plugged in. Take no calls. No visitors. We're keeping her!"

Sylvia shook her head sadly. "It's no good, Mike, and you know it. Brad knows it. So does she." She stood up. "We'd better get back to work."

Donna hung up the phone and started to pace. New York hotel rooms seemed to shrink year by year, she thought angrily. When she was bothered, worried, bewildered, or angry, she needed to walk in order to plan her course of action. They were here in town, now what? It was eight o'clock and she had called that apartment three times during the day, each time speaking into that damn answering machine, each time being ignored. Calling was useless. She knew she could not get past the security men in the lobby unless someone in the apartment agreed to admit her, and obviously no one there wanted to see any outsider.

"Damn you, Brad!" she whispered several times and stopped when she realized it was keeping her from thinking.

Jimmie Rivers was in town, her mother had said, and had supplied the name of his hotel and his room number. No doubt he was being ignored also. But how to get past the security men?

Brad and that ... that woman had gone tearing across the country with only the clothes on their backs, and little money. She knew that Brad was nearly broke; their last restaurant meal, that neither had been able to finish, had taken him down to practically nothing. Susannah would be without clothes, she thought, more slowly, groping toward a plan.

Presently she left her room and went looking for a women's store that was still open. She found one and bought a few things, and then she telephoned Jimmie Rivers.

"I'm taking a parcel to Susannah now," she said after introducing herself. "Mother sent it for her," she added. "I thought you might like to go along, just in case you've been having the same problem I have in getting through to them."

"Oh, yes, ma'am," Jimmie said sincerely. "I appreciate this a whole lot, Miss Murphy. We'll meet you in front of the apartment building in what ... twenty minutes?"

"Good. That's fine. I'll wait for you if I get there first. See you later, captain."

Satisfied, she hung up the phone and decided to walk over; it was a lovely evening.

❖❖❖

She had to tell him, Susannah thought miserably. Dinner was over and they were alone in the living room watching the city lights come on. There was no light in the room yet and it seemed to her that darkness was seeping out of the walls, rising from the floor, filling the room soundlessly. Mike, Max, and Sylvia had gone back to work, for a few more hours, Mike had said, and Sylvia had laughed and said make that all night.

She had to tell him. She had left a message at the desk in the lobby, if Mr. Rivers called, she was the one to notify, Susannah Rivers. And he would; within the hour, he would call.

She twisted the notebook diary around in her hands, over and over. After she told him, she would write in it, probably her last entry. He would not wait for Jimmie Rivers to show up, she hoped. It would be too hard if he waited. She would tell him and he would go out for the evening, take a long walk or something, and when he returned, she would be gone. That was the only way to do it. Anything else would be too hard, too cruel. She twisted the notebook, and now she looked at Brad, then away very quickly. He had been watching her.

"What's wrong?" he asked. "Wasn't it a great day! All the way through."

"Lovely. I'm amazed that you never took the boat ride before. I loved it." How flat her voice sounded, unconvincing, as if she were reciting lines.

"I never had anyone I wanted to go with."

"We should talk," she said after another silence.

"I suppose. What do you want to do tomorrow?"

"Brad, please. After...if someone comes for me...What are you going to do after...?"

"Sh. I don't want to talk about that."

"But I do. I think that after you get your Ph.D. you should take off a year or two and write stories, maybe a novel."

"Those were your stories, not mine."

"You wrote them!"

"But I didn't think of them. You did. I couldn't have done any of them without you."

"Don't be silly!"

"Let's not talk anymore."

They both stared at the city, the park, the traffic below.

"Brad?" Geneva asked from the hallway. "You in there?"

"I'm here," he said.

She turned on a lamp. "There's a lady in the lobby to see you. Miss Donna Murphy. She has some things for the lady. And some friends of hers."

He shook his head. "Not tonight. Tell her I'm not home."

"The guards already told her you're up here," Geneva said disapprovingly. "And miss, there's a gentleman to see you. A Mr. Rivers. The guard said you asked to be informed if he showed up. Well, he did."

Susannah felt her knees go strange. "Thank you," she said faintly. "Please tell them to let him come up."

"Let them all come up! Maybe they can round up some hoods from the park while they're at it!"

"Now Brad," Geneva said, and left them again.

"Who is he?"

"He says he's my husband," she said in a voice so low he could hardly hear it.

"How did you find out? Who told you?"

"I called Marlene. I told her to talk to him, tell him where I am."

"Why like this? Why didn't you tell me?"

"I wanted us to have one more good day. It was a good day, Brad. Thank you."

"You could have waited another day. One more day wouldn't have hurt anything."

"I thought one more day would hurt," she said slowly.

From the study they could hear Mike's voice raised in anger: "I drew him like that because that's the way he is! Look at those pictures again! And I wrote his dialogue like that because that's the way he talks, for Christ sake! You've made him too human! He's a robot!"

The doorbell rang and Mike cursed and stormed out from the study. "What the fuck is going on around here? Who's coming this time of night?"

Geneva admitted Jimmie, Felix, Anna Maria Lucia, and Donna in a group. Mike bawled, "Max, get your ass out here and take a look for yourself!" To the guests he said acidly, "All of you, out! This is not the railroad station, or the bus stop! And the concert is over in the park. Get!"

"Susannah!" Jimmie cried, and he walked quickly toward her, arms outstretched.

"Brad!" Donna said. "Oh, darling, I'm so sorry everything's ending like this. You poor darling!"

"Susannah, my God, how I have missed you. I was so worried..."

Donna and Jimmie both stopped short of Susannah and Brad who had not moved from the window wall. Now Donna reached out and took Brad's hand and held it. It was empty. And Jimmie grasped Susannah's shoulders and then pulled her to him in an embrace. She dropped her notebook as she pushed against him reflexively.

"Geneva!" Mike screamed furiously. "You're fired! You let them in here without telling me!"

"Now Mike," Geneva said, and left the group to return to her kitchen.

"Get your hands off her!" Mike cried and tugged at Jimmie who was still holding Susannah. "Honey, if you want, I'll call the cops myself and heave them all in the can or something!"

She shook her head.

"Do you know this man? Can you honestly say you know him?"

She shook her head again. Inside she was saying over and over, "I will not look at Brad. I will not look at Brad. I will not..." She knew she could not bear it if she were to look at him now.

"Then he's got no right to force his way into my house and manhandle you in any manner whatever. Just back the hell off, bub!"

Jimmie stepped back from Susannah. "I have all the proof I need," he said. "There's a marriage license, and pictures of us together, and documents of various sorts that will all testify to the fact that Susannah is my wife..."

Max had been studying him intently, now he nodded to

205

Mike and said, "Sorry. You're right. I'll go fix that last sketch." He trotted away.

Mike turned to Susannah. "You have free will, you're not mentally incompetent. You don't have to go with him if you don't want to. He's a stranger to you, for Christ sake! You don't have to go off with a stranger. It'll take time to check his credentials, to prove his claim. He could be mistaken."

"Mr. Berryman, thank you, but I talked to Marlene. It's all right."

"It's not all right, goddamn it! You're not going off to climb into a strange man's bed!"

"Mr. Berryman, I see that he keep distance," Anna Maria Lucia said firmly. "I agree. No stranger in anyone's bed is a good thing. I watch our little Susannah until she watch for self, until she remember everything, and after that she okay."

Mike turned to Brad and yelled, "Are you just going to stand there? Aren't you even going to try to do anything?"

"Mr. Berryman, I think we should all just leave now," Susannah said, not looking at Brad. "It would be best if we just go now."

"And I agree entirely with Susannah," Jimmie said. "I appreciate that this is a difficult situation for all of us, sir, but I have to register this little observation. It appears to me that you are not the person to be erecting any obstacles at all to the reunion of husband and wife. If anyone has a grievance, I really think, sir, that I am that person. You have to realize that I am willing to overlook the fact that my wife has spent two weeks in the company of your son, even traveling three thousand miles alone with him. And that, mind you, after he attacked her and did her bodily damage with his automobile. This is a grave situation, I don't deny, but if we'll all just keep our heads and not act precipitously, I am certain we can weather it with minimal further damage."

Felix said then, "I think what Susannah suggested is the best thing I've heard yet. Let's leave, Jimmie. Let's take Susannah to our hotel and talk over the problem calmly and rationally. And, naturally, the first thing after you arrive back in your own home again is to have a discussion of these various nuances with your attorney."

"Oh, for crying out!" Anna Maria Lucia screamed. "I think I go crazy! Come on, Susannah! Come on, Jimmie and Felix! Now! We go!"

22

Stones of power

Louis glared at Heinrich. "She has to come here, damn it! Where else can she go? Your name is the only one she knows in Cartagena! You work for the company, she'll come to you for help."

"For two days you've been saying the same thing, Louis. And for two days she hasn't come here. She's nowhere. What did you do to her?" It gave him pleasure not to tell Louis that he knew exactly where Leah was, holed up in the beach house of the red-haired American.

Louis pounded the desktop that was between them. Heinrich was fat, too fat to sit behind a desk. He was some distance from it, enough so that when he wanted to use the phone, or write a memo, or rummage in a drawer, he had to roll his chair several inches closer and turn his bulky frame slightly to one side. He was bald and even now at nine in the morning, he was too hot; sweat was oozing down his temples and he was red-faced.

Louis stopped pounding the desktop when it hurt his hand. He stood up. "She isn't my problem anymore. She's yours. She'll show up and I don't give a shit what you do with her. She's yours from now on."

Heinrich shrugged massively. All his gestures were oversized. "She won't show up," he said. "You've disposed of her some-

208

how. It doesn't matter. But I wish you had waited until after I had a chance to get to know her better. You promised, Louis, and you reneged."

"She wouldn't go along with it! I told you!"

Heinrich heaved himself up; it was a slow process. "It's time for you to go catch your plane. Goodbye, Louis. We won't be seeing each other again. It's just as well. Cartagena is bad for many people; the tropics can kill a man like you in a few months."

"You're not recommending me for the managerial job then?"

Again Heinrich shrugged. "It is for your own good."

"You bastard! Just because that little twit wouldn't play games with you!"

"Goodbye, Louis."

He went to the door where his suitcase and the little blue bag were side by side. He picked up his and started out.

"Oh, Louis. Take them both. When her body shows up, I wouldn't be happy to have anything to link her with me. Take them both."

At the airport Louis checked his own suitcase through, received his seat assignment, and had half an hour to kill. He was afraid that the half-hour was going to stretch out more than that; the plane had not arrived yet from Bogota. He went to the upper level bar to have a bloody mary, and decided to leave the blue suitcase there and be rid of it. The plane arrived miraculously only ten minutes late; a few people straggled into the terminal, and then his flight was announced. The bartender nodded at him, to confirm the flight number. He gulped the rest of his drink and hurried down the stairs, only to hear behind him an ingratiating voice:

"*Señor, un momentito!*" A young man was running to catch him, bringing his bag.

"Thanks," he said sourly, and hurried on.

There was no other chance to get rid of it. The terminal was large, and nearly empty, and military guards were keeping the peace, watching everyone closely. He went through the check-in, yielded with bad feelings to a superficial search that consisted of being patted up and down his body, watched as the blue suitcase was opened and pawed through, and then hurried out into the sunlight to cross the sizzling tarmac and board, along with no more than seven or eight others. Inside the plane he slowed down only enough to shove the suitcase into the storage closet behind a stack of other suitcases, boxes, and paper-wrapped parcels. The stewards and stewardesses were up and down the aisle taking drink orders; a baby was wailing, and two small children were crawling in the aisle playing a mysterious game. No one seemed to notice his hesitation at the storage area, and he knew that no matter what happened, he would deny ever having seen the blue suitcase in his life. Bitch, he thought in mild triumph, that would teach her to play her fucking games with him.

◆◆◆

"Brad, did you get any sleep?" Mike asked at nine that morning.

"Some. Did you?"

"Some. I read those articles about amnesia." He poured coffee and sat down at the table where Brad was shoving toast around on his plate. "Sorry I jumped on you. Nothing you could have done, I guess."

"Yeah, I know."

"You could keep track, and when you know she's back to herself again, you could introduce yourself..."

Brad nodded. "Yeah. This stranger comes to the door and says, 'Hey, we were friends for a while.' And she says, 'Come in and meet my wonderful husband.'"

Mike sighed heavily. "Goddamn it! Just goddamn it!"

"You're pretty busy now," Brad said, pushing toast back and forth. "I guess I'll go on down to Washington and do my work in the Library of Congress, get out of your hair for a couple of weeks."

"You'll come back by this way before you take off again?"

"If you don't mind. And there's Exxon. I guess I'll have to

take him back to California with me when I go. I could put him in a kennel somewhere for a while."

"Leave him here. I'm not through with him. He's not a bad sort actually."

Exxon was sniffing the furniture. He had prowled the apartment for an hour, investigating every room restlessly. Brad sympathized.

Geneva looked in the dining room. "Brad, that woman, Donna Murphy, is in the lobby wanting to see you."

"Christ," he said helplessly. "Tell her I've gone . . . Never mind, just let her come up. I'll tell her."

When Donna arrived, she was unbearably cheerful. "Brad, I know your inclination will be to mope and that's the worst possible thing you could do. I've come to take you out on a tourist's visit to New York. The Statue of Liberty, the World Trade Center, the Stock Exchange."

He groaned. "I'm not moping, and I don't have time for the tourist bit. I'm off to Washington, back to work. I've put up with all the interruptions I can take."

"Really? You're going back to work! Darling, that's wonderful. I'm so relieved!"

Mike stood in the doorway watching, and suddenly he knew what was missing from the new book. A plastic wife for the robot scientist, he thought happily, and ran to get his camera. He had been wrong about her, he admitted silently, loading the film pack.

"Miss Murphy," he said, returning, "I wonder if you'd like to see the rest of the apartment? We might have a little chat."

Without a backward glance she followed him, trying to control the triumph and jubilation she feared might show on her face.

Brad watched them go to the living room, and then he left the apartment, ordered his car, and tried to think of Washington, the Library of Congress, what it was that he had to do there.

He thought instead of Susannah, and then deliberately conjured an image of his father. The fury was gone, he realized, the resentment and anger had vanished. He still felt betrayed, but in a different way, not a way that threatened to make him join the Navy, or jump from a high building, or buy a gun and go look for him. He felt sadness for his father who had gone through life regretting a mistake he had made. The fact that he himself had a lifetime of regret to get through made him realize how his father had suffered, and almost, but not yet altogether, made him realize why his father had been so insensitive about the effect it had on others to appear in his dumb books. And now he was doing it again to Donna, who, innocent that she was, would probably never know. If she did find out, she no doubt would be mollified if the old man let her buy and sell a few stocks for him.

Every time his thoughts turned again to Susannah, he consciously thought about his father, about Donna, about his degree, anything that he could concentrate on for even a few seconds. In the end, his thoughts always turned to Susannah.

"Now, Susannah," Jimmie said, "I expect that now that you've had a good night's sleep, knowing you're back in the fold of your loved ones, no longer lost and homeless, your memory's probably starting to come back a little at a time. Isn't that right?"

She shook her head. She had not had a good night's sleep; she had slept hardly at all. For hours he had pressed her to remember, and now, the moment she got up, it was starting again. She looked at the breakfast they had ordered as if the table were covered with crawling things.

"You were a little sore at me," Jimmie prompted. "You packed two suitcases, your old big one, and the new little blue one that I gave you. Remember?"

She shook her head again.

"Now then, you got in your little car, a black VW bug, and you drove to a motel where a limousine was taking off for the airport. Remember? Try, Susannah, just give it a try."

"Stop it," she said wearily. "Please, just stop. I don't remember anything about it. I don't remember you, or them," she said, pointing to Felix and Anna Maria Lucia.

"All right. All right. Sometimes these things take a little time, I understand, but then all at once, it's over and, pop, there it all comes to you, fresh as a daisy. That's how it will be, any minute now. But meanwhile, I do believe, honestly — this is just my own intuition, not backed by any authority — but I really truly believe that if you'll just concentrate on it a little bit, that's bound to help. You know, I really do believe that there's nothing a person can't do, if you just put your mind to it and concentrate."

"Forget it, Jimmie," Felix said. "Leave her alone. We've got to check out and get to the airport. Maybe it'll come back to her when she steps out into that good old Florida sunshine. Susannah, are you going to eat anything?"

"I don't feel very hungry," she said.

"We really should leave then," Felix said. "There will be lunch on the plane."

Jimmie regarded Susannah with concern. "Is that really all you have to wear? Anna Maria Lucia, can't she wear any of your things?"

"No, she cannot. She is little where I am big, and long where I am short."

Susannah was wearing her jeans and shirt, the only clothes she had with her. She had no makeup on. Last night suddenly everyone had been hustling, and she had been rushed from the apartment without even her purse. She wouldn't need anything, Jimmie had insisted, tomorrow she would be home where everything was waiting for her. Not home, Anna Maria Lucia had muttered darkly, and the matter had rested there.

"Well, she'll have to go like that, but this is exactly what I mean about a permissive society, Anna Maria Lucia. Look at her, unisex clothes, unisex hair, you can't tell the boys from the girls in this society. It isn't good for the morals of a country if you can't tell the boys from the girls."

Susannah felt her eyes burning, and angrily she turned away.

"If we're going, let's do it," she said.

"See," Jimmie said sadly. "Dressed in her own pretty things, with her hair back to normal, a little makeup on, she'd never speak to me in that tone of voice. I tell you, clothes and hairstyle and all that do make a woman a woman. You can't get around that, no way."

◆◆◆

Louis was finishing his second drink, two hours into the flight when the terrorists seized the plane. For several minutes he could not grasp what was happening. Several kids had started to run up and down the aisles, and then an older man, in his thirties, had pulled a gun from somewhere, and now he was in the aisle telling them something or other in Spanish, which Louis did not know.

Someone screamed, a child began to howl, and for a moment Louis thought the man with the long gun, an automatic something, would start shooting.

A voice began to speak over the sound system. Even without understanding a word of the rapid Spanish, Louis knew it was the captain. He had that soothing rhythm. He finished his speech, then repeated it in English:

"Ladies and gentlemen, I'm afraid that we have been taken over by a group of people with guns. Please remain in your seats and remain calm. The attendants will continue to fill your orders, and I'm confident that if we all relax and stay calm, this problem will come to an end quickly. Thank you."

His voice was almost without accent, and very smooth, very reassuring. It gave Louis the shudders to listen to it. Terrorists! He was a hostage! He gulped down the last few drops of his drink and hit the attendant button.

It was Leah's fault, he decided bitterly. If she hadn't run off, he would have left Monday, be in his own apartment at this minute, thinking about the day's work ahead.

Four seats in front of Louis a man clutched at one of the terrorists as he passed. "Please, let me go," the man said.

"Please, I'm not political. I don't know anything about politics. Just let me go!"

"Go where?" the terrorist asked in astonishment. "We're thirty-seven thousand feet in the air!"

Now a murmur was spreading throughout the plane: "Iranians! They're Iranians!"

Louis could not tell. All those dark-haired, dark-eyed, dark-skinned people looked alike to him, and the lingo they all spoke was indistinguishable to his ears. Gibberish, all of it was gibberish.

❖❖❖

"Hi ya, Carl!" Jimmie said, sliding into the cockpit of the L-1011. "How you doing?"

"Hey, Jimmie! You a passenger? Didn't see your name on the list."

"Last minute change of plans. How's it going, Carl?"

"Real good." He introduced his copilot and then rang for coffee. "Make yourself to home," he said.

They talked baseball for a while, sipping their coffee, and then the copilot, who was monitoring the radio, held up his hand. "Get a load of this," he said to Carl, who slipped the headphones back on.

"Oh wow!" Carl said. He glanced at Jimmie. "We've got a bomb threat coming in on our heels at Miami. Due a couple of minutes after we land. They're talking about diverting everything after this baby gets home."

Jimmie shook his head. "Tough," he said. "What flight is it?"

"It's a Colombian flight, two-thirds Americans aboard. Yeah, it's tough." He was still listening and now he looked even more startled.

The copilot said, "My God!" and Carl and Jimmie both glanced at him reprovingly. He would never make captain that way.

"They have terrorists on board, they've taken the plane, and they've got a bomb threat that apparently has nothing to do with the terrorists," Carl said slowly, as if explaining the use of a set of blocks to an infant.

"Both? On the same flight?"

Carl nodded, listening. "They're allowing us to land, but then it's Katie bar the door," he said. He looked up at Jimmie, and added, "Oh, Jimmie, not a word, you understand. Not even a word."

"Sure, sure," Jimmie said and backed out of the cockpit. That was too much, he thought, a bomb threat on top of terrorists. There was simply too much criminal activity any more. No one was safe.

◆◆◆

Louis had heartburn, and a headache. The damn terrorists were searching each passenger methodically, men and women, even the babies, and all the bags and parcels. Louis wondered if he were having a heart attack, if this was how it started. Also he was going to piss all over himself if they didn't let him go to the john pretty soon. Up at the storage closet two men were examining all the carried-on parcels, the luggage, the clothes bags, everything. One had slit open six bags of coffee beans, spilling most of them, and now the cabin smelled of coffee. Four of them were making the passenger search, and it was not long before they got to Louis. They made him empty his pockets, dump stuff on the seat, and then they went over him thoroughly, more thoroughly than the people at the terminal had done.

"What are you going to do with us?" he demanded when they told him to pick up his stuff and sit down again.

"Maybe shoot those who talk too much," one of them said, and started on the next person, as the captain's voice came on to say that the plane was making its approach to Miami International.

◆◆◆

"There it is!" Felix said, standing at the wide observation window in the flight personnel lounge. Jimmie nodded. The flight from Cartagena was rolling onto the runway at the far end of the field. It would be directed to the parking spot reserved for bomb threats and terrorists, nearly half a mile from the terminal, while negotiations took place between the terrorists and the government.

Midway down the runway to its designated spot the plane came to a stop. "What are they doing?" several people in the lounge asked Felix, who was the only one with binoculars.

"Can't see a thing yet," he said. "Ah, yes. They've opened the baggage compartment, they're heaving out the baggage. I would assume that they failed to find a bomb and they are taking no chances that it might be concealed in the baggage. They'll dump all that stuff and then move away from it, that's my guess."

He continued to watch while all around him people were straining to see, squinting in the glare of the sun off concrete.

❖❖❖

Louis watched them go through the small stuff from the closet: coffee, baby junk, a few cases of duty-free liquor . . . Finally they came to the blue bag, and it flew open when it was yanked from the closet. Leah's pathetic belongings scattered.

"Whose is this?" one of them demanded, holding the bag up. He asked in two other languages before he got to English.

No one moved. He waited a few seconds, then tossed it down again, and he and two of the other men stood huddled over it suspiciously. Finally one of them knelt down by it and began to jab at the quilted and padded lining. Clearly they thought they had found the bomb, or whatever it was they were after, Louis thought in disgust. And if it were a bomb the idiots would blow up the plane and everyone in it. He started to yell at them to stop, that it was his, but at that moment one of the three men cried out some more gibberish, and all of them fell to the floor bowing to the little suitcase. Someone up front, a woman in a red pantsuit, stood up and looked over them to see what was in the bag.

"It's a king's ransom in jewels!" she cried for all to hear. "It must be a million dollars of jewels in there!"

❖❖❖

"They say they're students working their way through college in Tehran," a Delta captain said to the mob in the lounge. "They want five million dollars. It's a deluxe education they're after, I assume." No one laughed.

"I'll be damned," an American captain said, entering the crowded room. "Listen to this, they're letting all the women and children leave, and they want to be refueled. They say they're going back to Iran."

"When?"

"Right away. As soon as they get fueled."

"What about the bomb?"

"Nothing about the bomb. They've stripped the plane. No bomb." He had on earphones, monitoring a shortwave radio that he carried, and now he turned to stare at it intently.

"Hey, Jimmie, come here!" Felix cried. "Look what they tossed." He handed the binoculars to Jimmie. The side door of the plane was open, and on the ground a few feet away was the blue suitcase.

"It can't be the same one," Jimmie said calmly. "There's a mistake. It just looks like it."

"Yeah, it sure does. Even has letters, a monogram or something. Can't make out what it is. Can you?"

Jimmie could see what he meant, but the bag was turned in such a way that he could not make out the letters. He could clearly see that the lining had been ripped out.

"Shit," he said quietly and handed the binoculars back to Felix.

"How the hell do you suppose it got on that plane?"

Jimmie turned to look for Susannah, but the crush of people was so great that he could not find her. There were the uniforms of all the airlines — Delta, American, United, Eastern, Pan Am, Trans World . . . He tried to make his way through to where he had left Susannah and Anna Maria Lucia on the couch on the far wall.

"Listen," the American captain yelled. "They say they have the state jewels, the jewels that go with the Peacock Throne!

They say America has been caught trying to steal their most sacred treasure. They say they have shown the jewels to the women who will be coming off, they've given them Polaroid pictures taken on the spot to prove what they say is true. They'll let three reporters board to verify it, then they're taking off. They say the Ayatollah will guarantee them a place in heaven for returning the jewels."

◆◆◆

Louis felt dizzy and understood nothing of what was happening. Women were being allowed to leave, that was all he knew. Some of them were being given pictures to show to the news media. One of the kids that had been crawling around on the floor had picked up the jewels for the terrorists, who seemed afraid to touch them. The kid had put them in a little pouch and now sat with them in his lap. The terrorists were treating the kid and his mother like royalty. As for him, Louis, all he knew was that he was going to go to Iran. He stared out the window bitterly.

23

"We can't keep her and we can't turn her loose."

We have to find Susannah," Jimmie said carefully. "If she isn't in the restroom, then she's just wandering around looking at the sights." He glanced at his watch. "We have five or ten minutes to make our way down the concourse and meet our friends in the bar. That's plenty of time to pick her up on the way."

"And you hand her over?"

"Now, Felix, the way I see it, one of their people must have betrayed them. We tell them that Susannah was our contact here, that she carried the bag to Chicago and passed it on to someone there, who made arrangements to get it to Miami."

Felix looked at him in wonder. "That's crazy."

"Okay, we tell them the truth. Susannah stole the bag and we don't know what happened after that. One of their people got to her, I suppose. No doubt they will want to question Susannah, refresh her memory. I am not happy about this, but we have to do the right thing, demonstrate that the trust they placed in us was not betrayed."

"It doesn't matter what you tell them," Felix said gloomily. "They won't believe it. I don't believe it myself. They'll want our hides along with Susannah's."

Anna Maria Lucia returned from the restroom. "She is not there," she said.

"Okay. Felix and I will go through the shops, and you stay in the center of the concourse and we'll find her in a minute or two. Maybe she wanted a candy bar, or a Coke, or something. She didn't have breakfast, remember, and no doubt by now she has started to feel some stirring of hunger..." Still talking easily, he moved away from Felix and Anna Maria Lucia and entered the first shop, a men's wear store. Felix drifted into the next one, children's stuffed toys. Anna Maria Lucia looked over the people hurrying in both directions in the concourse, and slowly the trio began their search.

◈◈◈

Susannah had not understood what was happening in the lounge, and she had not been able to see anything; she had been crushed by the hordes of people, until finally she had left to take a walk. She looked at the window displays, and then stopped to read signs carried by a small group of men. "STOP ERA!" "GIVE US BACK OUR WIVES!" The men looked mean and obviously did not like her.

"Who took them?" she asked. "Are they being held hostage, too?"

"Slut!"

"Get a dress on!"

Shaking her head in bewilderment, she continued to walk. There was a table display that stopped her again. This one had a banner that said: "NUKE JANE FONDA! FONDA HAS NEVER PRODUCED A KILOWATT OF ELECTRICITY!" Another smaller sign, one that would fit a car bumper, read: "3MI PROVES THE SYSTEM WORKS!" Another said: "STOP OPEC! NUKES WILL SAVE US!"

"Will you sign the petition?" someone asked.

Susannah looked up from the sign she had been reading. The speaker was a pleasant-looking woman of sixty perhaps, gray hair, a nicely plump face with smiling eyes. "What petition?"

"We need nuclear arms," the smiling woman said. "We need nuclear power. This country can never achieve its former greatness unless we unite and prove to the world that the fearful few among us are not dictating our destiny. We will be strong and seize the initiative once more, take our place as the leader of the free world, a leader that the godless will not dare to cross in any way, because once more we will have the power to enforce our decisions. We need a strong armed America..."

Susannah walked on.

"Bet I have your favorite movie star in here," a beautiful teen-age boy said to her in a laughing voice. He was carrying a box. His hair was softly curled, his eyes candid and wide, with heavy lashes. He could have modeled for Michelangelo.

Susannah shook her head at him. "I don't have a favorite star," she said regretfully.

"Sure you do," he said, and this time he let the laughter bubble out with the words. He opened the box and showed her. It was filled with stickpins of Disney characters — Mickey Mouse, Donald Duck, Pluto... "See!"

"What are they for?"

"To wear. Or give to your best little friend. To keep. Take one."

"No thank you."

"This is our way to raise money for our church," the boy said confidentially. "You get something cute, something that's sure to please any child you know, and we get a dime, a quarter, whatever you want to give."

"I don't have any money."

"Then we give a dime or a quarter to you!" he exclaimed. "Can I buy you a cup of coffee, or a Coke?"

"Why do you want to?" Now she stopped. "Is this all you do all day? Sell those things and buy people something to drink? Why?"

"We don't sell them," he said, smiling. "We give them away, and accept donations. We do it because we want to reach out and help people who are lost, friendless, with nowhere to go. We do it because we love you, everyone."

"You mean you love me? Why? You don't know me. Do you? Do you know me?"

222

For the first time the boy seemed to hesitate just a little. "Of course I love you," he finally said firmly. "I don't have to know you to love you. I love everyone."

"Even those men back there, the ones who've lost their wives?"

He nodded.

"And the woman who wants to blow up Jane Fonda?"

He swallowed and nodded again.

Susannah began to walk once more. "I think if you love everybody you can't love anybody very much," she said thoughtfully.

"But love is limitless! The more you give, the more you have!"

She shook her head. "It's easy to say it, and to believe you mean it, but if you truly loved everyone, it would kill you. You couldn't stand to see those you loved suffering, going hungry, killing others that you also love. Love," she said positively, "is possible on a very small scale only, and even that is too much for many people to handle." She looked at him kindly then. "I don't want to discourage you, but if you love humanity, it's an abstract, you see. When it comes to people, individual people, it's altogether different."

"Let me buy you an orange juice!" he pleaded. "I want to talk with you. I want to tell you our goals. We need people like you to work with us, to help our cause. Please." He smiled prettily. "What's your name? What can I call you?"

"Marian," she said softly. "I was a student, like you. And God spoke to me and said, 'Marian, go to this place high on a mountain, and listen to the voice of the flowing waters.' I didn't know what that meant, and I saw a psychiatrist, who treated me for several weeks. But then God spoke to me again. 'Marian, why do you tarry?' And I said, 'I don't know where to go, Lord.' And He took me by the hand and led me to the mountain where a brook tumbled over rocks and He said, 'Sit here, Marian, and listen to the voice of the waters.' I sat there and nothing happened for days, and I became very weak from hunger, and the cold nights, and the heat of the days. I thought I would die by the little brook. I cried out: 'Lord, I am obedient, but now I will die here!' And then the voice of the waters chided me softly, lovingly. And I listened and forgot my hunger, forgot my weariness ..."

She paused. The boy was staring at her wide-eyed. "Do you believe me?" she asked softly. "It doesn't matter."

"Go on," he urged. "What happened then?"

"I lived by the brook until the summer ended, and I said, 'Lord, soon the snow will come and then I must return to my home, to the warmth of the fire, to shelter.' And the Lord said, 'Stay here, Marian, and listen to the voices of the falling snow.' And I thought then I surely would die, but the snow came and I listened to the voices of the snow, and I was warm."

He was nodding at her. "What did He tell you?"

"He told me that when He speaks to His people, He speaks to them directly, not through the voices of men who grow rich. He speaks through the voice of the flowing water, through the voice of the silent snow, through the voice of the wind —"

"Susannah! We've looked everywhere for you!" Jimmie rushed to her and caught her arm. "Come on, we're late for our appointment!" He drew her away from the boy who continued to stand unmoving until they were out of sight.

Someone bumped him and he shook himself as if he were waking up. He remembered the box he carried, opened it and looked at the Disney characters, and he walked to a planter with an orange tree growing in it. He put the box down on the edge of it and walked away. When he left the terminal, he lifted his face toward the sky, toward the wind, listening. There were too many people, sirens, traffic, too much noise. He would go to the beach and listen, he thought, and started to walk.

"We don't want you to say anything at all," Jimmie explained to Susannah, hurrying her toward the bar at the end of the concourse. "It wasn't your fault that you stole the blue bag and put it down somewhere. You weren't responsible, but they might think you were, and they might be angry with you. We're just going to tell them the exact truth, nothing else, only the truth, and if they are angry, and even if they say things that sound threatening to you, remember you are innocent of any wrongdoing."

"It's the curse," Anna Maria Lucia said. "Always a curse is fulfilled in ways that no one can comprehend. We are pawns the curse move here then there, no matter what we want or say. Always it is so."

"Anna Maria Lucia, I think you'd better not go into any of that with our colleagues when we meet them," Jimmie said. "I understand that it's your Italian nature, and I respect you for it, but they might take a different view altogether, you understand."

"Bah! They understand, just like me. It is you who do not understand such things. You see."

The bar was very dark, packed with customers watching the televised running account of the terrorists and the unfolding story. On the screen was the plane, and some distance from it a cluster of police cars, an ambulance, fire trucks, and a group of armed soldiers.

"Again, ladies and gentlemen, we are waiting for the three reporters to emerge from the plane. It's been twelve minutes and eighteen seconds since they entered, and so far there's no word. To recap these extraordinary events, as far as anyone knows at this point at any rate, it appears that a group of terrorists from Colombia seized the plane in midflight. At first it was assumed that they represented the terrorist group M-Nineteen, but as it transpired, they are Iranians, loyal to Khomeini, who demanded five million dollars in extortion. But, to complicate matters, there was a bomb threat to the plane, apparently a hoax, but perhaps not. Who can say at this point in time? The passengers who have been released are being debriefed by government officials, and there's been no official word yet from them, but according to a reliable source we have learned that they confirm the terrorists' statements that they found the crown jewels of Iran aboard the plane while they were conducting their search for a bomb. What an extraordinary story, ladies and gentlemen! The fabled crown jewels of Iran! Fabled and cursed. Priceless!"

"See!" Anna Maria Lucia cried. "I tell you that!"

"Sh. Do you see them, Felix?"

225

"I can't see anything in there," Felix said.

There seemed to be as many people trying to get into the bar as there were already inside. And then there were three men pushing their way out.

"Here they come," Felix said quietly.

Jimmie locked his shaky knees and took a breath. "Of course," he said. "They realize how hopeless the situation is now to try to carry on a conversation in these conditions..."

The men who were coming out were pale and more than a little wild-eyed. Suddenly half a dozen of the men who had been trying to squeeze themselves through the crowd, stopped pushing, and as each of the Iranians emerged, he found himself escorted by two well-dressed men who could have been stockbrokers.

"Ah, the FBI," Jimmie murmured. "Times like these it's good to know how fast they can gather their forces and take decisive action. They know as well as we do that those three Iranians were loyal to the Shah and would never have anything to do with religious fanatics and terrorists, but still, here they are, our men who never sleep, protecting us, risking everything..."

"Sh!" Anna Maria Lucia dug her elbow into his ribs.

"Let's not make any public fuss," one of the agents was murmuring as he passed close to Jimmie. "We just want to ask you a few questions, check a few credentials, that sort of routine."

"I think they were resigned," Jimmie said thoughtfully, gazing after the group of men. None of them had given him a glance as they passed by.

"They know it is curse doing all this," Anna Maria Lucia said. "But that does not mean they do not look for you later."

"Yes, well, I think we should rent a car and go home. Won't be any planes leaving the airport for hours maybe. You want to come over and discuss this little problem, Felix?"

"I think that's a fine idea," Felix said. "You know, old friend, I have over twenty thousand dollars tied up in this little venture of ours. We have many hours of discussion before us, and since my car is still at your house, I might as well go with you and get it."

"I know about your stake, old buddy, but you have to remember that I financed our little adventures all this week, all those flights, renting those little planes, motels...It has not been insignificant, old friend. I have kept very good records, and I can assure you, it has not been insignificant..."

Anna Maria Lucia looked from one to the other of them and sighed. "So we go now, no?"

❖❖❖

It was late; Susannah had been in her room for hours, and Felix had just left.

"So what you plan to do with poor little Susannah?" Anna Maria Lucia demanded.

"Well now, I have to tell you truthfully, I rightly don't know."

"She no good to you now. You send her away. She have money, a job, she be all right."

"We just can't do that, Anna Maria Lucia. We can't keep her and we can't turn her loose. She knows too much about our connection with that little business deal. And she tells everything she knows to anyone who asks. You heard her in the car coming home. Talking about the voices of the snow..."

"And then she sleep and wake up, poof, it all gone." Anna Maria Lucia frowned. "She will get sick," she said gloomily. "No appetite, no food. She look at food like it poison. She get sick, maybe die."

Jimmie nodded. "She just might," he said.

"You like that idea!" She drew away from him, aghast.

"Now, Anna Maria Lucia, take it easy. I'm not suggesting a doggone thing. You said she might get sick and die, not me. I don't want the poor little girl to get sick or die or anything like that. But it's true also that she's no use to us anymore. And she might talk. She's heard enough to make the FBI add us to their bag of Iranians for a few friendly questions."

"But she get well and forget all this. Mrs. Murphy say that is how this work."

"And then she might get hot again and decide to sue me for bigamy," Jimmie said resignedly. "You know I've had a few little business losses recently, nothing drastic, but still, a few thousand here, a few thousand there, you begin to feel the pressure. It wouldn't do to have any scandal at the company. No sir, it would not do at all. You know how important it is to keep a certain image when you have a position of trust. All those people in the sky have to have trust in their captain, or it would be chaos. And they have to have an image that permits them to trust."

"Jimmie, what are you getting around to?" Anna Maria Lucia asked. "Just say it."

"Anna Maria Lucia, let me just say this. I have a firm belief in choice, as you well know. I believe people have to choose for themselves, whatever the outcome. And take the consequences. I don't for a second believe anyone has the right to tell someone else you have to do this or that, no matter how good for them it might be. You simply can't choose for someone else. That's what I feel about poor little Susannah. If she chooses not to eat, to get sick, and even to die, I have too much respect for her as a human being to interfere in any way. It could be that deep down she knows that's the only way she can help me now, and she is still in love with me deep down, you can bank on that. Maybe deep down she is choosing, for my sake, for our sake, Anna Maria Lucia, and if she is, we have to cooperate with her. We can't stand in her way, not after all she's suffered. She deserves our help, Anna Maria Lucia."

The next day Susannah swam many laps and when she finished, she ate a large dinner, and then retired to her room once more. Anna Maria Lucia looked at Jimmie and cried, "Bah! Now I think of something!"

24

Poor little Susannah!

Where are you going?" Anna Maria Lucia cried as Susannah
entered the kitchen carrying a suitcase.

"I'm going to pack my things and leave," Susannah said. "I
just don't see any point in staying here, living like this. I'll get
a job somewhere."

"You can't leave! You're sick. You can't get a job."

"I can wait on tables, or sell shoes, or do something."

"Susannah, wait for tomorrow, for Jimmie to come back."

Susannah sighed and put the suitcase down. "Look," she said
quietly, "I'm not an idiot. I know about you and Jimmie, that
you're lovers and have been for a long time. I don't care. He's
a stranger to me. I'm in the way here and I'm not getting even
a little bit of my memory back. Maybe I never will. But I don't
intend to stay in this house and live like this any longer. It's
been ten days, and I can't take it. This isn't living, it's just waiting for something that may never come. It's waiting on Monday for Tuesday, and then waiting on Tuesday for Wednesday,
and on and on. I need to be doing something, keep myself
busy. I have money in the bank, enough to last a long time
even if I can't find a job right away. I can take care of myself.
And," she said slowly, "there's no way you can stop me from
leaving. I've been thinking about this, about what the doctor
in San Francisco told me. I'm a free agent. I can do what I

229

want. I just don't want to argue with Jimmie about it." She picked up her suitcase again.

"No, you are sick! Believe me, you are sick! You have blank outs, no? Times you don't know what you do, what you say. Susannah, what you do those times is criminal acts. You . . . you steal things. They put you in jail."

"I don't believe you," Susannah said faintly.

"But you don't know yes, you don't know no. You don't remember. This is what your friend in New York say to Jimmie, she must be watched every minute, or she go to jail. They don't want Jimmie to take you because they know he fly away all the time. I say I stay and watch."

Slowly Susannah walked to the patio, leaving the suitcase on the floor. It was true, she did not know what she did or said during those periods of blankness. She shook her head. It was aching again. But she wouldn't steal! She knew she wouldn't steal. As if it came from somewhere outside her own head a sly voice asked: How do you know that? Brad would have told her, she answered silently. He had watched her all the time, stayed at her side constantly. Had he been afraid of what she would do if left alone? Resolutely she tried to push him out again; she had promised herself not to think of him, to try to forget him in this lifetime, just as she knew she would forget him when she recovered her memory. Would he then be like Jimmie was now: a stranger that she did not even like very much? At that time would she find herself looking at Jimmie with love? Desire him? Bitterly she wished she had made love with Brad, and rejected the thought with even more bitterness. She knew she had been right in not yielding to the desire that had swelled, subsided, swelled even more, over and over. Right! She mocked herself, so right, so good and honest. And a thief during the blackouts? Maybe, she admitted then. Maybe that side had to come out too, and it emerged during those moments that she then forgot. She felt that her head might erupt into flames as the thoughts raced round and round.

She should have brought her diary, she thought suddenly,

vehemently, and just as vehemently denied that also. What good would it do to relive those days, renew the memories, keep them too fresh ever to fade away? Jimmie had paid her debts and the rest of it was a dream. You can't live in a dream, she told herself savagely. You can't return to a dream that has ended. Her headache flared, making her wince. That was what happened if she let herself think about the dream; it was like a scalpel scraping nerves.

"Susannah, are you okay now? You stay until Jimmie come home?" Anna Maria Lucia stood by her chair; she was dressed to go out.

Silently Susannah nodded, and her head throbbed almost audibly.

"I go shopping for dinner now. You promise you stay?"

"I'll stay," she said dully. She heard the sliding door open, close again, and then nothing. It was very hot, nearly one hundred degrees, and even though she sat in the shade, the heat was unbearable. The house was locked up, no one else was home, and it would be an hour before Anna Maria Lucia would return. Slowly Susannah pulled off her shorts and halter top, walked to the pool, and dived in cleanly with hardly a splash. The impact of the water on her aching head was like a cannon exploding too close to her ears. For a moment everything vanished, the pool, the sun overhead, even herself; she started swimming automatically, thinking of nothing.

Finally, exhausted, she climbed out of the pool and picked up her clothes, walked toward the house, then stopped. What was she doing back here? She shut her eyes hard and looked again. She was back in St. Petersburg Beach! But she had been in San Francisco, walking toward a hotel . . . She felt dizzy and held on to a chair back until the moment of dizziness passed.

Moving cautiously, like an invalid, she entered the house, pausing to listen every few steps, fearful of meeting anyone, more fearful of being alone right now. She had been in San Francisco. She knew she had. She could remember the cool morning air, the clouds, all the people on the sidewalks. She stopped again. That woman had come and told her about Jimmie! The wave of dizziness returned and she waited without motion for it to go away. When it did, she had the whole last evening back — running away, the various flights to Chicago, Denver, San Francisco... But what was she doing here?

She went to the bedroom and found nothing of hers in it. Jimmie's clothes were in one closet, the other one was empty. Her drawers were empty. Her confusion and fear increased until she felt nauseated. The guest room across the hall from the master bedroom had a woman's belongings, but they were not her things. Feeling near hysteria she searched for her own clothes, and finally found them in the guest room in the other wing of the house. She was shivering uncontrollably by now. Over and over she kept asking herself: How did I get back here?

She showered and pulled on a robe and returned to the kitchen, looking for a clue, anything to give her a hint of why she was back here again. She whirled in surprise when the garage door opened and that woman entered carrying a bag of groceries.

"Why did you come back?" Susannah cried. "How did you get in?"

"I tell you I be back in few minutes," Anna Maria Lucia said, looking at her suspiciously.

"How did you get in? Why are you bringing groceries into my house? How did I get back here?" Susannah heard her own voice go shrill.

"Susannah, you... I live here, don't you remember? I am your nurse, companion, what you call it. You haven't been anywhere. I don't know what you mean how you get back here."

"I was in San Francisco. And now I'm here. What's happening?"

"Poor baby," Anna Maria Lucia murmured soothingly. "Yesterday you say to me that you been to Tibet, and today you say San Francisco. Poor little Susannah." She started to put away the groceries.

"You came here and told me you were married to Jimmie!

232

You said he has other wives! I left him and went to San Francisco! Don't tell me I didn't!"

"Of course, I don't tell you nothing. Every day I tell you this: You have the what you say, the break-up? You see things and talk to people that are not here, no? You take the bad acid, maybe, the doctor say. You get better pretty soon he say. No more seeing things, talking to people we don't see . . ."

A breakdown? She had had a nervous breakdown? Hallucinating? Crazy! Quietly she slid to the floor in a faint.

◆◆◆

"Mrs. Rivers?" a voice called her from a great void. Reluctantly she opened her eyes to see a man sitting in a chair by her bed.

"I'm Dr. Felix Cornwall. Do you remember me?"

She shook her head.

"I thought you might not. It happens like that quite often." He leaned over the bed, gazing into her eyes. His hand groped for her wrist, and, she thought, missed the pulse, but he seemed satisfied. "Now then, tell me what you do remember?"

"I left my husband," she said clearly, "and went to San Francisco. And the next thing I was back in this house."

He smiled. "When did you leave him, Susannah?"

She had to think about the date. "It was Friday. Last Friday, whatever that date was."

"June?"

"Of course, June," she snapped.

"Susannah, this is July twenty-two. That was nearly a month ago."

She sat up abruptly. "I don't believe you!"

He showed her several newspapers. "I knew you wouldn't," he said cheerfully.

Then he told her how Jimmie had called him in from Miami that Friday night, how he had found Susannah irrational and incoherent. "I sedated you," he said, "and the next day you had no memory of any of it, but you still were hallucinating. I told Jimmie he couldn't leave you alone, that you needed hospital

233

care, but he refused to commit you, and we compromised by hiring Anna Maria Lucia, one of the best psychiatric nurses I know. I told Jimmie you would snap out of it exactly the same way you went into it, all at once, just as you did."

She stared at him in disbelief that slowly changed to bewilderment and fear. She had had a mental breakdown, she thought in wonder. For no reason she had gone bonkers, hallucinated, acted crazy. "But I remember going to San Francisco," she whispered.

"And from time to time you may remember other little bits of that fantasy life you led for several weeks, but gradually those memories will fade exactly the way dreams fade away with time."

He was so reassuring and kind, she thought, and found herself nodding with him. "Will it happen again?"

"Probably not. There's nothing physically wrong, nothing organic, that is. This was a little dysfunction of the cognitive synapses, a little mind storm that's blown over now." He laughed and patted her arm. "Now you get plenty of rest and just forget this little episode. No point in mentioning it in any medical questionnaire. People are too quick to pin on labels, and you needn't be stigmatized by something as harmless as this was." He stood up and she held his hand gratefully.

"Thank you, doctor. Thank you. You've made me feel much better."

"Good, good."

Anna Maria Lucia explained everything, Susannah thought late that night, sitting at her window watching the play of moonlight on the surface of the pool. Why didn't she have a purse and keys, driver's license . . . ? *You leave it in restaurant, don't you remember? Jimmie call but they no find it.* She remembered cutting her hair that night, but Anna Maria Lucia explained that too. *Poor Susannah, don't you remember? Every day you tie it in knots until I say to Jimmie I cut it and when you get well it grow again like before.* Susannah shuddered. Anna Maria Lucia had shown her the little blue suitcase that she remembered carrying to San Francisco, that the kids had snatched along with her purse. But the suitcase was in the storage room, on the high shelf, covered with a fine layer of sandy grit.

A sea gull landed on the pool, safe at last from sharks. She envied it. The last thing Anna Maria Lucia had said before going to bed kept repeating in her mind.

"Poor little Susannah, you get sick from too much fucking, I think. You marry older man, like father, to keep you safe from world, but you get confused then. Father, husband, who is he? You get sick so you don't have to think about it no more. That's what I think. That's why I move all your things to the other bedroom, so you don't have to think about it no more."

She sighed. Poor Jimmie, saddled with a mad wife. She should leave him, she knew, but the fear of another breakdown was overwhelming. What if it happened again when she was alone? They would surely commit her then, and she would spend the rest of her life in an institution of some kind, forced to watch daytime television.

She watched the gull float on the surface of the water, and in her mind's eye she began to see the limitless ocean, green, swelling gently, subsiding, and the depths where the green became darker and darker until it was velvety black, caressing and soothing, comforting those who found safety there.

25

Diary of a stranger

Sylvia looked at the living room with a sense of shock; for weeks now she had hardly seen it, and it was a rat's nest. The couches and chairs were clear, but the tables were still laden with notebooks and sketchpads, all the stuff Mike had searched through for an idea. Exxon glared at her from his perch on the window ledge; when she got too near him, he rose and stalked from the room with his tail aquiver. It wouldn't be long, she thought, watching him sadly. Brad would collect him and take him back home in a few days now. The miserable cat hated New York, hated the apartment, everyone in it. He sat on the ledge looking at Central Park as a prisoner might watch freedom through bars. Sighing, she started to pick up stuff. The book was in the final stages of artwork, another week and it would be done, and she was tired. They were all getting too old for marathons. She started to dump an armload of notebooks into a box, then sat down in resignation to go through them. No point in doing the same work twice, she thought, as she sorted them by date. Next year it would be the same thing, dig them all out, pore over them, reject them as useless, and fret until an idea came knocking at the door.

She had filled one carton and was starting on the next when she found Susannah's notebook, the diary she had written in faithfully every night. She put it aside to give to Marlene Murphy who was in town buying for her shop. She had said she would be keeping in touch with the girl, she could pass the notebook on to her.

Susannah felt her hands go clammy when Jimmie's BMW pulled into the driveway. She was wearing one of the long skirts he had bought her, and a halter to match, and she had on the high-heeled sandals he liked. She touched her hair nervously. She should have bought a wig, she thought in sudden despair. What must he think of her with such a short haircut?

He came in through the garage door and dropped his flight bag. "Hey, Anna Maria Lucia called me in New York! You're all right now?" He looked at her so anxiously that she wanted to weep. "You look wonderful!"

She nodded. "I'm fine now."

"Well, isn't that great! That headshrink said you would snap out of it and be yourself in no time, and look at you! Pretty as a picture again, all dolled up and everything!" He took several steps toward her and she found herself backing up. "My own sweet little girl again," he went on, reaching out for her. "Wait till you see what I bought for you."

"Jimmie, a registered letter came for you," she said in a rush. His little girl? Gray in his hair. That kind, loving, forgiving manner, the reassurance, telling her she was safe again. Bringing her presents, like a father returning from a trip. She ran to the kitchen table where she had placed the letter and thrust it toward him. "It must be important. Anna Maria Lucia was out when it came. She put your other mail on your desk. I signed for this."

He opened it and glanced at the letter, then said casually, "Where is Anna Maria Lucia now? I have to pay her."

"I'll call her," Susannah said quickly, and tried not to run from the room.

They went into his study, and Susannah sank down gratefully into a chair when the door closed behind them. He was

237

her husband, she thought in confusion; she must love him, or why was she married to him? She remembered last Friday . . . no, weeks ago, how excited she had been waiting for him to come home, watching the clock, listening to the television news, always so afraid there might be a crash . . . She did love him, she knew, remembering how he had calmed her fears during that thunderstorm when the plane had bucked and pitched, remembering his lovemaking. It was her illness making her so different now, she knew. She needed a little more time to recuperate thoroughly.

◈◈◈

"What is this thing?" Anna Maria Lucia asked, putting the letter down. "I don't understand this thing."

Jimmie was listening to Felix's phone ring and did not answer. He held a postcard. On it was a crudely drawn balloon with a happy face, punctured, sinking, the smiling mouth drawing down in a grimace. There was no message.

Felix answered at last.

"Ah, Jimmie here, old friend. I was just wondering if you got a little postcard recently?"

"Well now, Jimmie, funny thing is, I did. And, ah, Jimmie, I was going to call you later tonight. There's another little matter that's come up. Of course, there's nothing to it, nothing to worry about or anything like that, but it seems that I've been selected by the IRS for an audit. Wouldn't you think they'd have more things to do than harass a retired man?"

Jimmie sighed. "Yes, I understand how you must feel. Funny coincidence, though. Those random audits catch the guilty and innocent alike. Fact is, I had a letter from them waiting for me. As you say, nothing to it, but it's a nuisance. It is a nuisance."

There was a silence, then Felix said easily, "I thought I might drive over your way this evening, look in on Susannah, visit a day or two."

"Wonderful, Felix! I was going to suggest that very thing myself. See you around midnight?"

After he hung up, Anna Maria Lucia demanded, "You tell me what is new emergency. My God, no more emergencies!"

"Well now, Anna Maria Lucia, I wouldn't call it an emergency exactly, but like I said to Felix, it is a nuisance. Especially that part that says they want to see documentation about property ownership in foreign countries. That is the nuisance part of it, you see."

"How they know this?"

He picked up the postcard again and studied it for a minute, let it fall. "I'm afraid that our friends who were rounded up at the airport in Miami and more than likely exported may have decided to avenge themselves by this little practical joke. I would say that represents a last laugh idea, wouldn't you, Anna Maria Lucia?"

"Now we go to Costa Rica," Anna Maria Lucia said.

Susannah moved restlessly about the house. Anna Maria Lucia had gone out for the evening, to give them time together, she had said. But shortly afterward Jimmie had gone out also, a little business had come up that he had to handle, he had said. He would be back in a couple of hours, and then they would go have a wonderful dinner. She had kicked off her high-heeled sandals as soon as he left, but she kept stepping on the hem of the long skirt, and finally she went to her room and took it off, put shorts on instead. And it struck her that some of her clothes were missing. She sat down on the side of the bed and tried to remember exactly what she had put in the small blue bag that night, even while she reminded herself that she had not packed, had not gone to San Francisco. She had worn jeans, and her plaid jacket, a shirt. And she had packed all her old things she had liked before she married Jimmie, but most of them had gone into the big suitcase which she had left in the VW in the parking lot. She had already found them neatly put away. She closed her eyes trying to visualize the small suitcase, and slowly she began to remember what she had put inside it. Sneakers. Her old sneakers. She hunted for them and failed to find them. And her No Nukes T-shirt. It was gone.

It made no sense, she decided then. The blue bag was in the storage room. Grimly she went to the storage room dragging a chair to stand on to reach the blue bag. She pulled it down and opened it. Her missing clothes were inside in a jumble. She stared at them without comprehension. It didn't make any sense, she repeated. Only a crazy person would pack a suitcase and then put it high up on a shelf. A long shudder passed through her.

She did not believe it, and that, too, she realized, could be a symptom of her illness. She closed her eyes hard, remembering that other night. Jimmie had come in through the front door that night, and he had dropped his flight bag exactly the same way that he had dropped it this afternoon. And he had dropped a blue suitcase also. She started and opened her eyes wide, staring into the gloom of the storage area, seeing Jimmie drop two bags that night. Seeing Jimmie leave shortly afterward, out through the garage, picking up the wrong suitcase, the one she had left there. She went over it again and again and the only changes were more details that she had forgotten and now recalled.

Like a sleepwalker she returned to her room, carrying her own suitcase this time, and automatically she began to pack her old clothes from before Jimmie's time. It was nonsensical, and the more she tried to sort out the parts, the more nonsensical it all became. Why were they lying to her? Pretending she had not left when she had? Pretending she had been ill? But she had been ill, she reminded herself. There were over three weeks missing from her life, and there was that doctor . . . She began to hurry, for fear they would return before she was out, and Jimmie, with his snake tongue, would convince her that all this was another symptom of illness. Maybe it was, she admitted, but she had to go away, had to be alone to try to think through all the puzzle parts.

The doorbell rang and at first she tried to ignore it, but then, almost angry at being interrupted, she went to see who it was. Maybe something from her parents, telling her they were home again. She wanted them home so badly that tears came to her eyes at the thought of running to them, hiding in their house, being cared for again.

She yanked the door open to see a small, pretty woman with pale hair.

"Susannah," the woman said smiling. "Hello, how are you?"

Susannah shook her head. "I'm afraid I don't know you," she said slowly. "Do you know me?"

"Oh dear, this is going to be awkward, isn't it? Yes, I know you. I have something that belongs to you. I wanted to return it." She looked past Susannah. "Is anyone here with you?"

"No. Why?"

"I thought they might be keeping you here, hiding you away. I tried so many times to reach you by phone, but no one ever returned my calls. The answering machine swallowed them whole, I guess."

Susannah opened the door wider and moved aside. "Come in," she said hesitantly. "What do you have that's mine?"

"Your diary," Marlene said. "You left it in Mike Berryman's apartment." She handed a notebook to Susannah.

"When? I don't even know Mike Berryman. When was I in his apartment?"

"It's all in the notebook," Marlene said. Then, more gently, she added, "After you've read it, if you want to talk, please give me a call. My number is in there, too."

They were still standing in the hall, and she turned to leave. "I only have a short time before I have to catch my flight," she said. "I don't want to intrude, now that you're back to yourself again, back to normal. I probably can't tell you much that isn't in the notebook, but I'll try if you call."

"Wait a minute!" Susannah cried, remembering that Anna Maria Lucia was using her car. "Will you give me a lift to the beachfront motel section? I'm ready to leave!"

Marlene looked startled, then nodded. "Of course." She watched Susannah dash off down the hall clutching the notebook, and in a moment return with a suitcase, sandals under her arm, a skirt over her arm.

"I can dress in the car," Susannah said, opening the door.

"I'm not in that much of a rush," Marlene said.

"But I am! They might be back any minute now. I don't want to be here when they get home."

Susannah directed Marlene north along the beach highway. "They might look for me," she said. "But probably not this far north. And it's closer to the airport from Clearwater Beach." She did not start to relax until they were several miles up the beach. Then she asked, "When did we meet, and where?"

Marlene told her and she began to laugh. "I'm not crazy! They said I didn't go to San Francisco, that I had been crazy!"

"Who said?"

"Jimmie and a woman..."

Marlene's mouth tightened as she listened. When Susannah finished, they were pulling into a motel parking area. "Do you have any money?" Marlene asked.

"Yes. Oh!" Susannah had money in the bank, but no checkbook, no identification. "I can't get it out of the bank until tomorrow," she said. "I don't care. I'll sleep on the beach tonight."

"No, of course you won't. I'll register us both in, and say you're planning to stay on for a few days. You can mail me a check to cover it when you get around to it."

She saw Susannah to the room they were supposed to share for the night. "I hate to have to leave like this," she said. "Will you be all right here? Is there someone you can call if you need anything?"

"Yes," Susannah said. "There are some friends, and tomorrow I'll go to the bank, and I'll get a duplicate driver's license. I'll be okay. How can I thank you?"

"You can't. I'm off now. Keep in touch, will you?"

◇◇◇

It was eight o'clock when Susannah finished reading the notebook. She had laughed, and she had wept over it, and it was like reading the adventures of a fictional character; it had nothing to do with her.

26

A letter from a stranger

What was he doing here? For days he had looked up things like Harlow's critique of Edmunson's criticism of Winston's analysis of Beowulf. He knew what Winston had really said, but so what? He stared blankly at the stack of books he had yet to go through and realized that he was hungry, it was late, and for the third day in a row he had sat without reading anything, without making a single note. His bottom was sore from the wooden chair, his sinuses hurt from breathing dust and fungus spores, his head ached from the poor lighting, and he felt empty, mentally and physically. Hungry, he said to himself. He was just hungry. He picked up his notebooks and left the Library of Congress and walked to his hotel. He did not go inside, but went around to the parking lot entrance and gave the attendant his ticket and waited for the car to appear. Between motions he stopped thinking, and for just a second he was bemused by that, but then he stopped thinking about it. The Corvair came into view and he remembered that he had to pay his bill; he could not just leave. He told the attendant he would be right back and went inside and checked out, retrieved his suitcase, which he had not unpacked, and then got in his car and started to drive.

It was very hot and muggy, too hot to think about food yet, he decided, and it was nearly a hundred miles later that he thought of it again. He stopped and ate hamburgers, and then drove until he began to doze at the wheel. He pulled off the interstate at a rest area and slept. At dawn he woke up and drove until he found a restaurant, where he had breakfast, and then he continued to drive.

He thought of nothing, and only now and then realized that he was not thinking and concentrated on whatever came to mind for a brief time until the thought occurred to him once more that he was behaving like an automaton without consciousness. Then he thought for a while. He slept again for a few hours, and he was in Florida.

Now all the thoughts he had not considered raced to surface first. What are you going to do? She won't even know you. She'll look at you and see a bum and look away. What if you see her hugging the captain, laughing with him? They've probably gone on a trip together. He took her to Paris with him, afraid to leave her alone again.

It had been better when he was not thinking; now he could not stop. Bits of the trip across the country surfaced and sank — the chipmunks that had dared Exxon and had come to the table for scraps. The sun like a silver disk behind the tips of the fir trees. Her profile when she drove, intent on the twisting mountain road. The way she rustled her sleeping bag one last time, turning to her right side, before she fell asleep. The way they walked together, in step, faster and faster as they talked. How she swam in the ocean, shocked by the cold water, but not complaining. Never complaining. Not when he got them lost time and again, not when they were hungry, or cold, or tired, or too hot.

And you see her, then what? Then nothing, he said to himself. Nothing. I'll just look, and go away. The rolling pastures yielded to rolling scrub land, and then orange trees appeared in neat rows that marched to the horizon in both directions as the land leveled. Heat shimmered on the highway.

◆◆◆

Susannah was up at dawn. She had slept very little and felt logy. The beach was deserted and cool when she went out to swim; the gulf water was warmer than the dim morning air. After she showered and dressed, she thought about breakfast; at least juice she told herself firmly when the idea of food made her stomach churn. Still she dawdled, until she noticed the notebook and decisively picked it up and left her room. She would eat, and make plans for her future, and then carry them out. You could spend a lifetime hung up between two points if you didn't force yourself to move, she told herself severely.

She had coffee and opened the notebook, not to the front where she had written her diary every day, but toward the back to clean pages. She was not interested in what had happened during dream time. That was someone else's life, not hers. She had to start a new life now, alone, somewhere else . . .

She started to list the places she knew, pitifully few as it turned out, and she did not want to return to any of them. Her pen slid on a raised surface and she flipped through the pages to see what was tucked among them. There was a page of writing, heavy, firm lines, not hers, and there was a camp receipt from a state park in Iowa. She held it, turning it over and over. Then she read the page.

"Hello. You don't know me, not if you are reading this after your recovery from amneisia. (She smiled; amnesia was misspelled.) I don't know your name, or where you're reading this, or what your life is like now. I guess you've put things back together again and the blank spot is nothing compared to what you've found in getting back to your family, those you love who love you. I hope you're happy.

"It's strange that you don't know me when I know you so well. The real you, the magic you. Exxon knew from the start that you were magic. You are the only person he's ever trusted. It took me longer to find this out. The magic is real. You have your entire life back now and these two weeks we've been

246

together are meaningless to you. I have these two magic weeks and the rest of my life is meaningless. It's a fair exchange — if you're happy.

"I don't know why this is important to me to write you now. To tell you that nothing happened between us, that you were wonderful . . . Maybe I just want to be sure that I exist in your real life, even in this minor way. A letter from a stranger. We shared a dream and now you're awake and the dream has faded and gone, but I'm still in it and will always be in it. I wanted you to know that. They were good weeks, the best of my life. Thank you. Brad."

She read it again, then slowly turned to the opening page of her diary and started to read the whole thing over. Her food was brought and grew cold and was taken away, her coffee cup was refilled a time or two, and she noticed none of this as she read and reread her own words that had been written by a stranger.

She went back to the motel and sat under a palm tree and watched pelicans glide over the water, watched skimmers maintain their flights with their lower bills in the water, watched a crowd of sandpipers run before and after lacy wavelets . . . A hundred sandwich terns were holding a caucus and screamed angrily when an unkempt herring gull landed amongst them. Susannah watched them all with a curiously blank mind, as if waiting for an outside event to happen that would explain everything to her, as if somehow these birds, each intent on its own pursuits, held a clue that she would suddenly comprehend.

◆◆◆

If Brad had thought of it at all, he would have gloated that in his long solitary journey he had not been lost a single time, had not taken a wrong turn, had noticed when he needed oil and water, had in fact been an exemplary, if automatic, driver in every respect. But the Bay Vista subdivision, like most of the subdivisions up and down the off-shore islands, was not designed for automatic driving. It was a maze of winding streets, some ending in turnaround circles, some crossing themselves many times, some simply stopping and taking on new names in a whimsical fashion. Bay View Avenue mysteriously turned into Bay Vista North, and Oleander Avenue abruptly called itself Jacaranda. Brad long ago had decided to leave and reenter by another access street, but even that was denied him. He could not find his way out, and he could not find 1475 Bay Shore Drive, or even Bay Shore Drive with any number. It was all so neat, he thought, disquieted by so much tidiness. Not a blade of grass was unshorn, a hedge untrimmed; there was no one in sight, and he began to get an eerie feeling that no one lived here, it was a display village to tempt unwary buyers, a model subdivision with false fronts of houses and plastic landscaping. It was impossible to decide if he had been on any of the streets or not because the houses, although subtly different in trim, or window treatments, were more alike than not. He drove grimly, watching the street signs, but not all intersections had signs. He came to a stop at an intersection; through an opening in hedges and short trees, he could see the bay straight ahead. He turned left, determined this time to keep the bay on his right and follow its edge, which ultimately had to lead him to Bay Shore, or else the very name of the street was a practical joke.

Susannah had been to the bank, and she had her duplicate driver's license, and now she was in a taxi drawing up to the Bay Shore Drive house. She paid the driver and walked up the driveway steadily. She had gone over many different scenarios: Jimmie contrite and humble; Jimmie blustery and threatening; Jimmie explaining plausibly everything that had happened ... What she dreaded most was the last one, Jimmie explaining, forever explaining. All of the scenarios in which she talked at any length to Jimmie ended with her hitting him. She had been shocked and dismayed to find so much animosity

248

and violence within herself, but she had admitted that more than anything she wanted to hit him with something hard; it would have to be hard for him to notice, she had added. She had rejected that scenario also finally. All she really wanted was her car keys. No talk. No explanations. Nothing else, just the keys.

She rang the bell and waited, then rang it again, this time holding it down longer. When no one came, she went around the house, through the gap in the oleander hedge, to the back yard. The sliding glass door was locked, the first time she could remember such a thing. She hesitated only for a second, then picked up one of the aluminum chairs and smashed a bathroom window with it, swept the glass from the frame, and climbed into the house.

It was stifling; the air conditioner had been turned off. She had been moving cautiously, but now she realized they were gone, Jimmie and the woman, and they did not intend to come back. Everywhere there were signs of a sudden departure — drawers left open, papers scattered, Jimmie's closet half empty, all of Anna Maria Lucia's things gone...

Susannah looked in the garage and breathed a sigh of relief; they had not taken her little VW bug. It was too old to have any value, too old to be trustworthy for a long trip. Beneath notice, she thought happily, and opened the engine compartment, felt the side wall, and found the extra key she always kept taped there. She touched the horn and the garage door opened; the whale was going to spit her out again. She had checked out of the motel; she had cleaned out her savings account and closed her checking account, and now had everything she owned in travelers' checks and cash and a suitcase. Slowly she backed out of the garage.

Brad rounded the curve and saw smoke rising from a black VW bug. He slowed down more, then jammed on the brakes as Susannah got out of the car, and stood looking at it in dismay. She had turned off the ignition, stopping the smoke, which still hung in an ominous cloud over her and the car.

He did not know he had moved, had left his Corvair, until he stood at her side. She glanced at him, then regarded the car again.

"I thought it was on fire," he said, looking at her. She looked tired, he thought with a pang.

"So did I." She went to the rear and opened the hatch, released yet more clouds of dense smoke. Coughing, she backed away from it.

"It looks like there's no oil," Brad said hesitantly.

"I guess someone's been driving it without noticing the oil was low. I wonder if it's ruined."

"It sure looks ruined to me," he said.

She glanced at him again, now with a trace of humor. "You sound as if you know as much about it as I do. I'd better call Triple A."

She started to move toward the open garage, then stopped. She had no card, she remembered. She returned to stand by her car, frowning in thought. "I lost my card," she said. She became aware that he was watching her, and she gave him a sharp look. "I don't think there's anything you can do, but thanks for stopping."

The water sprinklers came on suddenly spraying them both with a dash of cool water. "Damn," she muttered and got inside. "I'm going to put it back in the garage," she told him, dismissing him. "Thanks again." When he didn't move, she said in exasperation, "You're getting soaked. Look, I'm going to put the car away and go inside the house and call a cab. There's nothing you can do." She turned on the ignition and the starter chugged and churned, but nothing else happened.

"It's frozen," Brad said. "I can probably push it, let it roll in."

Resignedly she got out and helped him push the little car until it began to move. They were both soaked by the time they got the car in the garage. She didn't know how to turn off the sprinkler system. "Come on in and dry off," she said and reached for the house door. It had locked automatically behind her. Sighing, she led him around the house and pointed to the broken window.

"Through the window?" he asked, startled.

"I don't have any keys. I lost them. It's all right, no one else is home."

"Are you going in?"

She shook her head. Water was running off her hair, down her neck, and now he could feel water on his back. He had been so hot before that it felt good.

"I don't want to dry off," he said. "First time in days that I've been relatively cool." He knew he was staring at her, and tried to look somewhere else, but his gaze returned again and again. She was different, the same, but subtly different. There was resolve and anger, or determination, something unyielding and decisive in the firm set of her lips, the level, frank appraisal of her gaze.

The glance she gave him now was annoyed. "Well, if you don't want to dry off, I'll be going."

"How? Can I give you a lift? Where are you going?"

She had considered entering the house to telephone for a taxi, but she did not want to go inside, even for that long. She looked at him again, then nodded. "Okay. Just to the corner where there's a phone. Where I'm heading is too far for a friendly hitch, I'm afraid." She started back around the house, and he followed.

"I have a suitcase in the car," she said, stopping at the edge of the spray. "I'll get it, won't be a minute." She darted through the water to the garage, and he was at her side still. When she glanced at him, he was grinning. "Just as well you didn't dry off," she said, and pulled her suitcase and purse from the VW. He took the suitcase and they left the garage. She touched the button to close the door behind her and ran through the water one more time; behind her she could hear it pattering on the metal door. At the Corvair she hesitated a second, looking at the car in bewilderment that passed quickly. She shrugged and got inside.

"We look like two people who got caught out in a storm," she said when he started the engine. Water was running down her back, down her neck; he was dripping. And he was grinning like an idiot. She felt an uneasy stirring that was not exactly fear, but she could not have said what else it could have been. All the warnings she had suffered through came to mind: Never get in a car with a stranger, no matter what. He was certainly a stranger, not only to her but also to the area. He was too pale to be a resident, too pale to have been visiting very long.

"Are you here on business?" she asked.

"Passing through."

"Passing through a subdivision? You should have turned at that last corner. The next one might work."

"Where are you going?" he asked, making the next turn.

"New York. I was going to drive, but I'll take a plane instead."

"I'm going to New York," he said.

"You just happened to be passing through our subdivision on your way to New York?"

"Honestly, that's exactly what I was doing."

She laughed deep in her throat, a hardly audible sound. "Take the next right, and then straight ahead to the beach road."

"Would you like to drive to New York with me?" he asked, clutching the steering wheel, staring ahead. He was not grinning now.

She laughed louder and longer. "Thank you, Mr. . . . But no thank you. Didn't anyone ever tell you not to pick up hitchhikers?" She looked at him. "My name's Susannah, what's yours?"

Staring ahead, rigid with tension, he said, "Brad. Bradford Hale. I . . . I know you, Susannah. I mean, I used to know you . . ."

"Brad," she whispered. And now she too stared ahead fixedly. "You followed the curve around," she said after a moment. "You should have gone straight. The only thing to do is turn around and go back."

He nodded and started a U-turn, then pulled over and

stopped the car. He looked at her. "You read the diary? All of it?"

She was studying him; she had not written a description in the notebook. She nodded at his question. "All of it."

"Why were you going to New York?"

"To meet your father, maybe, and thank him." She shook her head and more slowly went on, "I thought I might find you there, meet you. And thank you."

"Let me take you," he said quietly.

She shook her head again. "It . . . I don't think I should do that, not now."

"You were okay with me before."

"That was different."

"I know. You didn't know enough then not to trust me."

"How could I not trust you, after all you've done for me?"

"Then, let's do it."

"I would like for us to get to know each other," she said hesitantly.

"I know you, Susannah."

Slowly she nodded, and he grinned and started the engine. "We'll need a few things. A cooler, and some food to cook . . ."

"We could just stop at restaurants. I have enough money. I mean, I was expecting to drive and stop along the way."

"I have enough," he said. "I thought it might be fun to do it the same way as before."

"Exactly the same?" she asked, keeping her gaze on the winding street.

He looked straight ahead also. "Exactly the same."

❖❖❖

"You really don't remember any of it?" He knew he sounded forlorn.

"Nothing," she said, and knew she sounded miserable.

He drove across the bay bridge and joined the interstate traffic heading north.

"I called Dad a couple days ago. His agent has a contract for Leslie Knowles. She sold the story we wrote."

"Tell me the story," she said. She had not written it in her diary, only that there was one.

◆◆◆

"Those are live oaks and the stuff hanging from them is Spanish moss. They used to harvest it and use it to pad furniture, mattresses and things. I guess no one bothers with it any longer."

"Eerie," he said. "Like the cover of a gothic novel."

◆◆◆

"It doesn't seem fair that you don't remember any of our trip across the country. There were so many things we wanted to go see and we didn't have time for."

"I thought I might travel across the country by myself," she said. "I've always wanted to see the Rockies, and the desert."

"I have to go home, back to San Francisco. And I have to take the car, and that fool cat..."

◆◆◆

"I like your father. I don't quite understand why he treated me the way he did, but I liked it."

"He thinks you're magic."

"And Exxon, I feel that I almost remember Exxon. Isn't that strange?"

"Not at all. He had no doubts about you from the start."

◆◆◆

"Look, if we go south about thirty miles or so, we can see where William Penn lived. There's a restored pioneer village. Does that interest you? Do we have time?"

He laughed. "Nothing but time."

◆◆◆

"...wanted me to go out for the swim team, but I said no. I hate competitive sports, and I love to swim. I was afraid they'd ruin it for me..."

❖❖❖

They drove west, and north, and south, and more than once doubled back and headed east again, and they talked and talked, and at night each listened to the sleeping bag of the other make soft rustling sounds before the quiet settled over them both.

She whistled for Exxon, and drove while he relaxed and watched her face, and he drove while she made notes about the scenery, or simply looked with contentment at the unrolling landscape.

❖❖❖

"Tell me how we wrote the stories again," she said. "I can't believe I could come up with ideas so spontaneously."

"I know. I couldn't believe it either. I guess you must have read most of the books in your library. Whenever anyone asked who you were, what your name was, you'd tell a story."

"Try me now," she said.

"Who are you?"

"Susannah," she said without hesitation. "The scene: Florida, St. Petersburg and the outlying beaches, in late June when heat rises shimmering from the highways and sidewalks and all native life moves at a slow pace, while the tourists hurry..."

The car swerved and he yelped.

"What's wrong? What happened?"

"That's our story," he said. "A novel. Your story."

"But it will take a long time, months. And there are too many parts we don't know. What Jimmie was up to, where he went..."

"We'll make them up."

"There should be jewels, fabulous jewels involved, smuggled jewels with a curse on them."

"And the Mafia."

"The jewels have a life of their own, a story of their own, with many players who never know what happened to them or why . . ."

"And it has a happy ending," Brad said firmly.

"Does it?"

"Oh yes."